SUMMER SECRETS AT STREAMSIDE COTTAGE

SUMMER SECRETS AT STREAMSIDE COTTAGE

Samantha Tonge

An Aria Book

This edition first published in the United Kingdom in 2021 by Aria,
an imprint of Head of Zeus Ltd

A CIP catalogue record for this book is available
from the British Library.

ISBN eBook: 9781800241671
ISBN Print: 9781800246102

Typeset by Siliconchips Services Ltd UK

Printed and bound by CPI Group (UK) Ltd, Croydon CR0 4YY

Aria
c/o Head of Zeus
First Floor East
5–8 Hardwick Street
London EC1R 4RG

www.ariafiction.com

For everyone who's felt the need to ink their skin,
to use their body as the page for a story,

I hear your pain not from the needle but your past.

I hope the tattoo moved you forwards.
You are courageous.

Prologue

For every ten thousand clovers with three leaves
there is just one with four

Like most Monday mornings, my working week started with a client stripping off. Bill laid his t-shirt on a nearby chair. He'd done a good job of shaving the hair off his chest and I'd already prepared the carbon stencil and tore off a square of kitchen roll to clean the area with Dettol. Wearing latex gloves, I pressed firmly as I applied the design and waited a few moments. Slowly I peeled off the tracing paper to reveal the outline of his new tattoo.

'Let's double-check you're happy with the exact position.' He stood up from the bench and I guided him over to the wall mirror as we both studied the shape and size of my drawing. It nudged comfortably against the inked guitar that already went across his right pec.

'It's exactly where my Sheila's was.' Bill's scratchy voice

teamed up with his yellow fingers and signature tobacco scent.

'I didn't know she had a tattoo there.'

'No… her four leaf clover was silver-plated. Towards the end she never took that necklace off. It was my present to her on our twenty-fifth anniversary because marrying her had made me the luckiest man in the world.' He swept dyed black strands of hair back across the top of his head. 'She had the hereditary type, you know. It's just as well we never had kids.'

I reached out and gently squeezed his arm. I always reckoned my job was like being a hairdresser, the way people revealed things they might otherwise keep secret. Someone knocked on the door and Steve's head poked into view.

'Someone's asking for you, Lizzie,' he said.

'Cheers, Steve. Can you explain I've started? They can either wait or leave a message.' People were always dropping into the parlour to discuss designs before making an appointment.

Bill lay down and I prepared my machine, fitting the needle into the tube. I secured it and dipped it into the black ink. Normally we'd have joked about me being the only woman he got his kit off for, apart from Sheila. My foot pressed down on the pedal and as the needle moved, he chatted about plans they'd had for the future and how much Sheila had loved running the café opposite that I frequently visited.

Outside the door voices jostled to take centre stage and an impatient one took the lead. I heard my name and a gasp followed.

'Do you need to go for a minute?' Bill asked but I shook my head. It was probably a disappointed client who'd turned up unannounced expecting to be fitted in straightaway. Bill and I lapsed back into silence, experience having taught me when a client didn't want to talk.

'There. All done,' I said eventually.

He stood in front of the mirror. 'Sheila wore her necklace in the coffin. I wished I'd kept it afterwards but at least I've got this now.' His voice wavered.

Like many tattoos, this one's simplicity represented complex emotions. I taped cling film over my work and Bill sat down again with his takeaway coffee, draining the cold contents. He didn't need to tell me that it was exactly one year to the day that his wife had died.

Another knock sounded. 'Are you going to be much longer?' asked Steve. 'This woman...'

'Tell her I'll be there in a minute.'

Bill stood up, stretched and threw his cup into the bin. 'You get off, Lizzie. I know the routine by now. I'll buy a sachet of the aftercare cream when I pay and take the cling film off after a couple of hours, then it's a matter of washing and creaming around four times a day for two weeks – right?' His arms wrestled the inside of the black t-shirt.

'I've got you well trained.'

His head appeared out of his top and revealed a smile on his face. I walked around the bench and gave him a sideways hug before opening the door.

The treatment rooms of Kismet Tattoos were white and minimalist – the reception area anything but. As you came in, on the right, there were three black wicker chairs with mustard cushions, circling a low glass table bearing portfolios of our work. The blood red walls in that corner boasted framed copies of our most popular designs, from those inspired by the natural or fantasy world, to meaningful quotes in English, Latin or Aramaic. Music played in the background – my mentor, Katya's, choice today which meant hip-hop. Three treatment rooms led down the right-hand side, one of them for tattoo removals. Steve also did piercings and the shelving on the left, near the front window, displayed rings for an array of body parts. Straight ahead was the reception desk with a scanner by the wall. On top of the counter, in front of the appointment book, were sachets of aftercare cream in a glass bowl next to the consent forms.

Someone once told me that a reputable tattoo parlour should seem more like a doctor's surgery, with sterilising tools and licenses on display. Kismet Tattoos certainly looked professional and sanitary but not at the price of character with its neon sign outside and exotic reception interior. A middle-aged woman, with a neat bob, sat on one of the wicker chairs, rimless glasses balanced on her nose. She was much less colourful than our usual clients. A bus thundered past outside and puffs of cloud blotted out the July sunshine. I didn't want to keep her waiting any longer but needed to grab a glass of water after I'd seen to Bill.

Katya looked up from the appointment book. 'I think she's come a long way – you'd better go over.' Her voice was soft, her stare hard and I'd known Katya long enough to realise that combination meant this visitor was the bearer of bad news. Like the time a man had come back to complain I'd spelt his Latin quote wrong. Fortunately, I'd kept the printed out wording he'd brought in. I squinted across the room at the woman who studiously gazed into nothing. Curved arms folded underneath a generous chest causing the opposing buttonholes of her blouse to gape.

I said goodbye to Bill and strode over. The woman looked up and removed her glasses.

'*Aunt Fiona?*' My heart thumped and I blinked rapidly for a few seconds. 'I can't believe... it's so good to... is everything okay?'

Creases deepening, her face screwed up like a piece of paper and she got to her feet, looking shorter than I recalled. The proximity highlighted her smudged eyeliner.

'How did you find me?'

'I remembered the name of this parlour and Googled.' Her voice sounded thick. 'I would have called but... this isn't the kind of thing you say over the phone.'

The hairs stood up on the back of my neck. She followed me to the back, past the buzz of tattoo needles and colleagues who suddenly looked busy. Steve patted my back as I walked past. We climbed the wooden flight of stairs and, at the top, entered the flat that I rented, with its open-plan kitchen, the breakfast bar and the lounge – the largest room by far in comparison with the bedroom and bathroom. I grabbed Ash's pyjamas and my dressing gown off the sofa and told her to take a seat whilst I threw them in the bedroom. When I returned, Aunt Fiona sat amongst my colourful cushions and hugged one tightly.

'Can I get you a cup of tea? Coffee?' For some reason I felt sick. She felt like a stranger. More than ever I felt the ache of it having been five years since I'd last seen her and my parents.

Aunt Fiona shook her head, took out a handkerchief and wrung it between her hands.

I hadn't expected to see a member of my family. Not yet. It seemed too soon, normal time having been skewed by the fall out.

'Are… are Mum and Dad thinking of moving back to London?' Aunt Fiona doted on her sister and such plans wouldn't have pleased her. Perhaps… perhaps my parents wanted a reconciliation.

'I told the investigating officer it would be better coming from me. Now I'm not so sure.'

Investigating officer. What could be wrong? Was Uncle Jack ill? Why were the police involved?

'It was a beautiful sunny day. Your parents couldn't resist taking a dip. Nothing pleased them more than swimming away from the crowded beach but they'd misjudged the tides…'

Like hives allergic to words, red blotches appeared on her cheeks. My forehead tightened. Getting back to the beach must have been an Olympic challenge. They would be exhausted. Or perhaps it got late and they caught pneumonia. My mind went into automatic. Katya would give me the time off work. It would only take me ten minutes to pack. Within a few hours I'd be by their side in hospital. I'd stay a few weeks until they were fully recovered – start to make up for the last five years apart. We'd be a family again and—

Her voice shook as she rose to her feet. 'This is all your fault.'

My voice caught. 'What do you mean?'

'They were swept away by a freak current. Your mum… it was all over by the time the rescue services found her.

Later that night they found your dad's body washed up on the shore.'

No, Aunt Fiona must have got it wrong. My throat ached. I couldn't move. For a second her face softened and she sat down once more. As she told me all the details, tears streamed down her cheeks.

I couldn't cry – couldn't feel.

I couldn't speak.

The room span for a moment and my hand flew to my mouth. I charged into the bathroom and crouched on the floor before everything went black.

I

Now

The Latin word for tattoo is stigma

Arriving in Leafton, I drove past a straggling estate on the left and over a junction. Quaint grey stone cottages edged the small village high street. A poppy-red letter box provided a splash of colour. It stood outside a post office that was situated within a small supermarket. I read the twee names of the few businesses – Blossom's Bakes, The Pen Pusher, Styles by Stacey. There was one pub called The Tipsy Duck and an estate agency on the corner.

I stopped at the traffic lights and glanced at my phone. Google Maps directed me to take the next left, an avenue that ran alongside a stream. Its row of cottages became increasingly spaced out until I came to one right at the end. It was set back and surrounded by overgrown lawns. My heart thumped at the thought of what I might find here.

I parked the car on the road outside Streamside Cottage. Despite its uncared-for appearance I could tell that, once tidied, it would look like the front of a touristy box of fudge with its thatched roof and honey and white coloured stone dash. Window boxes hung underneath the ground floor windows although the plants inside them had shrivelled. The glass panes were each divided into six by white bars and needed a wash. The front door was cornflower blue although the colour had faded, with ivy sprawling up either side as if reclaiming the stone for nature.

This looked like a family home that begged for children and a pet dog, for visiting grandparents, for football kick-abouts and vegetable patches. Ash would have liked it here. I swallowed and tried not to think of what happened with him and how that had pushed me to finally check out this place. I focused on the building that looked so isolated. Lonely even. I got out of my car. The stream carried on straight and then cut left and flowed along the property's back garden which looked onto a forest. The gentle babble of water played in the background. I wasn't used to such quiet. After Aunt Fiona's visit last year, on that July Monday morning, the busy London soundtrack had provided a welcome distraction from the news she'd broken.

I stepped forwards and a shed came into view in the distance, behind the driveway on the right. Oak trees and weeping willows stood tall at the rear, by the water. It was such a picturesque garden I almost expected Mr Darcy to wade out of the stream. I went through a wooden gate and the gravel gave a satisfying scrunch beneath my feet as I walked along the drive. At the front door a black plaque with the cottage's name dipped on one side. Carefully I corrected it, as if straightening a tie.

I ventured around the side of the building and strolled

towards the stream and as the countryside enveloped me, I homed in on its finer sounds. The quack of ducks instead of the tattoo parlour's recorded singers. Buzzing came from bees instead of ink machines and leaves rustled in the breeze like clients flipping through my portfolio's pages.

My jeans felt too thick for the June sunshine, despite the holes torn in them for effect. At least I was wearing my sleeveless t-shirt. The weathermen were predicting another heatwave. I stood at the water's edge, in front of a wired fence that went all around the nearside of the water. A cluster of ducklings formed a queue behind mum.

'You can do it,' I said to one struggling to keep up, at the back.

Leaf-dappled light added sparkle to ripples and crests of white water formed around the occasional boulder. Small fish flexed their bodies from side to side, in the calmer shallows, as if doing dance moves. In the middle the stream turned onyx as its depth increased. On the opposite bank a squirrel froze before darting into bushes. I couldn't help smiling as my shoulders relaxed.

A dragonfly hovered nearby. It was one insect I'd never done a tattoo of. I stared at its metallic-looking blue and purple hues and translucent wings and my paint box came to mind and the gift cards Ash had encouraged me to design.

'There's nothing you can't do, Lizzie,' Ash had once said. 'You really should take your painting to the next level. You're a natural – one hundred per cent it can be more than a hobby.'

My boss, Katya, had even started to sell my cards in the parlour this last year. Despite my city upbringing, nature had always inspired me the most and my work reflected urban wildlife with watercolours of foxes, pigeons and blackbirds. As I gazed around the garden I felt overwhelmed by the textures, shapes and colours. I'd never seen so many different shades of green.

I ducked under the hanging leaves of the weeping willow planted right by the water's edge and ran my hand over the bark. In capitals someone had carved the word Earl and next to it a number eight, drawn lopsided as if the bark had made it difficult to chip out vertically. I pushed the branches aside and ventured out into the open again. A voice called out hello and I turned to face a woman who was all lipstick and tailored edges. A postman stood behind her. He wore baggy black shorts and red top accessorised with an apologetic expression. I walked up to them, for some reason unable to take my eyes off him.

'It's her,' said the woman, her eyes moving from my ripped jeans, to my Doc Martens boots and finally snagging on my candyfloss pink hair. With her grey trouser suit and clear nail varnish she looked like a sketch waiting to be coloured in. A whiff of heavy perfume filled the air and her eyes darted to the side of my head where the hair was shaved.

'I'm the local estate agent. We've handled the renting out of this cottage for years. This is private property.'

'I'm just—'

'You shouldn't be here without an appointment,' she said.

'Wait a minute. Let her explain.' The postman stepped forward and ruffled his russet spiky hair. It was unruly, untidy – I liked it. 'Hello, I'm Ben and this is Caroline. Lovely garden, isn't it?' He stared at the running water. 'The stream is much darker at this point. It must be the shade from that magnificent weeping willow.' His eyes flicked up and down and left and right then narrowed as if he were hunting out the things people don't usually see, like the effect of light and shade and how colours, once scrutinised, aren't as simple as they first appeared. He turned around to study the building.

'Are you an artist?' I asked.

'I love photography.'

'Our Ben's had his shots used by BBC weather forecasters,' said Caroline, momentarily thawing. 'Leafton is very proud of him. Were you here to view the property, because, like I said, you really should have rung the estate agency first?'

'Actually, I—'

'Because, you know, we take trespassing very seriously in Leafton. Last week I had to report a scruffy so-and-so hanging around the church car park and only yesterday—'

'By the looks of the outside this place needs a bit of work,' Ben said hurriedly, glancing between us, 'but still, it's got plenty of character.'

'It's well past its best – even I don't romanticise about that,' said Caroline. 'This beautiful garden is the highlight. The thatched roof has leaked and upstairs there's a problem with damp. We've done our best as the letting agent, but tenants have mostly been short-term and never treated the place as their own. Although, in my opinion,' she said conspiratorially, 'it's just as well some of them didn't hang around. One lot were Buddhists and another... well, I'm not one to tittle-tattle.' She straightened up. 'Anyway, I've just had to let it out for a month.'

'That really is a short contract,' said Ben.

'It's always better that a property is occupied,' Caroline

said, holding my gaze, 'the last thing Leafton needs is someone squatting. It was a shame when the last tenant left so abruptly.'

'Perhaps I should introduce myself. I'm Lizzie, the new tenant you talked of.' Mustn't laugh. She wasn't to know that. 'I think we've spoken on the phone, Caroline. Thanks for checking up on the property. It's appreciated.'

Ben looked away, eyes twinkling and biting his lip. My stomach gave a tiny flip.

Mum and Dad had both worked in insurance and the cottage must have been one of their investments but I couldn't understand why they'd never mentioned it to me, not even before the fall out, six years ago now, when we were close.

They'd always told me about everything; their holidays, like the romantic trip to Santorini and where they'd lived, like the flat they'd first stayed in when they got married, next door to a favourite restaurant and above a cellist whose playing they loved hearing… and like the properties they owned as investments in Bournemouth and Spain. Nothing else about their will had been a surprise, such as all of their trinkets and Mum's jewellery – I'd seen them before and knew the stories behind each one. And in any case, they'd taken me through their will when I was in the Sixth Form, explaining their assets and everything I would inherit, and what they wanted to go to charity out of their estate.

I'd asked their solicitor, George, for more information about this property and he'd reluctantly revealed that they'd bought the cottage a couple of decades ago and sporadically rented it to locals – so it had been in the family for a long time. He said it was situated in a Hertfordshire village and they'd given instructions for Aunt Fiona to inherit it. That's how I'd found out, I'd overheard her talking to Uncle Jack on the day of my parents' joint funeral. She'd hissed that she didn't want anything to do with the place – that the agency could just carry on looking after it.

I tried to ask her more but she'd turned away from me, crying into Jack's shoulder. All George could tell me was that for some reason my parents hadn't wanted to sell it, that's why they left it to Aunt Fiona instead of instructing him to put it on the market on their passing.

I'd done my research online and found out the cottage was being let by Caroline's agency. I kept putting off any trip to Leafton, but as the summer approached, I now felt strong enough to investigate and rang Caroline on the off-chance, without telling her I was related to the owner, hoping I could take a look-around and hoping my offer of paying for a few weeks would appeal. I'd done my best to persuade her.

I'd turned up a day early. Once the date had been set to finally see this place, I became impatient. And… and it wasn't as if there was anything to keep me in London at the moment. Things at work weren't going well. I hadn't wanted to be away for so many weeks but Katya had insisted. She'd been so accommodating since Aunt Fiona's visit last year. Her gran had passed a few months previously. She'd sold her car to raise the airfare back to Sofia, to pay her respects. She understood. And I'd managed okay at first, organising the funeral, and putting my parents' home in Devon up for sale.

But then questions that had surfaced became bigger and bigger. It was hard living without answers. And Ash and me... six months ago... that confirmed I'd never move forwards without closure.

I'd done my best to adapt to a life without Mum and Dad over the last six years and all this time I'd been working towards showing them, one day, how I could manage and be a success... but now that would never happen, so what was the point? I became distracted and almost made a mistake and coloured a tattoo in the wrong colour. And slowly, over recent months, I'd found my creativity dwindling. It had become harder and harder to feel I was producing exactly the concepts that my clients wanted. I found myself falling back on ideas I'd already used. That wasn't me. I'd always prided myself on coming up with something unique and individual for every appointment.

'The flat remains yours for the moment and I'll keep your job open for when you've sorted yourself out,' Katya had said. 'But you'll have to take unpaid leave, Lizzie, you can't work in this state of mind – it's not safe, or fair on the clients. A change of scenery, away from city life, will do you good.'

I gazed past Ben and Caroline, towards the cottage. I needed this visit to make me understand, to give me a sense of peace. I'd worked so hard to build my life in London. It was all I had. I couldn't lose it.

There were only two things I didn't understand about my parents: why they'd cut themselves off completely after the argument and why they'd kept this place secret. That's why I'd had to visit Leafton, hoping this cottage might provide an answer to both riddles.

'Ms Lockhart? Oh, right. I just didn't expect... Okay... well, you can't be too careful these days.'

'Yes, sorry. I am a day early. I've got a sleeping bag and can spend the night in my car if moving in now isn't convenient.'

She hesitated before reaching into her pocket and passed me the keys. 'I had the electricity reconnected a couple of days ago. Would you like me to show you around inside? Of course, I've had cleaners in but the previous owners and the current one who took over a year ago... none of them have been the most approachable sort, so it's been difficult to progress a discussion about getting repairs done. That's why it's not been rented out regularly over the years. Although the last tenant, an author, was very insistent he wanted to stay there – well a bit like you.' She smiled. 'But apart from that it has had periods of standing empty. You know, there's a lovely little hotel on—'

'No thanks, I'll be fine and this place is perfect,' I said. 'A little dust or a few cracks here and there don't bother me.'

'Good for you,' said Ben and his eyes crinkled.

My mouth curved into a smile.

'I'll contact the agency if I need any help.'

'Right, I'll leave you to it then,' said Caroline as she smoothed down her trousers and turned to go.

'It's so beautiful here,' I said, 'I don't understand why this cottage has been so neglected.'

Caroline paused before facing me again. 'I started working for the agency around twenty years ago, when this place first came onto our books. I'd been told that we were never to contact the owners – the original ones – of Streamside Cottage if there were any issues. Their solicitor was always our point of call. I just assumed they were very busy people, but then... it's probably nothing but...'

'What?'

She leaned in and lowered her voice as if the trees and flowers might spread any gossip. 'The thatched roof caught fire a few months after that. I was still a trainee. It had been a hectic day and I got flustered. There had been a bad storm, you see and lightning hit near the chimney. There was a lot to sort out. The property would have to stand empty for several months whilst the repair work was done. Insurers had to be called... In a rush I accidentally rang the owners. The solicitor drove up from London the very next day and erupted with anger at my mistake.'

George? It didn't sound like him.

'A woman had answered when I rang. I told her who I was and before I could finish, she told me not to ring again before hanging up. She was clearly very upset. The owners, they didn't let the cottage go, despite not wanting anything to do with it. I've never understood why.'

2

Now

A butterfly's story is one of transformation
and new beginnings

Caroline's phone rang and she left as she answered it. Ben readjusted the bag on his shoulder as we walked to the front of the house. 'Sorry about that. Caroline wanted moral support and I didn't want her entering the property on her own in case she ran into trouble.' He smiled. 'She means well but can be a bit... dramatic. Leafton is a small place. Anyway, I live three doors down so if you need anything, feel free to knock.'

I glanced in the distance at a cottage smaller than mine with a lilac door. Lace curtains filled the windows and ceramic dragonflies decorated its front. The small lawn was mowed and the well-stocked borders indicated the owner was an experienced gardener. An ornamental cat slept by the front doorstep and a coral coloured Fiat 500 was parked out the front.

'Your place puts this one to shame.'

'If it's any consolation the tidiness is nothing to do with me. Apparently, some scientist said messiness is a sign of genius so I wouldn't be too worried.'

A comfortable silence fell for a moment. I noticed the freckles on Ben's face, all different shapes.

'There's a decent teashop on the high street called Blossom's Bakes. You must be thirsty after driving all this way.'

I nodded.

'Tell Tim, the owner, that I recommended him.' Ben turned to go. 'You should get a discount.'

I wanted to talk to him for longer. It sounded odd but this Ben made me feel less like a stranger. And I could have stared at that smile all day...

I gave myself a little shake. I barely knew him. The sun must have gone to my head.

I grabbed my small rucksack from the car and gazed back, keen to explore the building. But Ben was right, I was thirsty, and hungry after the drive. I passed the estate agency on the corner and headed right, into the centre of Leafton, afternoon sun scorching my pale skin. The stone cottages had such short front doors, opening straight onto the pavement. I stopped outside Styles by Stacey and looked through the window at the simple pastel decor, a framed sketch of Elvis on the wall, a rotary dial phone on a desk and a rudimentary price list on the window that didn't mention Brazilian blow dries or extensions.

It was as if my journey here had hit a time warp and oddly that was a reassuring thought.

A grey-haired couple walked past, the grandfather

proudly pushing a buggy, the toddler waving a large lollipop at me and I winked. His gran shot me a proud-as-punch look. Further down the street a pensioner with a knotted handkerchief on his head had placed a deckchair outside his front door and was stretched out, watching the world go by, whistling a merry tune as I passed, blissfully unaware he was blocking the way.

I surveyed the handful of locals on the opposite side, with their conservative hair and unsurprising clothes. The scene took me back to my younger years, with the perfect braids and shiny shoes. A teenage girl passed by and we smiled at each other. I crossed the road and reached The Pen Pusher – a stationery shop. Its front was comprised of brown painted wood framing two bay windows – one either side. Set back in the middle was a white door to match the letters painted across the shop's top. Inside, on the left, I could see practical shelves bearing students' essentials. The right couldn't be more different with colourful displays showcasing colourful gift cards.

Next door to that was the teashop. It had a glass door and the front's wood was painted sky blue. To the right of the door an ornamental bicycle with a shopping basket full of flowers was attached to the vertical slats underneath a window. A door entry bell announced my arrival.

An old man in a flat cap and untamed eyebrows looked up from his sandwich and wiped his mouth with the back of his hand before going back to it. He was the only customer apart from a woman gazing out of the front window. I walked to the counter and was hit by the smell of baking bread. Cloths embroidered with pink blossom covered tables. Pale pink walls were decked with framed paintings of wildflower scenes. Cheerful piped music played from a retro wireless to the left of the till. Despite the lack of customers, the floral theme made the room feel full and welcoming.

'Can I help?' asked a man in a beige apron and styled comb-over. 'We close early on Wednesdays, but The Tipsy Duck, two doors down, serves food until three. If you hurry, you'll just get there in time.'

'Oh. Ben the postman recommended you. It's Tim, right?'

'Yes.' He hesitated. 'If that's the case... I suppose one more order won't hurt.' He smiled as my stomach rumbled.

I consulted the chalked menu on the blackboard ahead and ordered a sandwich. There were only two versions of coffee available – with or without milk – and I found the simplicity refreshing. It arrived within minutes in an old-fashioned teacup and the food quickly followed. I sat on the same side as the woman near the window.

I was struck by the remoteness, the unworldliness of Leafton. My parents hadn't much liked the countryside, preferring the city or a sophisticated seaside. In fact, a programme about rural living came on the telly once and it featured a farmhouse next to a stream. I was young and wanted to watch about the chickens and goats but Dad turned it off straightaway, cross that I was so insistent.

On my right the woman was now staring at her companion – a large slice of plain sponge with jam and cream slathered in the middle. The dull frown didn't fit her cheerful yellow patterned top and matching long skirt. Her chin rested on one hand, arm bent at the elbow that pressed against the tablecloth.

She looked at me and gave an almost imperceptible nod. 'Just passing through?'

'Kind of.'

'Take a look at the forest, if you've got time.' She rubbed her forehead and a silver Buddha ring stood out, on her little finger. Around her wrist hung a bracelet with a charm in the shape of a butterfly. My wrist bore the black outline of one with striped wings and long antennae. Katya had done it for me that first year after my fall out with Mum and Dad and a couple of years ago, when watercolour tattooing became really popular, I asked her to add a splash of pink around it. I liked tattoos representing nature whereas ambitious Katya favoured skulls – as a memento mori reminding people that life was short.

Half-heartedly she jabbed the cake with her fork. 'So you're travelling? My son, Will, also enjoys visiting new places and couldn't wait to go inter-railing when he turned eighteen. He's worked as a holiday rep in Rhodes since leaving university.'

'That sounds wonderful. How adventurous.'

Her face brightened as if someone had run it through an Instagram filter. She introduced herself as Trish and pulled the latest postcard out of her bag and tentatively handed it over to me. I turned it over and saw a list of islands. 'The other ones he's been to,' she explained.

Tattooing had turned me into a good listener.

As she talked about her son's escapades abroad her pride should have warmed my heart but, instead, it left me feeling cold. She clearly loved this Will to bits. My parents had loved me too, yet they would never have supported me heading abroad on my own as I became a young woman. I never understood why they needed to keep me so close.

She put down her fork and pushed away the plate. 'Have you come far?'

'From London, it's just a short visit.'

I finished my lunch. Trish sneezed and muttered that her hay fever was bad at the moment. She paid her bill and left. I stacked my plates before taking them up to the counter and Tim wished me a good day and gave me a gap-toothed smile. I went outside. Trish stood by The Pen Pusher holding a cluster of keys.

'It's a great name,' I said. Like the hairdressers, it looked like a longstanding business with its Victorian feel.

'It's stood the test of time since I moved here with my husband.' She selected the right key. 'So, where exactly are you staying?'

'It's past the estate agency, turning left at the top of the high street.'

'I haven't walked that way for a long time,' she said.

'It's called Streamside Cottage.'

The keys fell from Trish's hands. I darted forward to help and handed them to her.

'Silly me,' she muttered.

'Do you know the place?'

She glanced at her watch. 'Sorry, I didn't realise it was so late, I have to go... enjoy your stay.' She entered the shop, closing the door behind her.

3

An open birdcage symbolises independence and freedom

With a last backward glance at The Pen Pusher, I hurried to the end of Leafton high street and the post office within a supermarket. I shivered as a gust of air conditioning blew my way, before picking up a shopping basket and looking for essential items – milk, bread, cheese, coffee, biscuits, air freshener, cleaning products... definitely chocolate. A young woman with a name badge saying Neve sat behind the black conveyor belt. The navy-rimmed glasses looked too big for her delicate frame and pixie face, circled by a short blonde bob.

'What a beautiful tattoo,' she said and stared at the top of my arm.

'Oh, um, thanks... open bird cages are a popular theme.'

'Are you a tattoo artist?'

I nodded.

'That must be such a satisfying job.'

The manager walked past and she and him exchanged glances. His name badge said Alan. From behind, the athletic body contradicted the bald head. He must have been around thirty.

'I only mention it because I love history books,' she continued, in a bright tone, 'and am currently reading about Otzi the Iceman. He was born around three thousand BC and found in an Austrian glacier. He had over sixty tattoos – made by incisions filled with charcoal. They weren't on parts of the body that would show so experts decided the tattoos were therapeutic and not for decoration.'

I couldn't help smiling at her enthusiasm.

'Imagine getting to touch someone who had walked this earth so long ago.' She went on to ask me why I'd become a tattoo artist and how long I'd been doing it. I mumbled a couple of short answers before swiping my card.

'Sorry, I'm always getting told off for too much talking. It's just so lovely to see someone new in the village. You'll call in again?'

My phone ringing meant I couldn't answer and I went over to a nearby chair. I realised it was a wrong number, but then I shouldn't expect Ash to call.

I put the rucksack on my back, glad for the bottle of water in the front pocket, and decided to explore a little more before going back to the cottage. The church was Tudor style surrounded by a well-maintained cemetery. On from that was a tarmac car park with a sign saying Churchgoers Only. I pushed forwards into the forest and a breeze ruffled my hair and caught the perspiration – I never even thought the word *sweat* as Mum had hated it. A small bird flew past with a bluish head and orange chest. The smell of bark and soil accompanied me as I trod on twigs that snapped, and a floor of decomposing leaves. Trees creaked conversations to one another as I headed towards a sunny clearing. I sat on a log and admired toadstools growing up its side like stacked meditation stones. Trees towered around boasting a variety of soft-shaped and pointed leaves and a mouse scuttled into the undergrowth.

I couldn't remember the last time I'd been somewhere so secluded. Ash and I visited London parks but often their signature was noisy ice cream vans, passing traffic and the pounding feet of fitness fanatics. My mind turned back to the loud house clearance van in Devon. It was run on diesel and rock music belted out of it. I'd sold off most of my parents' belongings on the cheap. When I got home, I didn't eat for two days. Instead my stomach was full of memories as I sifted through clothes I recalled them both wearing.

I'd let Aunt Fiona select personal items. She took bits of jewellery, a few ornaments and the photo albums. I took a bottle of perfume and one of aftershave. Sniffing them was the only thing that took me back to happy places, like nights out at the theatre and my proud Mum and Dad attending my Duke of Edinburgh award ceremony. I'd lain in bed, back at the flat, hugging their clothes, rueing the fact they'd died before things had been resolved. It all felt so unfair.

That's the thing with funerals. You're not supposed to speak ill of the dead. It's an unwritten rule. So where was I to go with all the anger? I'd gone to my drawing book – except this time to write not sketch. I scribbled into the night, asking the questions, listing recriminations. I should have gone down to Devon sooner, to sort things out whilst they were still alive. They'd been forty when they'd had me, their careers having always come first, and had been approaching seventy when the accident happened.

That was the worst part of losing the other half of a conflicted relationship. Guilt insidiously crept into your mind. Your self-righteousness couldn't compete with the fact that they'd lost their life. Guilt about the past, guilt about the future – they'd never visit their favourite French restaurant in Chelsea again or meet potential grandchildren.

I reached into my rucksack and pulled out a sketch pad that I always carried with me. I gazed at peeling bark, a pile of soggy leaves, spider webs and spongy moss. A bush caught my eye, punctuated by bright tangerine berries. A rabbit darted behind a tree trunk and a bird flew down a couple of metres away. It had a beautiful fawn speckled chest. I wanted to draw but still something held me back.

Drawing tattoos was less freestyle but the creativity hit came not from transferring to the page exactly what I saw, but instead what was imagined inside the client's head. I felt as if I'd failed at that during recent months.

The sun had begun to set. I would have liked to find the bank opposite the cottage's garden but I wanted to get back before darkness. I walked back past the church and onto the high street and eventually passed the estate agency. Caroline must have been working late. She stood outside, arms folded, smoking. We caught each other's eye and nodded as I continued along the avenue, breathing in the stream's fresh algae smell – a pleasant change from car fumes. Twilight stars had emerged, already distinct without the orange glow of city lights to compete with. A car passed my house and almost blinded me as it turned. Its lights were set to full beam and an animal bolted towards the water.

Gravel felt uneven under my feet as I walked down the drive, my phone's torch highlighting the way. I was just about to get out my key when I noticed a stain on the ground, smeared across the entry. It was red. I bent down and picked a leaf, pressing it against the thick liquid and lifted it to my nose. It smelt metallic – like blood.

4

Three years ago

During World War I women showed support for their men
by getting a tattoo of their regiment

I lay flat on the tartan blanket, head up, chin resting on my hands.

'You could make your staring less obvious,' said Ash and looked sideways at me. His mouth twitched at the corners. 'I'm not the jealous type but you've not paid me two minutes' attention. Come on. Focus please. Sunday is one of our precious days off and it's not often we enjoy a picnic.'

Birds issued warnings and joggers' thumping feet navigated the park's meandering paths. The smell of sun cream wafted over from a nearby family and dogs barked. Overhead an aeroplane momentarily drowned out a toddler's crying. I was listening but I was only seeing one beautiful thing.

Captain Awesome.

'Lizzie!'

I rolled onto my side to face Ash. I reached out a finger and gently tapped the end of his nose.

He grinned. 'It's only a car.'

'Did you say *only*? No, Captain Awesome is so much more than that.' I sat up. So did he. 'I paid the deposit outright myself and after a difficult two and a half years I'm financially independent, I've got a flat of my own and job I love – and now, at last, a car. And that shade of red… it's like tomatoes just before they ripen – distinct yet not too attention-seeking. The boot's a great size and the interior just needed a good clean. And as for the way it drives, I never—'

'Enough already. I get it. Although naming a car is really a step too far, but I'm really proud of you, if not a little annoyed you've got wheels before me.'

Ash had secret dreams of one day owning a Maserati.

'You've been studying and it means a lot that you insisted on paying my first year's road tax, especially as it was out of the money your great-uncle left you.'

'As I told you a hundred times, Deepal wouldn't have had it any other way. He was a practical man. He didn't have much to leave me and my brothers but would have thought that was his money well spent. For some reason he adored you – despite your tattoos.' Ash smiled. 'And what's mine is yours, you know that.' He took my hands. 'We've got something special and solid – a future. I'll finish my postgraduate course next year and then we can really start to make plans. I'll start my career and we'll have a decent joint income. We'll buy an amazing house and enjoy exotic holidays in places like Bali and Dubai...'

One thing that had always attracted me to Ash was his unassuming confidence. He wore it like a cloak visible to everyone but himself. I rubbed my thumbs over his palms. I'd felt drawn to him the very first day we met. It was at university in the art society. I sketched constantly as a child and had begun dabbling with watercolours. Thanks to YouTube videos and gut instinct I taught myself. Before his current postgraduate course Ash had been studying textiles and design. In line with my parents' advice I'd embarked on a business studies degree.

I'd never met anyone like him. Yes, he was good-looking with his muscular frame and dark bed hair and nothing looked sexier than his long, lithe body stretched across a snooker table, but it wasn't just that. Along with his kind nature and infectious laugh, I soon discovered an irresistible quality: Ash could see the real me desperate to break through the conservative appearance.

Within the first week of meeting we'd gone shopping together and he'd taken me to an indoor market.

'Go on, fit on those Doc Martens, I can tell you like them,' he'd encouraged.

He helped me see that I was a grown adult who could follow her own path. This had felt like news at the time.

'That's what my grandparents have taught me,' he'd said, 'they were determined to come to Britain in the sixties. It meant leaving their families behind and people tried to dissuade them – even Deepal, before he changed his mind and moved here too – but despite the upset they embraced their own destinies. I believe that's what we all have to do, otherwise what's the point?'

I gave a shiver as the sky darkened.

'What are you thinking about?' he asked, pulling me back to the present.

'You, us – how lucky I am.' A lump formed in my throat. Ash was the nearest thing I had to family now.

We packed up the sandwiches and drinks as spits of rain turned to torrents. I drove back to my flat and parked around the back of Kismet Tattoos before letting us in. Ash filled a pan with milk whilst I changed into dry clothes. Despite his damp jeans he fell asleep after the hot chocolate, having been studying especially hard lately. He was similar to my parents in that he had high aspirations to be a success and earn money – I was happier with the simple life, but it would be boring if we had everything in common. I took out my drawing pad and a charcoal stick and did my best to catch the determined line of his jaw softened by long eyelashes. By the time he yawned and opened his eyes the portrait was done.

He took the pad, studied the lines and shook his head. 'You've got such talent.'

His hands enveloped my shoulders and turned me around. Gently he massaged, knowing they'd feel stiff after a sketching session. Instinctively he knew the spots that needed a harder rub. Just before finishing he kissed the crook of my neck.

'I love you, Ash Kharal,' I said.

'Enough to get my name tattooed on your arm?'

'Almost,' I whispered.

This had become a private joke. One of the first things

I'd learnt from Katya was that inked lovers' names almost always ended up with laser removal and were to be discouraged where possible.

He went for a shower whilst I tidied away our mugs and then padded back to the front door. On the way in we'd stepped over the post, being too keen to get out of the rain. Bills, junk mail, a postcard from a university friend volunteering abroad... Tension returned to my shoulders as I recognised the handwriting on the front of a white envelope.

I slumped onto the sofa and held it for a few seconds. I lifted it to my nose, disappointed I couldn't detect a familiar scent. It was sterile, just like the two I'd received since we last spoke. Ever efficient it had been posted one week early.

I tossed it to one side and then picked it up again. I thought about putting it straight in the bin but instead reluctantly ran my finger along the seal. I tugged out the card and read the words Happy Birthday on the front, before studying the illustration – a cake candle. It couldn't have been less personal. Rolling my lips together, I opened the card afraid of what I would – or rather wouldn't – find inside. Just like the previous ones it simply said *from Mum and Dad*. They hadn't written my name, nor *Best Wishes*, let alone *Love*.

Why did they keep marking this day? Every May it was like picking a scab. Yet, deep down, once a year those cards fuelled a flicker of hope that my parents wanted to finally meet and make up. I'd planned it in my head. When Ash landed a great job and we got a bigger place, when I was earning more, I'd invite Mum and Dad over, they and

Ash would get on so well. We'd cook them meals from scratch and they'd admire our wallpapering skills and be so impressed.

I had to believe in that.

I'd cried a lot during the first year my parents and I were apart. Night after night I'd lain awake, telling myself I wasn't a bad daughter. Yet those cards meant my parents hadn't abandoned me completely – and I couldn't abandon those cards. I kept them safe, in a box.

Ash appeared in the lounge, a white towel wrapped casually around his waist.

'I didn't realise it was so late,' he said. 'How about I make us an omelette?'

Dad made omelettes using oak-smoked cheese and caramelised onions. They'd turn out rubbery but the flavours outshone any faults. His mum had been a high-end chef in London and this meant he knew how to cook but grew up lacking practice as she'd always commandeer the kitchen.

I missed the conviviality my parents and I used to share, we were never apart then. The first night I ever spent away from them was when I was twelve. A school trip that I'd actually been allowed to go on, once Mum and Dad had thoroughly checked the health and safety aspects. Before then I'd never even been away for a sleepover with a friend.

I breathed in and out, pushing the weight of my memories away.

'Lizzie? Don't tell me, you're still dreaming about that hatchback.'

I met Ash's teasing gaze. 'Yes. Accept it. Captain Awesome's The Man. You're no longer my number one.'

With a flourish he pulled off the towel and let it drop to the floor. 'Are you sure?'

5

Now

*Self-professed catman, Dennis Avner, has had full-body
tattooing and whisker implants*

I put down my rucksack and cast around the ground
with my phone's torch. There, further along the wall,
was a ball of bloodied fur. Poor thing. Perhaps it was a
large rat. I jumped back as it hissed and stripes became
visible. I touched the soft hair and a head lifted up and spat
objection.

'It's okay, I'm not going to hurt you,' I said as my heart
swelled. I didn't need to run my hand down the kitten's back
to see how thin it was. I stood up. It couldn't stay out here,
not injured, with dogs about and it might die with the night
chill. I opened the front door and threw my rucksack inside
the cottage, then stood for a moment, in the darkness. I
switched on the hallway light and immediately I liked what
I saw – the mahogany beams, the solidity of the walls. I
noticed an old cardboard box to the left of the front door

with an empty bottle of cleaning spray in it. I took out the spray, picked the box up and went back outside.

Wishing I had gloves I took a deep breath and gently slid my hands under the kitten's body. It weighed nothing. It spat once more but had no strength to fight. I lay the kitten inside the box which I carried inside with one arm underneath. I walked along the hallway to the kitchen that loomed to the right. It was tidy and clean but dated. I searched for a saucer in the pine cupboards. My luck was in and I placed it into the box and poured in some of the milk I'd been carrying in my rucksack, then I had second thoughts. I knew nothing about cats. Water might have been a better option so I replaced it.

The kitten didn't even raise its head so I'd have to risk the germs or a bite. I dipped my finger in the water and hesitated a moment before pushing it into the mouth.

'Come on, try to have a little, you'll feel better for it.'

The kitten jerked its head and a small tongue licked my skin so I repeated the process several times, trying not to jump as the teeth nipped. I couldn't work out where the bleeding was coming from. Perhaps Ben or his wife knew of a local vet. Leaving the light on I hurried out, walked the three doors down and knocked on the front door. No one answered so I tried again and it opened. Ben stood there yawning in jeans and a t-shirt. He smoothed down his hair looking much younger out of his baggy postman uniform.

'Lizzie? Everything all right?'

'What? Oh, sorry, um, I won't keep you a minute. Have you got a vet's number as I've found an injured kitten outside my house? Maybe a car has knocked it over.'

Ben took a phone out of his back pocket. 'I'd be surprised.

No one races up and down here. It's a cul-de-sac that ends about ten cottages further on.' He scrolled through his contacts. 'We've got a cat. I'm good friends with the vet, he's on my round, let me ring him.'

'It's okay – if you just give me the number I—'

'I don't mind, honestly,' he said. 'Let me find out what the procedure is for emergencies.' He raised an eyebrow and I nodded. Ben came outside in bare feet. I liked that. He pulled the door behind as he made a call. I glanced up the road at the silhouette of the cottage.

'Right, shall we go?' Ben had bobbed back inside to put his shoes on.

'Sorry?'

'Matt, the vet, he's stayed late tonight as one of the patients unexpectedly gave birth. He says if we can get there in twenty minutes, he'll take a look. It's not far.'

'That's very decent of you but I don't want to put you out.'

'No problem. I'll drive as I know the way.' His tone turned this into a question. I nodded again, finding it hard to resist Ben's help, he made everything sound so simple. 'Great, you get the kitten and I'll start the engine.' He walked past a cream coloured Fiat 500 and I wondered who lived with him. Ben opened the door to a hatchback almost as old as mine. After removing the saucer, I carried the cardboard box outside, got in the back of Ben's car and put the box next to me.

As Ben drove dappled moonlight fell on the kitten's face and its gunky eyes. Now and again it meowed. I wasn't sure what to do or how to make it feel better. I carried the box into the vet's whilst Ben parked up. I sat in a tiled waiting room, silent apart from a distant dog's whine. Bags of animal food filled wall shelves, along with manuals and toys to promote pet care. A man in a green overall called us into a treatment room that smelt of disinfectant. He lifted the kitten out of the box as little claws flexed. Matt ran a hand down each limb and opened the mouth, he examined the fur and got out his weighing scales. Eventually he called in a nurse who took it away for a clean-up. He pulled off his latex gloves and suppressed a yawn.

'That's one lucky little fella, there's no serious injury as far as I can tell. He's been mauled and is in shock, probably by a fox. It's a miracle he isn't dead.'

'I saw an animal run off.' He must have been scared by that car's full beam before it could do any real damage.

'We'll check for a microchip but I've no doubt he's a stray. He's so weak because he hasn't eaten for a few days.' He shook his head. 'I don't know what's wrong with some people, he's barely ten weeks old and will only have just been weaned. Whilst he objects to being handled, I've seen worse and think he's used to human contact and that he's recently been abandoned. It happens a lot during kitten season, by owners who haven't bothered getting their cats neutered. His eyes are infected and his back left leg is swollen and sprained. We'll keep him in tonight, get him eating and on antibiotic drops. The nurses will de-flea him.'

'And then what?' asked Ben, concern etched across his face.

'A rescue centre if I can find one that's not full. I'm sorry to say we can't keep him here for long. He'll need plenty of love and attention.'

'Good luck to whoever tries that,' I said and smiled.

Matt shrugged. 'It's usually the feistier ones who need more one-on-one. This chap will have been looked after by his mum and suddenly thrust into the world on his own. That's a proper little fighter you've got there.'

I pictured it again bloodied, outside my house, alone and helpless – despite the spitting. Fate had torn my parents away from me twice. I could relate to it being ejected out into the world on its own, without the experience or confidence to cope. Living with my parents had felt so safe when I was younger. They'd never open the door at night without a chain and set the house alarm even if they were just popping around to a neighbour's. As I got older, I realised the way they lived their lives must have had a lot to do with their work in insurance. For years I'd heard them talk about something called underwriting. Eventually I learnt that it meant assessing and evaluating risk. Suddenly their personalities made sense, it explained why they always looked for the negative – for the things that could go wrong. Opening a door at night? That could have let in a burglar. Not unplugging the switched off fan heater? That might have caused a fire.

Although just occasionally they let their reservations slip, like the time they danced at a party until two in the morning, even though they had work the next day. They'd walked two miles home in the dark, eating take-out kebabs – it was all very unlike their usual healthy hours and diet. Their loud laughter with the babysitter had woken me up and the next morning, despite the tiredness, they looked somehow younger than usual. It was as if I'd glimpsed a hint of different people altogether.

I looked at Ben who cocked his head and stared at me

just before he drove the car onto the main road. I could read what that meant, but Streamside Cottage wasn't where I really lived and pets weren't allowed in my flat above the tattoo parlour.

'No way,' I said to him airily in the car.

'What?' he asked, and shot me a grin. I couldn't help grinning back.

'I've only just landed in Leafton myself. From what Caroline says the cottage isn't one hundred per cent habitable for a human, let alone a vulnerable, ill pet. I'm only here for a month and what with the claws and shedding fur – I'd rather look after a snake.'

'You don't think you'll want to stay longer?'

'No,' I said firmly and looked at him. I gave a shrug. 'Long story.'

Ben didn't push me to explain.

'I can't take him. You should see our Smudge chase other cats out of the garden.' He turned past the estate agency. 'At least give him a name,' he said, the corner of his mouth twitching.

'It's not going to work, you know,' I said, trying to maintain my superior air.

'A name, where's the harm in that?' The false innocence on his freckled face felt so familiar, he was so easy to be around and my stomach fizzed a little.

He pulled up outside his cottage and I got out. 'He's a bit of a devil,' I said over the roof of the car. 'How about Taz?'

'Perfect.'

'What did Matt say?' called a voice from the doorway to Ben's cottage.

Lit by the porch light a slim woman stood in three quarter length denim trousers and a sensible white round-neck t-shirt. She drank out of a floral-patterned mug and I walked around to Ben's side, our hands accidentally brushing as I passed.

Did he feel that heat too?

I headed over to the woman with her mouse hair that was tied back in a ponytail. There was a freshness about her face with the lack of make-up.

'I'm Jill, you must be Lizzie. Ben told me about the kitten. Poor little mite, is it okay? I'd have come out to take a look but was in the bath when you stopped by.'

So, a girlfriend? Wife? She must have been at least ten years older than Ben. A small part of me felt as if it were sinking inside. Katya would approve, her last boyfriend had only just left college.

'They're keeping it in overnight,' said Ben. He stood by Jill. 'Would you like a drink, Lizzie, before you go?'

'Yes, come on in, I'll rustle up biscuits as well. You're surely not sleeping in the cottage after all these months standing empty? Although I noticed a team of cleaners in a few days ago and I must say I love its understated prettiness.' She wrapped an arm around Ben's waist and his body stiffened before he pulled away awkwardly.

'It's fine, thanks. From the little I've seen of the place it's not in a bad state and I might just give it another once-over.'

Jill gazed at me for a second. 'Okay... well Ben can give you a hand if you like, when he finishes tomorrow. I'm at work.'

'Mum, Lizzie may not want that,' he hissed.

'I thought you two were partners or married,' I said before

I could stop myself and couldn't suppress my laughter at Ben's horrified face. Jill joined in.

A black and white cat came out from their hallway and wound its way around her legs. Its pink diamante collar stood out and didn't fit with Jill's modest appearance. Now I could see the likeness between her and Ben. She had freckles, just sprinkled more sparsely, and they both had the same broad nose.

She tilted her head. 'Look... it really doesn't seem right you sleeping up there. Streamside Cottage hasn't been lived in for six months.' Her brow furrowed. 'At least let me give you some blankets although you're really most welcome to sleep on our—'

'Stop fussing,' said Ben in an exasperated voice.

Jill rolled her eyes. 'Well, we're here if you need anything and seeing as you're staying for a few weeks it's my birthday on Friday – we're holding a small party in The Tipsy Duck and you're very welcome to join us,' she said. 'It's always nice to see a new face around here.'

Ben took a visible breath and said, 'Goodnight, Lizzie. Any other problems, you know where we are.'

As I walked up the road a chink of light came out of the lounge of the cottage opposite. An old woman stood looking out before she finished closing the curtains. I put my key in the lock and hovered before stepping back. Moonlight shone attention onto cracks in the woodwork and loose thatching. With a deep breath I let myself in and switched on the lights.

I rubbed my eyes and walked down the narrow hallway and into the kitchen where I sat down for a few moments, hardly taking in my surroundings as tiredness washed over me. Then I went upstairs and did a quick sweep of the rooms and, not bothered about the musty smell, settled on the biggest bed at the front. Before drifting off I peered into the darkness before burrowing into my sleeping bag. I would unpack properly tomorrow and explore. With ease I closed my eyes. The property felt neither too big nor too small, neglected but forgiving, as if it had been waiting for someone to arrive and love it again.

6

Now

It's estimated that 10,000 people got the memorial Manchester bee emblem tattoo after the city's 2017 arena attack

I woke up late, to loud bird song and sunlight streaming through the window. I got out of bed and stretched before making my way down the stairs, standing at the foot of them. The house looked more alive in daylight. To my right, opposite the kitchen, was a drab study, with dark laminate flooring, the perfect room for a snooker table, I imagined Ash saying as I went in. It was empty of furniture and my eyes narrowed as I stared at the wood looking for some kind of sign or clue. Further along, on this side, was a small lounge, its fireplace had a woodburning stove and was set against brickwork. The walls boasted a smooth buttercream wash. I ran my hand along the top of the threadbare beige three-piece suite that looked unappreciated and plain against the different textures of the building. My hands slid between the cushions, unsure why, or what I thought I would find. Nothing.

Next, I ventured across the hallway and into the large kitchen come diner. Warm pine gave this room a welcoming feel, despite a cobweb hanging in the French patio glass doors. It looked as if the agency had arranged for someone to give it a quick clean but it wouldn't have met Mum's standards, she liked everything completely spick and span. There was a pine table with four matching chairs and a welsh dresser. Gently I searched the cupboards. I looked behind the fridge and carefully pulled out the cooker.

The wood beneath my feet creaked in a friendly way as I went back up the narrow, twisting staircase. There was the simple black and white tiled bathroom I'd used briefly last night and three bedrooms, all with low mahogany roof beams. The mattresses tried hard to hide their lumps and I ended my search in the largest where I'd slept. I opened a window to combat the room's stuffiness and looked under the bed. I went over to the wardrobe that was built into the wall. Running my hand into any accessible space, I worked my way from its top to bottom. About to give up I lay on the laminated floor and stretched my arm out, pushing right into the far left, bottom corner. Here the back panel had loosened. My fingers scrabbled against brickwork and touched dusty ground. I was just about to give up when they brushed up against… smooth, pliable card. I gripped it and tugged. It came free. I went over to the window.

An old photo.

I blew away dust. It was a street, the shot focused on

a pavement and an ordinary looking building. A group of youngsters were walking along in flares and platforms – this must have been from the seventies. I squinted, the front door had a huge brass knocker in the shape of a pine cone and to the right was a gold plaque with G & B written on it. The property next to it was half visible – a pub called Best Inn.

I couldn't help feeling disappointed and returned to the kitchen, placing my find on the table, willing the photo to talk to me. As I gazed out onto the back garden a sense of calm and contentment washed over me. A flash of turquoise dipped gracefully into the stream and emerged with a fish in its beak and again I felt a strong urge to sketch – an urge I hadn't felt for such a long time.

I wondered if Taz was eating properly and gaining strength at the vet's. The fridge whirred comfortably as if the cottage enjoyed company and was willing me to stay. I used to feel my first car was a friend. Ash used to chuckle when I called it Captain Awesome and I felt silly until I read an article about how in some parts of Japan there were funerals for inanimate objects because energy, wherever it was, in an item or living being, was seen as being connected, all of it worthy.

I pulled on some clothes and considered looking around the garden again. There wasn't much here after all, and I should head home, back to London. But, despite thinking yesterday that this would only be a quick stay, I now didn't feel quite ready to go.

My phone buzzed and I pulled it out of my pocket. The vet had promised to ring me with an update. I looked at the screen but it was just a Facebook notification about

Katya's most recent design. Maybe I'd wait for him to give me the latest news on the kitten and just nip out now for a sandwich. Then I'd decide what to do.

Humming, I walked into the village and down the high street. The Pen Pusher was closed even though all the other shops had opened up. I entered Blossom's Bakes.

'Hello there, again,' said Tim and he smiled. 'I hear you're staying in Leafton, in Streamside Cottage?' He put down a knife, his comb-over as smooth as the butter he'd been spreading.

'Just for a while.'

Tim talked about the stream whilst he made my sandwich. We both agreed how picturesque it was although he said its innocuous appearance was deceptive as it had quite a strong current and for that reason young children loved playing Pooh Sticks in it.

He passed me an iced bun. 'Have this on me, love – because you're a friend of Ben's.'

Eating the bun, I made my way back to the cottage. Still no word from the vet. I rolled up my sleeves feeling I could make this place feel a little less unloved. I found a hoover and dustpan and brush in the kitchen cupboards. I scrubbed the floors and polished shelves, just to give the cottage a bit of added shine. The team of cleaners hadn't done a bad job but I felt this place deserved to be treated like a home. I washed the windows until they sparkled and as I removed each sign of neglect I felt as if I were getting closer to... I didn't know... some sort of truth.

Long after lunchtime I sank onto a chair in the kitchen and devoured my sandwich. I'd enjoyed a good sleep last night despite having never slept alone in a large property before. My parents wouldn't leave me overnight, not even in the Sixth Form. They worried about hob plates left on and unlocked doors. When I started university, I wore my room key on a piece of string around my neck. Dad said it was a good idea in case I ever lost my bag. A flatmate had laughed and said she used to do that in the lower years of High School, as both her parents worked.

Until my A levels were completed, Mum fitted her work hours around me. I'd been grateful for that when I was little. We'd hold hands walking back and have a juice and cake when we got home. After she died, I'd study mothers and daughters out together shopping, watching them in shops laughing at each other's choices.

I remembered once when Mum seemed to throw caution to the wind. She bought pointed shoes she'd probably never wear and super glittery eyeshadow for me. I loved those glimpses of a more carefree parent that didn't often emerge, like when I dared Dad, once, to do a handstand. The three of us couldn't stop laughing when he toppled over, his chuckles being the loudest of all.

I toured the cottage with the spray can of air freshener I'd bought to eradicate any dank smells. As I walked on them, newly shined floorboards groaned their appreciation. As a thank you the windows gave me an even better view of my new surroundings. I collapsed onto the old sofa and, in return for me airing its cushions, it eased the twinges in my back. With everything really clean now it was easier to imagine the cottage as it deserved to be, with sheets on the beds and colourful cushions brightening the chairs, with attractive lampshades protecting the rooms from light bulbs' glare.

I didn't understand why but I felt protective towards this run-down place.

My oatmeal crockery would fit perfectly into the sunny pine kitchen. I imagined what it would be like to live here if Mum and Dad had left the property to me instead of Aunt Fiona. Various watercolours I'd done over the last few years would add flavour to every wall; not that I considered myself to be an accomplished painter. But that didn't matter. Like my tattoos, those paintings encapsulated a period of my life that I'd always remember, like the first time I'd attempted to capture Ash on canvas. Anyone else might not recognise him but the picture summed up everything that appealed to me, like his bed hair that felt so soft between my fingers and the wide mouth that slanted sexily on the left. I'd added light to the eyes – that's how they looked when he teased. He said he loved it and so did his mum. She had a photo of it on her phone and would show it to her friends.

My phone rang and I pulled my mobile out of my back pocket to see that the veterinary surgery was calling.

Taz had improved but they hadn't managed to find a rescue centre. Financially and space-wise they could only keep him a couple more nights. As it was, the day had been busy and apparently, he'd not had the attention he really needed.

'So what happens then?' I asked.

I heard Matt pause at his end. 'It's one of the hardest parts of my job, putting down healthy animals.'

'But surely…' Just for a second I lost my breath.

'It's the kitten season. The people we're in contact with who foster cats are overrun. If he didn't need so much attention at the moment it might not be so much of a problem – but with those infected eyes he can't go near other cats.'

'Right.'

'If someone could just foster him until his health and weight improves, well, it might be a different story in a couple of weeks, but in his present condition…'

'Can I see him?'

I didn't bother getting changed but jumped in the car and got to the vet's just before five. That gave me an hour. The nurse brought Taz into the treatment room in a cage. He said it was up to me whether I opened it and gave me a towel in case the kitten ended up on my lap. When we were left alone I looked into Taz's eyes. They'd cleared a bit to reveal a bright sea blue. But you've hardly lived yet, have you? I said to him, in my head. Taz gave a small meow as if he'd heard. I opened the cage door. What should I do? Would he like me to stroke his back? I directed my hand towards him and feebly the kitten swiped. His ears went flat.

His head rested on tiny paws. Out of curiosity I persisted and eventually he let my fingers tickle behind his tiny ears. I looked at the towel on my lap. If anyone could bear a few scratches it was someone who'd had several tattoos. As I scooped my hand under his stomach, his head turned and he nipped the side of my hand.

'Bite all you like, Mister, whether you like it or not I'm lifting you out.'

Despite the protests I placed him on the towel. He was still too weak to stand up – and to stand up for himself. I scratched around his cheeks and the soft sensation of fur felt oddly addictive. Gradually the eyes turned to slits.

It was a physical closeness and companionship I'd missed in recent months. Until this moment I didn't realise just how much and it sounded odd but I'd sensed that the cottage felt the same.

My hand moved away and down his back and the scrap of fur relaxed. Instead of using fingertips, I changed to my palm, going near the underbelly and even though his eyes were closed a paw swiped my way. I couldn't help smiling and relaxed into the chair. The nurse glanced through the door's window. Taz and I must have sat like that for half-an-hour. My phone rang but I didn't bother answering it. Every now and again he emitted a faint noise, a kind of vibration and for some reason his purr gave me a sense of achievement.

Matt looked in. 'Just five more minutes, Lizzie. We need to get him settled for the night.' He closed the door. Taz lifted his head.

'Don't look at me like that, I can't take you home, I'm not staying around.'

Taz gave a meow.

Oh crap.

Where could I hygienically keep the litter tray and what if he still had fleas? Now and again I slipped into the old groove of thinking like my parents.

'Right, look… it's just a temporary measure until the vet sorts out something more permanent. Is that absolutely clear?'

A roller purr.

What was I thinking?

I felt another vibration as Matt came back in and saw

George Dolan's name flash on my phone. Mum and Dad's solicitor? What could he want?

'I'll pick him up Saturday, Matt, he can stay with me for a few days.'

Matt didn't say anything as he gently returned Taz to his cage.

'You win,' I said.

'It's not me who's the winner,' he said and gave me a knowing look.

7

A tattoo needle penetrates the skin up to
3000 times a minute

I looked at the clock. Half past six. Ash would be here any minute. He'd gone to visit his eldest brother straight after lectures – or, more pertinently, his niece who'd started primary school last week.

I set up a bowl of crisps, on the low coffee table, along with olives and a bottle of champagne. It wasn't the proper stuff – what my parents used to call cheap fizzy plonk would be a better description. I helped in the tattoo parlour as much as I could, increasingly shadowing Katya. I was time-restricted due to working in a clothes' shop to pay bills. Kismet Tattoos didn't pay me – but then didn't charge for teaching me a craft either. I made the coffees and cleaned up, answered the phone and took appointments. My income was small but I managed.

I sat on the sofa impatient to share my news, yet Ash's key didn't turn in the lock until almost half past seven.

'Sorry I'm late,' he said and threw his light jacket across the sofa's arm. It was designer; he'd been thrilled to be able to afford it in a sale. His presence took my breath away, the physical attraction still felt so strong. I ignored a tiny niggly voice that bobbed up into my mind and questioned how compatible we were long-term, with his yearning for the high life – compared to my jaded view having grown up with the big expectations attached to that lifestyle. He gazed at the wine glasses and half-empty crisp bowl. 'Are we celebrating? You're not pregnant, are you? I don't think I could cope with kids after visiting my niece.'

I held out my hand and pulled him down for a kiss. I breathed in the last traces of his citrus aftershave. He applied it religiously every morning. It was expensive and a present from his brother. Whereas I couldn't remember the last time I'd bought perfume. Perhaps it was the wine but momentarily tears threatened. My parents' silence had lasted eleven months now. Mum had taken me shopping for my first ever scent – we'd visited a fancy department store. It was my sixteenth birthday and we went for afternoon tea afterwards. I'd felt so grown-up even though I was only allowed to wear it on special occasions unlike friends who sprayed theirs on for school. So much had changed in the last year but I bet she still wore her favourite in the black and gold striped bottle.

He collapsed onto the sofa and intertwined his long fingers with mine. My parents had always implied abstinence was the best contraception. However, at university I'd learned to trust my female flatmates' reassurance that the pill and condoms were just as effective.

'Everything okay?' I asked.

'Sure. Now, what's all this about?'

I squeezed his hand. 'Why has the visit to Ismail upset you? Is little Alena okay?'

'Oh nothing. I'll tell you later.'

'Ash?'

He pulled away his fingers and his hands interlocked. 'Ismail and Leah are worried. Alena's been at school a week now and has hardly spoken about how it's going. I like to think I'm her favourite uncle...' He managed a smile. 'So I tried to get her to talk but any question about school was simply answered with a yes or no.'

'Maybe she's finding it hard to make friends.'

'It's worse than that. I got her to do a drawing – with crayons. Well two. We both did them. I said it was a game. First of all we had to each draw a picture of the best thing that had happened since we last saw each other a few weeks ago – hers was a zoo visit, ours was the tour of that new art gallery. Then we did the worst. I drew me talking to my lecturer when he challenged me for handing my essay in late. He looked cross and was shaking a finger. I thought it might prompt something from Alena if she wasn't getting on with her teacher.'

'And did it?'

Ash leant back. 'She drew herself and three other girls. They were bigger and had their hands curled into fists. She'd drawn big tears running down her cheeks. It looks as if she's being bullied. From what I could gather they were jealous of her new trainers that lit up at the heels and it started with that.'

'Oh Ash... at least you got to the bottom of what was the matter. Well done.'

He straightened up. 'It's helped me decide something I've been thinking about for a while. After finishing next year, I want to do a postgraduate course in art therapy. Working with people who are traumatised or ill – helping them deal with their problems through drawing or the use of other textiles.' His eyes lit up as he described the courses he'd researched and the modules on using imagery as a form of psychological expression – and the excitement he felt at helping people use images to gain insight, where words failed. How eventually he dreamed of setting up his own practice, helping people and making good money, the perfect combination for him.

'That's just brilliant. You'll be brilliant. It's perfect.'

Gently he pushed me. 'A lot of it's because of you. Watching you blossom into your real self... it's shown me what a boost of confidence can do; how people can change and become the people they were always meant to be. How they can overcome their past – you are so inspiring.'

I poured wine for him and we clinked our glasses together. 'And today I'm celebrating because of what you've already helped me accomplish. I did my first proper tattoo.' It still didn't seem real. I'd finally inked on skin that didn't belong to me or fruit. I'd always remember this day in September. It was one of those firsts, like the first time Mum took me to an art gallery. Little did she know it would contribute towards me longing for the career I followed now.

I'd had no one else close to tell about those firsts, not even siblings. It didn't matter, said a voice in my head, you aren't doing this for validation. Instead you are fulfilling your destiny. But I'd so wanted a sister or brother, especially as a young child and I remember often playing with my reflection. I'd stand in front of a mirror and pull funny faces and pretend the funny face looking back was another girl.

Ash stopped drinking. 'Wow. On a client?'

'No – I've got a long way before that – but Katya let me do a letter on her sleeve of artwork, there was a small gap. That's how she lets all her apprentices start. I had to do L for Lizzie.'

The dark eyes I loved so much shone. 'Were you scared?'

Yes. I'd been putting it off. A while back Katya said my practise lines, shapes and writing were getting really good and it was time to proceed to the next level, but my parents' voices, in my head, hadn't just disappeared because we'd broken contact. Week by week I'd had to readjust to life without them, after twenty years or so of hearing their advice and talking through the smallest thing. They'd always been there to edit my ideas and point out the risks. Me putting a needle to someone's skin went against everything they taught me in terms of career aspirations, health and safety, in terms of risking being sued and going to court or possibly prison. In terms of being seen as respectable and fitting in.

Although one month ago I had done an outline of a small rose on the inside of my leg, but that didn't feel so risky as drawing something on another person. I loved roses, always had and as a little girl that particular flower covered notebooks and duvet sets and as I got older featured on t-shirts and pendants. I'd always make Mum a handmade card every year for Mother's Day, bearing a big rose on the front.

'Yes, my stomach was in knots, but you know what finally made me do it? You. All this time you've just listened without telling me what to do and suggesting I follow my heart, being so supportive of whatever course of action I've chosen.' I kissed his cheek. 'You're going to make a fantastic therapist.'

'*You've* done it, Lizzie,' he said softly. 'No one else can take the credit.' His lips twitched. 'Does this mean we can finally stop buying up the local greengrocer's?'

'No, I'll still need to do lots of practice on banana and orange peel, unless you'd rather I go to the butcher's for pig skin.'

'The greengrocer's it is and talking of food, I'm going to make tea. My way of saying I'm proud of you, Lizzie.'

We wrapped our arms around each other and kissed before heading over to the kitchen. Ash looked in the fridge and pulled out a tub of yogurt, chicken breast, mushrooms, potatoes and carrots.

'That yogurt's out of date. I meant to bin it,' I said.

Ash took off the lid and inhaled. 'It's fine.'

He peeled carrots without rinsing them and didn't wash the chicken. It was as if the universe had sent me the complete antithesis of my parents.

8

Now

Charms were worn as amulets in ancient times to ward off evil and cure disease

I sat on my sofa, next to Katya. We both drank tea, mine milky, hers black. I was all pastel hair colours and nature whereas Katya was skulls and night-time shades. It felt strange being back at the parlour with me not working here, with Ash not sitting on this sofa, watching his latest Netflix obsession. I eased off my Doc Martens and caught sight of the bracelet I'd had inked on six months after Mum and Dad died and one month after the huge misunderstanding with him. So far, the chain had two charms – a little rose and sketching pencil.

After a phone call with George last night I'd driven back to London to visit his offices. It was only an hour and a half each way and it made sense to pick up some things if I was going to stay in Leafton for a little while longer.

'So why this visit to the solicitor?'

'George was very apologetic. Dad... I can't believe it but he wrote me a letter a few months before he passed. Somehow it ended up in another client's file. George has only just found it. He feels terrible.'

'What's it about?'

'He doesn't know.'

George had offered to post it but I couldn't wait that long. I didn't sleep last night. The prospect of contact with my parents gave me hope. The hope I'd had a couple of times over recent years. Once or twice someone had called and just listened to my voice before hanging up, having withheld their number. My parents didn't know my landline details but by its own definition a miracle didn't need to be logical.

'This is huge,' said Katya and stared at me with sympathy. For years she'd had limited contact with her parents, staying close only to her late gran. Every month she sent back money for their medicines and heating yet they couldn't be happy for their daughter leaving Bulgaria for England. They still had phone calls and she tried to get home for Christmas but they couldn't understand their daughter's aspirations.

I nodded, not knowing what else to say and I chatted about the weather, the traffic jam on the way down, how London had welcomed me back with market traders' cries and car horns and how I hadn't seen a single person in Leafton with a tattoo.

'Your tattoos are pretty – I wonder what the village would make of mine. What's this Leafton like?'

'Olde worlde. Conservative yet friendly. Everyone knows each other. And we're talking basics – there are no branded shops and what's there is limited but I kind of like it. I've met a neighbour, Ben. Well, he's the postman too and has been really friendly.'

Katya raised an eyebrow.

'It's nothing like that!' I put down my drink, pushing away thoughts of Ben's intense eyes and boyish freckles, my cheeks feeling hot. I didn't dare catch her eye. She might work out that Ben was increasingly on my mind. Which was stupid. I wasn't looking for love and he was simply being neighbourly. 'Anyway, I'm only there for a few weeks.'

Katya looked at my luggage.

'I just want the place to look more homely.' For its sake more than mine.

'It's cool. Take as long as you need. You know what that most common and unoriginal of inkings says.'

Carpe Diem.

'We've got a really good freelancer covering your shifts – but there's no one here, now, who understands like you did that a cup of coffee is no good without a biscuit.' Katya smiled and reached out to touch my arm. 'I miss you, Lizzie and can't wait for you to come back to work when… when you're feeling better.' She looked at her watch. 'You'd better get going if you've got to see the solicitor and get back for a party. I'll help you carry everything downstairs before my next client arrives.'

I washed up our mugs without replying.

'Do you want me to come with you and we'll read the letter together?' asked Katya gently as she stood up. 'I can cancel my client.'

A lump swelled in my throat. 'I can't believe it,' I whispered. 'What if Dad's just repeated all the things they said that awful night of Mum's sixtieth party? That I'm a huge disappointment and unbelievably ungrateful and—'

'Then that will say more about him than you.' She held the sides of my arms. 'Look at yourself – you've got a career. You're a caring person – I know your tattoo sessions take so long because you listen to those clients who want their stories to be heard and I remember that first year you shadowed me and all the times you tried to win your parents around. The roses you sent on Mother's Day, hoping your Aunt Fiona would pass them on. That time you mustered enough courage to send them a letter, asking if you could all meet up, even though you knew your note would probably come straight back unopened, which it did.'

Aunt Fiona didn't even write down the address I'd put on the back of that envelope and to find me last year had to Google the parlour.

Katya kissed me on the cheek. 'There's nothing this letter of your dad's can say that will reflect badly on the Lizzie I know.'

Fifty minutes later I was sitting in George's office. I gazed at a framed print ahead – a poster of a mountain with some cheesy quote about reaching your peak. My relationship with my parents had probably reached a peak when I was ten, before I was at high school and exposed to new friends who enjoyed more freedom. At that age I basked in being seen as a good girl, keeping my room tidy and helping Mum weed the garden. Occasionally I wished I could have my best friend over more often but my parents were never keen. Looking back, I realised it was because they'd found out her mum was a recovering alcoholic. It didn't seem to matter to them that she'd been sober for five years or that she was on the school parents' committee.

But I didn't question their reasoning. At that age you think parents can be unfair but not wrong. That's one of the biggest shocks about growing up – realising they have as many weaknesses as everyone else.

'Elizabeth? Lovely to see you. It's been a while.'

George stood over me in his usual uniform – a three-piece suit, walrus moustache and holding a pipe. I followed him into his office, with its wooden panels and sage green wallpaper. George sat at his oak desk littered with family photos. The room would have shouted old-school masculinity were it not for the framed cross-stitch of a floral garland. We'd talked about art during one of my appointments last year. George's grandma had taught him to sew as a small boy and effectively taught him to worry less about the teasing opinions of others. These days he found the cross-stitching to be a perfect stress-buster.

George leant forward and handed over an envelope. 'Once again, huge apologies for the delay.'

Pulse racing, I took it, trying to second-guess what Dad could have written.

'Do you want me to leave you to open it in private?'

I stared at the white paper. My mouth felt dry and a noise in time with my heartbeat whooshed around my ears. I'd worked so hard at trying to pack away my grief, I was scared that this letter would unwrap it. Opening this envelope wasn't just about reading words, it was about opening the past, opening the hurt. And opening a puzzle that now couldn't ever be solved – unless his letter gave me answers.

For a second, I considered asking George to burn it. Instead I stuffed the envelope into my rucksack.

'My head's full...' I looked up. 'Sorry. It's just... I need plenty of headspace before reading this.'

'I completely understand. Ring me if I can help in any way once you've read the contents.'

'Thanks. In fact, there is one thing, George, that I hope you won't mind explaining.'

He put down the pipe.

My cheeks flushed. 'I've visited Streamside Cottage.'

His eyes bulged but he didn't say anything for a moment. Then he got up and paced the room. 'You parents were quite clear – you were never to know about that place or have anything to do with it and I feel bad enough that I confirmed what you heard your aunt say after the funeral. Did she suggest you take a look at it?'

'No, she still won't speak to me and has no idea I'm there. I've rented it for a month,' I blurted out.

He raised his palms in the air. 'Why, Elizabeth? Your parents must have had good reason to keep it secret.' He rubbed his forehead. 'I don't like this... I don't like it at all. I understand your curiosity but some things are best laid to rest.' His voice softened. 'Why put yourself through this?'

'I- I have to, otherwise I'm never going to be able to move forwards.'

He sat down again and squirmed in his chair.

'What I wanted to ask you... when I arrived in Leafton, the estate agent, Caroline, talked of how you turned up, years ago, when the roof had caught fire. Caroline accidentally rang Mum when she shouldn't have and Mum hung up. You were furious and went all that way to make sure it never happened again. What was the big deal?'

George flushed. 'I remember and probably owe this Caroline an apology. I was young and keen. A kind friend of mine recommended me and my rates to your parents and they duly moved their business. I was determined to impress as they were my first big client. When she messed up it reflected badly on me.' He picked up the pipe. 'I don't know why your mother reacted like that – and sorry Elizabeth, I truly wish I could help. Your father had been so adamant that they never wanted to talk of the cottage or speak to anyone from Leafton again. His tone – I've never forgotten – it was full of... foreboding, warning me never, under any circumstances, was that rule to be broken.'

9

*Cosmetic facial tattoos include freckles to give the
appearance of youth*

Back at Streamside Cottage I positioned my cushions on
the sofa and immediately it looked more cheerful. I'd
packed my hammer and nails and spent a while deciding
where to hang my watercolours. Originally the sheets of
paper had been stuck to the walls of my flat with Blu Tack
but Ash had framed the ones he knew I was most proud
of. In the cottage's lounge I hung my favourite – a pigeon
standing in the snow. Those birds' proportions had always
fascinated me, their tiny heads looking as if they still needed
to grow. In the hallway I hung a picture of a squirrel nursing
an acorn between its paws and in the kitchen a frame that
featured the first designs I'd tattooed onto paying clients.

I put fresh sheets on the beds upstairs and set out my
toiletries in the bathroom. In the study downstairs I stored
my tattoo and painting equipment and an array of old gift

cards I'd made. I'd brought a handful of books for shelves in the lounge. Minute by minute the cottage stood taller as it transformed into a home.

Okay. So this was over the top for a property that wasn't mine but I felt a compulsion to give this place the furnishings it deserved. It wasn't as if Aunt Fiona would ever find out. Next to George's office was a small florist's, and on a rusty bracket that was already out front I placed a colourful hanging basket I'd bought.

'That's brightened the place up,' said a voice behind me. 'It looks as if someone is planning to stay for a while after all.'

My pulse raced a little and somehow the day instantly felt a little brighter. Ben. Hair appealingly ruffled. Tight jeans, and a sharp tan shirt that lent itself to his robust frame and accentuated his freckles. He carried an old cat bed and two plastic bowls, a camera swinging on his shoulder.

'These are for you,' he said and handed me the bed and bowls.

'Wow. Forget flowers and chocolates – you really know how to spoil a woman.'

We grinned at each other.

'I've spoken to Matt and spent last night trying to convince Smudge that she could do with a kitten to look after,' he continued. 'To no avail, I'm afraid, so you're stuck with the little devil.'

'These are such a help, thanks. And I'm sure that by the time I leave Taz will have another foster carer or maybe even a permanent owner.'

'You'd better make the most of your last night of freedom.

I came to see if you wanted to come to the party, seeing as you're here.'

There was something about his smile and the way his eyes crinkled that made me feel as if he genuinely wanted me to go. It was hard to resist even though I wouldn't really know anyone there. And it would mean... the letter... I couldn't face opening it yet. A party could be just the distraction I needed.

'I haven't had anything to eat. You get off. I'll try to be as quick as I can.'

'I can wait.' He followed me in, accompanied by a musky aftershave scent. 'Don't worry about eating, there's plenty there, we've pulled out all the stops for the Big Four O.'

'Sounds great, okay, I won't be long. Seeing as you're here... would you mind looking at this kitchen cupboard for me?' I pointed to a pine door. 'I was hoping brute force might straighten the hinge but perhaps you'll have more luck.'

Forty? Ben looked as if he were in his mid-twenties like me, but must have been younger. Jill looked fantastic for her age with her glowing, make-up free skin. Ash's mum always used to say the number of crow's feet she had were directly proportional to her number of sons but then she did have four to worry about.

I left him in the kitchen, had a quick wash and changed into a black lacy knee length dress. I wore it with Doc Martens and pink lipstick to match my hair. I completed the outfit with a narrow diamante nose ring and a determination to push my visit to George out of my mind for the time being. I used to chat to Ash's mum about parenting and she said there were many challenging aspects – colic, weaning, nappy rash, failed exams, bullies at school, restricting computer time, setting fair curfews for nights out… but that there were two things much harder than anything else. The first was accepting your offspring were not you – two of her sons drank alcohol and dated non-Muslims. Secondly, that the time came to trust them to make – and learn from – their own mistakes. My parents had believed the opposite. With their happy successful lives they'd unquestioningly wanted exactly the same for me – a reliable career in finance and dating someone from a similar background. They expected it.

I stared in the bathroom mirror. Yet who was I to criticise? I'd only ever had to look after myself.

I came downstairs, fighting the pull of the letter from Dad. I'd left it on the sofa. It had waited this long to be opened, it could wait a while longer. Ben pointed to the frame of tattoos on the wall of the kitchen as we headed out.

'They're fantastic. Are you a tattoo artist?'

'Yes.'

'That's amazing, Lizzie. I bet it's one of those careers where you never stop learning.'

'So true. A few months ago I learnt all about working with skin that doesn't hold ink well, for example if it's aged or oily. And there are always new trends that clients ask for…' I chatted for a moment, surprised to feel a twinge of inspiration again that I hadn't experienced for a while, back in London, and the desire to sketch a design overwhelmed me.

'Photography's the same. There's still so much I don't know on the technical side about angles and lenses… and then there's the artistic aspects. I've learnt a lot by not trying to chase the perfect shot.' He told me about a project he'd set himself last year, focusing on buildings in Leafton – unusual roofs, different types of doors. He made it sound so interesting and promised to show me the collection of photos.

'Secretly I think my mum's always fancied having a tattoo done,' he said, looking at the frame of tattoos again and he glanced at his watch. 'And talking of her, my life won't be worth living if we're late!'

That's the other thing that struck me about Leafton. People lived near their families whereas my mum and dad had moved away from theirs. I'd barely seen my grandparents on Dad's side before they died and Mum's parents had retired to Provence. Other properties in Leafton must have held secrets passed down through related generations. With such a turnover of tenants, Streamside Cottage might have nothing deep-seated to hide.

I closed the front door behind us, taking one last look at the envelope in the lounge. Ben and I strolled into the village and he briefed me about people going to the party – shop owners, staff from the school, Jill's colleagues and the vicar who'd christened her. He knew most villagers well from his round.

'Apart from the resident who's always waiting to grab the post when I push it through and the Rottweiler owner who encourages his dog to snap at my shoes...' Ben grinned. 'Plus the pensioner who reads tarot cards, she sometimes tells me my fortune.' We turned onto the high street. 'Then there's the hoarder whose son punched me for delivering junk mail...'

'The cute cottages and twee shop names are clearly a distraction from a very disturbing side to the village. I hope my trip here isn't going to end like some horror movie. That friendly expression of yours isn't some mask, is it?'

He pulled a monster face and I couldn't help giving a belly laugh. I hadn't done that for what seemed like months and my stomach gave a big clumsy flip like a gymnast back on the beam after being injured.

'You've never lived out of this area?'

'No. Never felt that pull. I like Leafton. I know everyone and enjoy my job. It doesn't feel like work, really – I speak to so many friends on my round. I travel away sometimes to take photos but I guess I'm kind of old school. Mum could never afford holidays abroad but I wasn't jealous of school friends' stories of Spanish beaches or Greek food. We used to go camping, maybe in Devon or Cornwall. Mum would let me take a friend. I loved rockpooling, and eating fish and chips outside at night, under the stars.' He gave a smile. 'Some might call me boring.'

'I don't think that. I travelled the world with my parents and I'm grateful but it wasn't always fun being in a fancy hotel as an only child, unable to run through corridors or eat meals that didn't involve at least two different sets of knives and forks. Sometimes I'd envy my school mates who stayed in England and spent their summers mucking in on a farm or living amongst nature in a log cabin.'

I'd always thought Ash and my parents would have loved holidaying together, having the same high-end taste when it came to destinations – a taste I didn't share.

We crossed the road and I glanced up at the sign bearing an illustrated dancing duck with a cigar in its mouth. Ben opened the pub's door and side by side we went in. Even though I was a stranger to Leafton, it was the oddest thing but he made me feel as if I kind of belonged.

A well-polished oak bar swept the width of the room with a huge porcelain green and brown duck in the middle, by the till. Oak tables were dotted across the room with matching chairs and a tiny vase with a yellow rose in each one. On the far right were the toilets and a small flat-screen television hung in the far upper corner. By the side window two elderly men sat playing dominoes. Paintings of farm animals hung on the buttercup walls. Dad loved nothing more than spending an evening with board games. He'd seemed as proud as me when I finally beat him at Scrabble, and Monopoly was another favourite. Although one time he threw the board in the air when he lost, paper money and card properties flying everywhere, before he very quickly tidied up. I loved those so occasional, wilder flashes of his sense of humour. Mum would join in the game so long as she could play with the top hat token, in honour of her favourite movie tap dancer, Gene Kelly. Once she put on a movie of his and pretended to tap dance along, eyes closed, hair falling down. She had looked so at peace until the CD jumped and jolted her back to the present where she smoothed down her dress and turned the stereo off.

Jill waved from the left-hand side of the room, next to reserved seating. Her hair hung in carefully crafted curls and a hint of apricot highlighted her lips. She wore jeans and a satin grey blouse with sleeves down to the elbows. The overall effect was modest. Behind her were a small dance floor and a large table inviting us over with plates of food. Hits from the sixties played in the background. On this side of the bar, was a large glass jar that bore a small scribbled sign saying *church repairs donations*. Tim chatted to other men his age. Jill came over.

'Lizzie! So lovely to see you again. I've been secretly fretting no one would turn up. You know what people are like – you tell them the party starts at seven so they don't turn up before half past eight.' She guided me to the table, at the end of which were drinks. 'What would you like?'

I lifted up a glass of wine. Ben was already taking photographs of camera-shy guests.

She lowered her voice. 'Can I just say you look lovely? I wish I had the nerve to be more adventurous with my hair.'

'Thank you!' I pulled a small present out of my bag and a card.

'Lizzie! What a kind gesture. You didn't need to do that.' Carefully she undid the wrapping as if it were as valuable as the gift. She examined the earrings. They were studs, cat faces in oceanic blue and silver, made by Steve. I'd picked them up for myself this morning in Kismet Tattoos but then when I decided to come chanced that Jill might like them.

'Oh my days. Ben, look at these.' She beckoned to him. 'They are just perfect, you thoughtful girl.' Jill opened the card. I'd sketched a neighbour's cat in Finsbury Park a while back – a ginger tom with a black-studded collar and claws that would do more than ladder tights. She looked at the back and saw my name next to the copyright sign. 'Aren't you talented? This will have pride of place on my mantelpiece. Trish, come over here.'

Trish was fully focused on everything Neve was saying, the cashier from my first day. Jill called her name again and finally she turned. Her face looked paler than the other day and concealer had been thickly applied under her eyes. Slowly she approached, her demeanour contrasting the cheerful lime jump suit.

Jill lifted up the card. 'Only yesterday you were saying The Pen Pusher could do with some new gift card stock. Here's your answer.'

Ben shot me an apologetic look. 'Lizzie might not want—'

'Don't be silly,' said Jill. 'It's the perfect solution. You could do local views, I'm sure the villagers would snap them up.'

'I'm only here for a few—'

'Fingers in lots of pies, that's the key to success. It'll give you an excuse to visit Leafton after you've gone back to London.' She beamed and pushed the card into Trish's hands before walking off to greet another arrival.

'Sorry, Lizzie, it wasn't my idea,' Ben mumbled as he followed Jill with his camera.

Trish studied the card. A feather earring hung from one of her ears. 'I do need new stock. My ex-husband used to be good at sourcing cards from local artists that proved popular.'

So she was divorced, yet she'd stayed in Leafton with all the memories of her marriage. Perhaps this village was one of those places that slowly wrapped its arms around you, like the cottage was doing with me.

'He was good on the marketing side and pitched our products to the local school. We ended up supplying them.' Her lips pursed. 'In case no one here has already told you, in time they supplied him with a new wife.'

'I'm so sorry.'

Not a muscle in her face flinched. 'It happened over

twenty years ago. In the end I was glad to see the back of him.' She looked at the card again and her face softened a little. 'Anything to do with nature goes down well. Does it take long to draw something like this?'

'Not at that size but I'm picking up a kitten tomorrow so won't have big chunks of time to spend outside for a few days – not before he's settled. But until I get into the forest you could look at my old stock and I could do scenes of the stream and trees from the back garden. Why don't you come around and—'

'A kitten? So you're going to be here for a while?' she said. 'You... you like living there, then? You feel... safe at night? I mean, it has often stood empty over the last couple of decades.'

I took a deep breath. 'The cottage used to belong to my parents.'

Her cheeks looked even paler than before.

'They died last year. I haven't mentioned that to anyone because it's been hard coming here. Things were difficult between the three of us at the end and...'

Trish bent the card. 'I see. I'm so sorry for your loss.' She'd dropped the card and I picked it up, almost colliding with Ben's chin as I straightened up. Trish had gone.

'Sorry about all that,' he said. 'Jill gets carried away.'

Was it my imagination or was something off with Trish when it came to me or the cottage – or both?

Jill appeared at his shoulder. 'You know I don't like you calling me that.'

Ben rolled his eyes. 'Sorry, Mum.' He caught my eye and smiled as Jill disappeared. 'Never thought I'd be living at home again, but I split up with my girlfriend six months ago and have struggled to find somewhere affordable to rent near my round.' He sighed and gave a lopsided smile. 'I thought a broken engagement might mean a new beginning – instead it seems to have sent me back in time.'

I stared at him and then Jill. 'Gosh, engaged? That makes me feel positively ancient at twenty-six.'

'That's only one year older than me.'

'Oh, sorry... I thought... what with Jill being forty...'

'Mum had me when she was fifteen. My dad didn't stick around.'

'Oh, Ben, that can't have been easy for either of you.'

'No. But then sometimes life isn't – like moving back home at my age. It's as if time has turned back ten years. She opens my mail, answers my phone and looks at my credit card bills. In fact, I'm sorry if I was a bit abrupt yesterday, of course I'm happy to help you tidy up the cottage – it just niggled because Mum offers my services to people as if I'm some kind of cub scout. She doesn't seem to realise I'm a grown-up with a life of my own and a job. Don't get me wrong, I'm grateful for her taking me in but...' He shook his head. 'Lately she's just gone too far. Last night she tried to cut up my pork chop.'

His eyes crinkled and I surprised myself with another belly laugh. Following it I suddenly thought I might cry.

I excused myself and headed to the toilets, quickly, before anyone saw. I sat down in a cubicle and pressed my fingers firmly over my eyes. I hadn't felt such a joyful sensation for so long, not since Mum and Dad... not since Ash...

A noise from the cubicle next door pulled my hands away from my face and I sat up. I knew that sound well from those first nights after my parents and I fell out, when

I'd often leave Ash in bed and sneak into the bathroom. I left the cubicle, washed my hands and dried them on a paper towel. Outside the toilets I waited and was just about to give up when the Ladies' door opened to reveal a vision of lime with a red nose and eyeliner smeared at the edges. Trish made her way through the crowd and disappeared outside.

10

Now

Gregory Paul McLaren is 100% tattooed,
even inside his eyelids

'Hi there... Lizzie, isn't it?'
I turned to see a Hawaiian t-shirt. The young man looked nervously around the room before smiling at me.

'My name's Ryan. I'm Tim's son...' He jerked his head over to the owner of Blossom's Bakes.

I nodded.

'Is it right that you're a tattoo artist?'

'I'm not working at the moment, but yes.'

He swallowed. 'Would you mind following me for a moment?'

I hesitated, but he looked so worried.

'Where are we going?' I asked, still thinking over Trish's sudden departure.

We bobbed outside, into the porch, and he undid his buttons and pulled down the left-hand side of his shirt.

On the top of his shoulder was the black outline of a pineapple.

'Dad will kill me if he finds out, I had it done in Ibiza last month, after a few beers. I'd just finished my A levels. It's… it's pretty cool, right?'

'You were lucky, Ryan. If the artist was unethical enough to ink whilst you were under the influence, they could have used dirty needles.'

His ears turned red. 'But everyone gets tats when they've been drinking.'

'Not the clients where I work.'

Ryan cleared his throat. 'The thing is, it's still itching.'

'Did you follow the aftercare regime properly and avoid going into the pool or sun too soon after you had it done?'

He looked sheepish.

'Just for your peace of mind, Ryan, I'd go to the doctor in case there is an infection. The itching can last for a while, and that's normal, but this does look red. And be more careful next time with where you get one done and how you treat it afterwards.'

He smiled. 'Don't worry. I'm not having another.'

I'd heard that before.

When I was a young girl my and Mum's styles couldn't have been closer. Like children in the fifties, I simply liked to dress like her, unlike my friends who wore glittery clothes bearing slogans about girl power and unicorns. Sometimes, if I held her hand, she'd let me walk up and down her bedroom wearing her heels. I used to think she looked like a princess when she and Dad went out for business dinner dances.

But then the teenage years arrived and I became keen to develop my own look. My parents did take me shopping in stores unsuitable for them but they made strict rules about the length of skirts and tightness of trousers. Mum had read somewhere that skinny jeans caused nerve damage. My friends' parents never seemed as bothered. As I got older, I dreamed of the outside reflecting my true personality, hence the dreamcatcher tattoo down the middle of my back. I got it done to celebrate Katya agreeing to mentor me.

Ryan and I went back inside. Tim had baked an amazing botanical themed cake as Jill worked in a garden centre and the top tier's lawn was made up of a dyed green desiccated coconut. Ben took several different angled shots and then he led me to the buffet where I enjoyed a plate of food. I teased him for the fact that every single thing on his plate was coated in pastry so he insisted I try the sausage rolls and vol-au-vents and I had to admit they were tasty.

Projecting a strong eighties vibe thanks to shoulder pads and sprayed hair, Caroline came over.

'Hello, Ms Lockhart—'

'Please, call me Lizzie.'

Caroline turned to her companion. 'This is my boss, Julie.'

We chatted about the cottage and I asked them both about the buildings in the old photo I found.

'I've never heard of a company called G & B.' Julie shrugged.

'Best Inn used to be a popular restaurant chain years ago,' said Caroline. 'Oh for the days when you could smoke indoors when eating out.'

'Hear, hear,' said Julie.

As the evening came to a close, I sat with Jill, the two of us in front of large slices of the green birthday cake.

'Is Trish okay?' I asked. 'She seemed upset before leaving.'

'She's recently received bad news. I'm not sure exactly what. I must invite her around for a meal next week.' Jill picked up a fork. 'Trish hasn't always had the easiest of times but she's always held things together. She's practically brought Will up on her own but never complained and always offered others a helping hand. I remember babysitters letting me down at the last minute and Trish would always insist Ben go to hers for a sleepover on those occasions.'

'She told me about her husband and his affair.'

'Trish threatened to kick up a fuss in the playground and embarrass the school where his mistress worked, unless he agreed to her divorce terms.'

As guests began to dissipate, we ate the sponge that tasted more traditional than it looked and melted in the mouth.

'Would you mind if I came over to see Taz?' Jill asked when she'd cleared her plate.

'Sure.'

'That'll be the first pet that cottage has ever seen, apart from a couple of clandestine farm animals.'

'Have you ever got to know any of the residents?'

I wondered if she could tell me anything about the history of the cottage and my parents' purchase of it.

'Ben played with various children over the years – that gave me a connection. But it wasn't always occupied so I haven't got that many stories. One couple were avid gardeners. The cottage looked beautiful whilst they lived there. I'd let them know if we had any sales on at the garden centre.'

'Has there ever been any drama?'

'Leafton may not be London but it doesn't mean we're without skirmishes... but talking about it in private might be better.'

I didn't speak much as Jill, Ben and I walked back. Despite his complaints about her before, they linked arms and chatted affectionately. And surely that was normal for families – to have disagreements but get over them? Dad's letter was my very last point of contact with my parents. I thanked Jill and Ben for a lovely evening, waved goodbye and headed indoors, stomach twisting.

11

*Glow-in-the-dark tattoos made from "invisible" UV ink
have become increasingly popular*

Humming, I turned up the festive CD. Katya and Steve
downstairs in the parlour didn't approve of my music
choice but I'd bribed them with our favourite brownies from
the café opposite. I walked over to the window. Shoppers
hurried past bearing bags and stressed out expressions. I'd
moved in just under two months ago, not long after Mum's
birthday celebration. Christmas hours meant I could work
longer shifts in the clothes shop and the manager said there
was a possibility of keeping them after December. Somehow,
I managed to free up enough time to shadow Katya and
pay the rent.

Although me shadowing actual tattooing wasn't exactly
the truth, not yet. I cleaned and topped up the containers
full of surgical grade soap and Dettol. I replenished stocks of
kitchen roll and petroleum jelly. I made drinks, answered the

84

phone and logged appointments. Last week I'd been shown how to sterilise the equipment. But I'd already learnt so much about the different inks and needles and every spare second was spent practising my own designs.

My creative skills had been needed this Christmas. I'd made my own bunting out of paper and painted it green and red before adding a sprinkling of glitter. Ash's older brother gave us fairy lights that his wife hung in the lounge all year round. They'd replaced them and were going to throw these away.

The letter box sounded. Katya was good about sifting my mail if any got mixed up with the parlour's instead of being delivered to my private entrance door around the back. I was on my lunch break and finishing off a painting I was doing for Ash's mum. She didn't celebrate Christmas but had been so welcoming I wanted to show my appreciation. She was very proud of her Pakistani roots so I did some research and found out that the attractive Chukar Partridge was that country's national bird. The family had a large cage that was home to two budgies so I thought something avian would be perfect. I was nervous of showing it to her but Ash had encouraged me.

I put down my brushes at the breakfast bar and wiped my hands. There was one week to go until Christmas and last week – seven days ago precisely – I'd made and sent a card to my parents. I'd thought it best to give them some space after the party and now seemed like a good time to break the silence we both held and give them my new address. I'd wished them a Happy Christmas and suggested meeting up in the New Year. They liked traditional scenes so I'd painted a reindeer in snow.

I'd got used, over the years, to giving them – or rather Mum – some space. Not after arguments – we rarely had those – and never for so long. Just for a few days. Over time I worked out it was usually once a year, in the summer, that she'd become morose and go to bed. Dad would say she'd been working too hard and needed to rest. Occasionally she'd leave all together and, on her own, visit her parents in France but as I became older, tear-stained eyes couldn't hide from my growing awareness. I asked her about it once. It was just after my GCSEs and one warm, sunny day I heard her crying in her room. She said it was nothing for me to worry about. Dad got cross when he found out I'd disturbed her so I concentrated on making it easier for them both by keeping quiet and doing the housework.

Since sending this card I'd been hoping for a reply. Like a child excitedly anticipating Santa on Christmas Eve, I'd wait for the postman to call every day.

'They may need more time,' Ash had said.

What worried me was that time had no deadline.

My heart pounded as I spotted a card on the floor. I picked it up. My stomach lurched.

Return to Sender. It was the card I'd sent. *No longer at this address*.

There had to be some mistake. I checked the address I'd written. Everything was in order.

That left only one alternative. Dare I phone my old home's landline?

A wave of nostalgia hit me as Silent Night rang out. I'd always go to church with Mum and Dad on Christmas Eve, even when I'd started to question whether I believed or not.

The twenty-fifth without my parents would be like holly without ivy, like Christmas Day without the Queen's speech and turkey without stuffing. I picked up my phone and took a deep breath.

What if Mum or Dad actually answered? Would they hang up? Or maybe they'd be glad to speak to me. I'd practised the words so often in my head. *It's me. How are you? It's been a while. I'm sorry about the party. I love you.* I'd lain in bed at night, imagining our first meeting. The hugs and apologies; how we'd fill each other in on the weeks we'd missed of each other's lives.

I stared at my phone and paint-stained fingers. The Chukar Partridge had the most amazing red ring around its eye. I'd wanted a tattooed ring on my finger but Katya wouldn't do it because the ink fades and wears off too quickly on that part of the body. However, I loved the paintbrush she'd agreed to ink down the inside of my left arm, a few weeks before Mum's party when I decided, for sure, that I couldn't spend my life doing business studies; that I was an artist and had to follow my heart.

The idea of my future career had crept up on me slowly since starting at the University of London. No one in the Sixth Form had a tattoo – at least not to my knowledge. But during that first term away I'd seen new friends' tattoos on lower backs, wrists, down legs, across shoulders. They'd fascinated me and each told a story, whether it represented a difficult time the person had got through or simply a fun holiday. Increasingly I thought how amazing it would be to have my art on a permanent, living canvas; commissioned art that would mean so much. I began to create my own designs and show them to friends. By the end of that first year they were asking me to draw their ideas to take to tattoo artists.

'Tattooing isn't real art,' Ash would sometimes say, with a sideways glance.

'As an art form it goes back much further in history than any style you've ever appreciated,' I'd hotly reply, my determination strengthening. 'You can think what you want. I'm not going to stop.'

Ash was clever like that and I often thanked the universe that I'd met him, that very first term.

New trends in the tattoo world were always appearing, such as creating designs made from white or UV ink. Watercolour tattoos were my favourite, perhaps because I also practised the brush-to-paper form of that art. They were less pronounced than traditional tattoos, with subtly merged colours that weren't solid. Their wild aspect appealed because they were freeform. My finger hovered over my parents' number and I studied the old-school paintbrush tattoo on my arm. The brush's handle was slim and dark brown. It was about fifteen centimetres long and ran down to the wrist joint where the inked wood turned into a point of bristles.

If only I could paint a cosy reunion with Mum and Dad and bring the picture to life. Wishing I'd got a drink of water, I pressed dial and sat down on the sofa, the card next to me. The number rang out and I fought the sudden desire to run away and hide under my duvet.

'The number you have dialled has not been recognised. Please check and try again.'

I took the phone away from my ear and looked at it.

I pressed dial once more. The message repeated.

My fingers clutched the edge of the sofa. What if the house had burnt down or they'd lost all their money and the phone had been cut off? I got to my feet and paced up and down. Aunt Fiona. She'd know what was going on. I turned off the music and wandered over to the window. It had started to snow. As a child I'd impatiently wait whilst my parents dressed me in boots, a scarf, hat and gloves. I wouldn't be allowed to sledge down hills on my own but they'd take it in turns to sit behind me. That was more fun anyway as we went quicker. Then we'd rush back home for hot chocolate with marshmallows on top and Mum would run me a bubble bath.

One time, however, they took me ice-skating and I begged them to allow me to have a go on my own. They'd looked at each other and then, reluctantly, Mum let go. I zoomed off, only to topple forwards and graze my face on the ice. My parents never took me ice-skating again.

The winter seemed to be their favourite season, all of us cosily, safely, holed up indoors. One especially cold Christmas – I was about seven – they'd bought me a microwave heatable soft toy. It was a penguin in a green hat. I called it Jimmy Jammy after a friend I once had and carried it around the house the whole time. My parents said it was a silly name for a penguin and made me change it even though I got upset. It didn't make sense. My teddy bear was called Fruity Tooty which I thought was much sillier, but they'd been adamant. It sometimes felt, even then, that I didn't know them entirely, that I couldn't reach them in some way.

My phone rang out.

'Good afternoon,' said a polite voice down the line.

'Hello. Aunt Fiona. It's—'

'Elizabeth.'

'How are you?'

'What do you want?' Her voice was cool. Perhaps it was snowing in Devon as well.

'I- I sent Mum and Dad a Christmas card but it's come back, so I rang the house. What's happened? The number wasn't recognised.'

Silence.

'Aunt Fiona?'

'You've got a nerve.'

'I—'

'It's not that long ago you broke their hearts.'

'They broke mine too,' I said in a small voice.

'Well, yours must be more resilient because they don't want any contact. They've got new mobile numbers as well as a new address.'

'What?'

'They've moved down here, to Devon. Their house wasn't on the market for long. A couple without a sales chain bought it for the asking price.'

Why had they cut themselves off so completely? And that… that was our family home.

'But what if—'

'You can get in touch with me, Elizabeth, but only in an absolute emergency.'

'What about if they ever need to contact me? I can give you my new address and landline number to pass on. I live above Kismet Tattoos now where I work and—'

'They won't.'

'Aunt Fiona. Please. Let's sort this out. This is crazy.'

'It's too late.' She sucked in her breath. 'You've no idea how much you've hurt them, especially your mother.'

'So tell them I called. Surely we can work this out? Please. I don't understand...'

'Your mother deserves to put herself first after too many years of blaming herself.'

'Years? What do you mean?'

The phone went dead. With clumsy fingers I rang again but no one picked up.

12

Now

Some cultures used urine mixed with coal dust to make tattoo ink

It was time. I sat down on the sofa, took a deep breath and opened the envelope. The letter shook slightly as I read Dad's words.

Dear Elizabeth,

Remember when you were little and argued with friends? We always told you to be the bigger person and apologise first – even if the disagreement wasn't necessarily your fault. And if they still wouldn't talk to you or were mean – if they couldn't forget the argument... remember that phrase of ours?

'Those who mind don't matter. Those who matter don't mind,' I whispered.

Oh Elizabeth. You matter more than words can say. And we shouldn't have minded so much about what happened at the party. You reached out afterwards but we didn't reach back. It's just that Anne... she's been through so much. I had to put her first. I hope one day you'll understand when you meet someone who becomes more important than your own happiness.

Last week I had a heart scare and have been put on medication. It's made me realise that anything could happen without warning...

My throat felt as if I'd swallowed broken glass.

Anne misses you as much as me. Last week I caught her drinking warm milk in the middle of the night. Remember her making that for you when you couldn't sleep? She caught my eye and simply said your name.

I'm sorry about the things we said. That boyfriend, Ash – over time I've thought how he seemed like a decent chap, supporting you like that. And we should never have let Aunt Fiona get involved. You were never a disappointment.

When I'm feeling stronger it's time for us to be more open — about so much... There are things we haven't told you which might explain things a little more. What happened in a little village called Leafton and how the Strachans badly affected your mum and... how... how we did a terrible thing... but I'm rambling now. Sorry.

None of this must seem to make sense to you, Elizabeth, but I promise that one day we'll talk about everything and how Leafton is a place we'll never forget.

I'm feeling tired now but I'll write again. These letters are just an insurance policy in case the worst happens before things get sorted. You'll probably never get to read them, but if you do, never doubt, we both love you very, very much.

Dad X

Several times I turned the paper over, scouring both sides. They missed me? They loved me? I *wasn't* a disappointment? *A terrible thing...* what did that mean? A single tear dropped onto the page, diluting my name at the top so that only the letters *beth* were visible. Mum never liked my name being shortened. I rang George who listened, even though it was late, and I pretended I wasn't crying. He had no idea who the Strachans were. I didn't ask him about the *terrible thing*. I don't know why. Those two words scared me. He suggested I rang Aunt Fiona but I knew that was pointless. I'd sent her a card this last Christmas in the hope we could meet and talk things through, six months after the funeral, but just like the card I'd sent my parents six years ago, it came straight back unopened.

I flicked off the light and lay down, sinking into the sofa's cushions that felt as if they were trying to hug me better. The cottage's floorboards creaked goodnight as they contracted after another warm day. I fell into a fitful sleep and dreamed of the younger reflection of me in the mirror. I also dreamt

Dad was still alive and visited. A knocking rapped loudly at the door. I opened it. We hugged and the years of being apart melted away between us.

But the knocking didn't stop. I opened my eyes. What if the funeral had actually been a mistake and Dad was still out there somewhere and he'd come to find me and...? Logic returned as I took my bearings. I picked up the letter that had fallen on the floor, face tight with dried tears. I stumbled into the hallway and opened the front door. Ben wore his postman uniform and his bag was empty.

'What's the time?' I mumbled.

'Midday. You must have partied harder than I thought. Do you want me to drive you to pick up Taz? That way you could sit in the back with his carrier on the way back and... Is everything okay?'

I rolled my lips together.

'I don't know about you,' he said brightly, 'but I'm parched. How about I make us both a cuppa?'

I went back to the sofa. Ten minutes later he appeared with two mugs and the remains of a packet of biscuits. He put them down on the coffee table and sat next to me. Just his presence made me feel a little better.

'What's happened?'

The tea tasted sweet and hot.

'Is there anything I can do to help?'

I shook my head.

'Are you unwell? Shall I call the doctor? You look—'

'Like crap?'

'You don't look yourself, and certainly not in the frame of mind to pick up a kitten. I know Taz is spirited but you don't want to frighten him.'

I smiled and straight after my eyes filled again.

I shoved the letter into his hands. 'My parents used to own this cottage. They both died last year. I got this from my solicitor yesterday. Dad wrote it not long before he passed away.' I told Ben about the day they went swimming, how a freak current had carried them out to sea and neither had survived. 'We hadn't been on good terms, my family... everything was messed up. I never knew about this place but this letter shows that Dad wanted to explain why it was kept a secret.'

'Lizzie, I'm so sorry.' He rubbed my arm and then read the letter. 'If it's any help Strachan is a particularly Scottish surname – a colleague is called that and is very proud of his roots.'

I thought hard. 'Mum spoke of a good Scottish friend she made at university but her surname was McDonald. I remember because she used to get teased about being called the same as the burger restaurant.'

'Did your parents ever live here?'

'No, it was just part of their investment portfolio. Their will instructed that the other properties be sold off, some of the money going to me, some to charity. This place was left to my Aunt Fiona but from what I can tell, she didn't want it.' I shrugged. 'It's all so confusing.'

He read the letter again. 'And this terrible thing...?'

I shrugged.

'I don't know what to say.' He shook his head. 'But from personal experience I know that family life is rarely straightforward. My dad might have stayed with Mum but didn't thanks to... complications caused by other people.

Dealing with that used to be hard enough. I can't imagine what you must be going through.'

'They died before I had a chance to apologise, face to face... before I could tell *them* that yes...' The words choked. 'That I still loved them too. This letter... finally it sounds as if they were ready to meet and—'

'Who knows?' A hard look crossed his face. 'That was only your dad talking. Maybe things would have worked out, maybe they wouldn't. There's no point fretting about what might have been, believe me, I've been there and it screws you up.' He handed the letter back and ate a biscuit whole. Vigorously he chewed before knocking back his drink. 'You get ready. I'll rustle up some lunch. Then you and me can go and get Taz.'

'But—'

'No arguments, Lizzie. Humour me. It's sheer joy to boss someone else around when most of the time it's my mother doing that to me.'

I used my arm as a handkerchief. 'I meant to find a pet shop this morning. I still haven't got in a litter tray or kitten food.'

'The big out of town supermarket has got a pets section. We'll drop in on the way. Not much smells worse than cat urine in your carpet. Right, get going.'

I sniffed and went to get up but before I could he drew me into his arms and hugged me tight. I relaxed into his body and sobbed quietly feeling somehow safe to do that in his arms – safe in a way I hadn't for so long. It didn't make sense; Ben and I didn't know each other well, but he felt solid, strong and yet so gentle as he ran a hand over my hair. It reminded me of how it used to feel when I was little and Mum and Dad would hug everything better. I didn't want to let go.

Eventually I pulled away slightly. I liked how he'd let me decide when the closeness was over. We stared into each other's eyes, his full of concern; I noticed the especially dark freckle at the corner of his lips. For a second, I wanted to press my lips against his and lose myself, forget my life that had become such a mess. My pulse raced as I felt a magnetic pull.

A cold shower was exactly what I needed and I came back down in fifteen, the water having diluted my sense of shock. I'd grabbed a t-shirt and jeans and pulled a brush through my hair before searching for a notebook and pen. I sat at the table thinking how much the cottage must appreciate the delicious smell of frying eggs, after so many months of the kitchen standing bare.

'It's time I got practical. There's clearly a story behind Streamside Cottage so I'm going to investigate.' I sipped the fresh cup of tea Ben put in front of me. 'First of all, I'm going to need to interview Jill.'

Ben found cutlery and placed it on the table. He put down two plates of eggs on toast and sat opposite. Everything about him was so easy.

'Thanks. This looks great. Now, at the party your mum hinted that there's been plenty of skirmishes here – her words – over the years.' I dug my knife into one of the eggs. A rich yellow puddle pooled across the plate. I took a mouthful and reached for the pen. I opened the notebook. 'Then there was the fire Caroline told me about and...' Furiously I scribbled.

Ben's large hand covered mine. 'Eat, Lizzie. All that can wait a few minutes.'

I stared at his arm as my hand tingled. 'Your freckles… they're incredible, the different shapes and shades of colour…'

'Are you having a laugh?' Ben took away his hand.

'Of course not. Sorry, I didn't mean to…'

He paused. 'It's okay. Guess I'm a bit sensitive, I've never thought about them as being attractive. Red hair and freckles are made fun of at school. Teenagers and all that.'

'I think they're lovely.'

Ben gave a tentative smile and our chat moved onto the party. I mentioned Trish's early departure. He didn't know what her bad news was.

'What's the story with Neve?' I cut the toast, butter dripping onto the plate, each mouthful feeding my determination to find out what my dad had been trying to say. 'She was with someone at the pub – I think I saw him at the supermarket where she works. Have they been dating long?'

'That's Alan – he's the manager there. Neve was due to go to university a couple of years ago but her dad lost his job, so she took a gap year to help out with bills until he found his feet. She never left in the end.'

We chatted about other shops in the village until I finished and pushed away my plate. I ran a hand over my notebook. 'What can *you* tell me about Streamside Cottage?'

Ben picked up his mug with both hands and slowly drank from it. 'It's old – about two hundred years. You'd have to check the deeds.'

'Good point. I've got a box filled with all their paperwork, although it's back at my flat. I had no idea it had been built such a long time ago.'

'It's bigger and been around longer than the rest in our road. A bomb landed during the Second World War and decimated the area. This was the only building left standing, although there are some cottages from the same era if you carry on over the junction at the top of the high street. I'd bought one with my last girlfriend but when we split up neither of us could afford the mortgage on our own and that's why I had to move back here, not that Mum's happy about taking rent money. I insist even though she was left our cottage by my great aunt.'

'It must have been hard – buying your dream home and having to let it go.'

'Not really. When we decided to sell, I was surprised at how relieved I felt. It had stretched us to buy it and I hadn't been sure, but my girlfriend had her heart set on a detached property with a conservatory. My needs are more basic – in fact the smaller the property, the better. Housework isn't my forte.'

I smiled.

'Looking back, we rushed into things. It'll be a while before I let someone new into my life.'

For some reason that comment made my stomach knot. Could Ben sense that I'd felt like kissing him before? He must have been making it absolutely clear he wasn't interested in anything romantic. Which was fine, of course, I wasn't ready either.

'Do you think I could drop in tomorrow to see your mum?'

'She'd love that. In fact, I know she's dying to see Taz.

How about I ask her to drop around to yours after she's finished her morning shift at the garden centre? And talking of the kitten, we'd better go and pick him up.' He put our dishes in the sink. 'Prepare to have your life turned upside down.'

13

Now

A Commemorative Tattoo is made with ink containing a loved one's cremation ashes

I went over, bent down and attempted to tickle Taz's head as the doorbell rang. He swiped. We'd both eaten and he'd slept. Matt had given me ointment to administer instead of the fiddly eye drops used by the nurse. I'd placed the litter tray near the French patio doors and his bed on the tiled floor, the other side of the kitchen by the Welsh dresser. Ben had encouraged me to buy a stick with a feather on the end. Neither me nor Taz were sure what to do with it.

The doorbell rang again and I shut the kitchen door behind me before answering it. Sunshine streamed in and wildflowers in the long grass that needed mowing politely tipped their heads in the breeze. I caught sight of the silver and turquoise cat earrings Steve had made. Jill came in.

She brushed soil off her shorts and t-shirt. 'I would have changed but couldn't wait to meet your house guest.'

'He's not particularly friendly.'

She closed the door and slipped off her dirty trainers. We went in the kitchen.

'Oh my goodness.' She stood still. 'Aren't you adorable?'

Taz looked up at her high voice.

'Yes you are.' She sat on the floor and lay down on one side. I liked how relaxed Jill was. She tickled under his chin. Eventually Taz closed his eyes.

'That's the first time he's purred since Ben dropped us off yesterday. It seemed much easier when he was at the vet's.'

Jill sat up and went to lift him.

'Be careful, he might—'

'Aren't you so beautiful?' She kissed Taz on the head and held him to her chest.

'He wouldn't let me do that.'

'Did you try?'

'Yes. Well… I mean… I'm not used to animals.' I sat down at the table again. 'To be honest I feel completely out of my depth. I've spent the whole morning in here to keep him company but he just sits, eats a bit and then uses the litter tray. How do I know if I'm doing the right thing?'

'What do your instincts tell you?'

'To give him physical contact but every time I go near—'

'Show me.' Jill put Taz back in his basket.

Like before, I went over and started to bend down.

'That's your first mistake,' said Jill. 'Cats' instincts tell them to beware of anything in the air as it could be a flying predator. So your hand coming down from a height is a threat. It's why many cats don't like balloons. You need to get down to his level.'

I sat crossed-legged on the tiles and gingerly held out my hand.

'And don't show you are nervous, he'll pick up on that and it will put him on edge. Try to look confident, even if you don't feel it. Go on, just stroke his head.'

I couldn't help smiling to myself as Ben's hard done by face popped into my head, him talking about Jill being bossy.

Without hesitating I tickled his cheek.

'Talk to him. Tell him how handsome he is.'

'Who's a gorgeous boy?' I looked up. 'I feel stupid,' I whispered.

'The fact that you just whispered proves you know he's taking in every word.'

'Are you Taz? Are you extremely clever as well as handsome?' The kitten tilted his head so that I could reach the right tickle spot.

'Oh bless. He really is striking,' said Jill. 'Just look at those stripes and the M above his eyes. He's going to be a right heartbreaker.'

I took a breath and lifted him up.

'Support his bottom and back legs. Now use the other hand to stroke.'

Taz's heart beat rapidly against my chest. Instinctively I buried my face in his fur. A fresh and woody smell filled my nostrils as his paws kneaded my body.

'That's because he's missing mum,' said Jill. 'Moving paws like that – it's part of the suckling process.'

'Is that bad?'

'Adult cats do it as well. I think it's a comfort thing.'

I breathed in his scent and a memory flashed into my

head. Jimmy Jammy. I was with my friend Jimmy Jammy. Why did I call him that? We must have been close for me to name my toy penguin after him. We'd just started school I think – the memory was vague. He was holding a ginger cat and we were in a garden. It was a large one for London but then my parents were high-end – we only lived in exclusive areas. I remember giggling. We must have smuggled it into my bedroom because my next memory was another one of me playing with my reflection that was now holding the cat.

Remembering the reflection always made me feel happy. It made me feel as if I wasn't alone – or hadn't been, at least, as a child. She felt like family.

'How about I make you a cup of tea and chicken and stuffing sandwich?' I'd made a Sunday roast. It felt different living here. Back in London I'd happily have grabbed a toastie but this kitchen deserved to be filled with the soundtrack of cooking – the creak of the oven door, the boiling of water, the chopping of knives... all that was missing from the family vibe was Dad's out-of-tune whistling.

Living here with a garden, with space and two floors reminded me of my earlier London childhood. They were cheerful times, filled with visits to museums and parks. On days out I'd walk in between my parents, one of my hands belonging to each, arms swinging timelessly to and fro like a clock's pendulum. I remember Dad stealing Mum's scarf once, on a cold day. She'd chased after him screaming. They both returned out of breath and looked more sparkly than they ever looked day to day. It was as if I'd glimpsed how, perhaps, they'd been as a young couple. Carefree. Spontaneous. The opposite of how they'd brought me up.

'That sounds delicious, thank you.' Jill stared at the

framed tattoo designs on the wall and then sat at the table. With a bobble from her wrist she tied back her loose hair before reaching out her arms and taking Taz.

'Oh.' I'd expected her to sit back down on the floor near his bed.

'What's wrong?' said Jill.

'Nothing… it's just… don't take this the wrong way but isn't it unhygienic to have him near where we eat?'

'Lizzie, no love. Obviously you'd have to wipe down the table if he trod on it, but he's been defleaed, right? And he's not going outside yet. This little man is as clean as you and me. Once you're a hundred per cent happy he's not going to have accidents you could let him into the other rooms – as long as they are suitable without wires he might chew on or surfaces he might scratch and ruin. A plant sprayer filled with water lets a cat know pretty effectively if they are flexing their claws somewhere you'd rather they didn't.'

Heat flooded my neck as I unwrapped a loaf of bread. 'Mum and Dad… pets… they said there were too many health risks.'

When I was small, as an only child I'd longed for the company a cat or dog might provide but my parents talked about bites, about moulted fur and allergies. Finally, they compromised and allowed me a goldfish as long as I wore long rubber gloves when I cleaned it out, having read-up about the possible transmission of bacteria.

Ash had opened my eyes to the irrationality of my parents' concerns by just being his laid-back self. He used public toilets, shook hands with homeless people and always trusted me to get back safely if I went out for a girls' night.

'Ben told me that your parents had passed. I'm sorry for your loss.' Taz stretched upwards and rested his neck by Jill's neck. 'What did they tell you about Leafton?'

'Nothing. I didn't know about this place until they died, or that they left it to my aunt. I only found out about it by accident.'

'Really? Why was that?'

'I have no idea. I don't know if Ben told you – my parents and I… we hadn't talked for several years. But I've just found out Dad left me a letter and in it he talked about a secret he wished he'd told me connected to here. I came here to find out more about my parents and that letter confirms I did the right thing.'

Whilst she ate, Taz sat on my lap and I wrote in my notebook as Jill spoke about previous residents. Eventually the paws ended their pumping action and his curled-up body relaxed. Every now and again I stroked him and challenged myself to carry on eating biscuits without worrying about washing my fingers. That's what life had been like during the first years of leaving home. I'd observe other students and challenge myself to follow behaviours my parents would have considered full of risk. It never ceased to surprise me how unpleasant consequences rarely followed. Like leaving my bedroom window slightly ajar at night – no one broke in. Like walking in the dark on my own, as long as it wasn't too late. In the winter, right up to the Sixth Form, Mum or Dad would drive me in the car rather than let me go it alone after sunset, even if it wasn't teatime yet.

At university I learned to assess my own risks in a way I hadn't been allowed to before.

I became my own underwriter.

It felt powerful.

'Some tenants used the place as a stopgap until the homes they'd actually bought in the area became available. One lovely retired couple were waiting for their bungalow to be built.' Jill swallowed the last mouthful of her sandwich. 'Whereas the longest staying residents, let's see, it must have been around 2010, the Jones family, they lived here for about three years, with twin sons at primary school, cheeky little things. They always seemed to know when I was baking and would knock at the door for a cake.' Jill stroked Taz. 'I missed them when they left.'

'Why did they go?'

'It was all rather odd, they just up and left one night. A rumour did go around that he'd been sacked for laundering money. Just goes to show appearances can be deceptive. Another family did the same, years before, when Ben had just finished the reception year. They must have been some of your parents' first tenants. The mum and dad spent a lot of time at work. They had two children and left Leafton without saying goodbye. It was such a shame because Ben got on really well with their kids.'

'Did they have a Scottish surname by any chance?'

'I can't clearly remember.'

Two children. A family of four. That had always seemed perfect to me. It seemed balanced, symmetrical – as nature should be, according to da Vinci's drawings. Three was an odd number, there would always be someone left out, if the child was closer to Dad or closer to Mum or if the parents put each other first... It never occurred to me, when I was little, that parents might consciously decide to have just one child. I found it hard to believe a friend who lapped up the attention of both her parents and prayed she'd never have a sibling.

'An ambulance turned up late one afternoon,' continued Jill. 'The family disappeared the next morning. Professional packers emptied the house of their things over the following days.'

'What were the rumours about that?'

'None, it was just really strange – like in the movies, as if a secret organisation had been paid to go in and remove all traces of some crime.' Jill drained her mug. 'Unlike Carrie and Tyler who were a friendly pair of youngsters, but I always wondered how they could afford the rent. Free-spirited types they were, totally against modern living and earning a pay cheque. They grew their own vegetables and wore home-made clothes. A police car turned up one day. Turns out they'd been growing marihuana on a big scale and had set up grow rooms upstairs. I always assumed the blackout curtains were because they didn't sleep well.'

Page by page my notebook filled.

'I can't really remember the others clearly, there were so many periods when the place just stood empty – apart from the last one, he left about eight months ago, Frederick Fitzgerald, a good-looking guy in his forties. You might have heard of him? He's a well-known thriller author. He rents out different properties to write each book. His bestselling novel was behind that movie Talking Doors.'

'The cottage must find me very boring – I've not brought any drama, I'm not famous,' I said and smiled.

'He chose Streamside Cottage because he'd done research and believed it was haunted.'

I sat upright. 'Really?'

'His new manuscript was a ghost story. It's all nonsense, of course. I think I'd have noticed if ghosts lived three doors up.' She smiled. 'But I don't mean to scare you.'

I smiled back, liking Jill more and more each day. I imagined, just for one second, what it would be like to have her as a neighbour, to move to Leafton, to become part of a small community.

'Don't worry, my job requires a pretty thick skin – no pun intended. A not inconsiderable part of my week is spent creating images of skulls, snakes or zombies. And I've inked with ashes mixed in, to comfort bereaved clients.' Jill grimaced as I explained. I'd also slept with my parents' ashes in the flat. After the funeral I told Aunt Fiona I'd keep them for the moment. Everything had happened so quickly and I couldn't decide what would be for the best... to bury them at a crematorium with no family connections or to think of somewhere more meaningful.

Aunt Fiona's brusque tone told me she'd rather things be done properly – a burial, a memorial plaque, their names written into a remembrance book but her fight had all gone by the time I was ready to leave. I'd driven down a couple of weeks later to fetch the nondescript wooden box. For the first few weeks I kept it by my bed.

For a long time, late at night I'd talk to it and chat about the good times we'd had, like holidays abroad, the luminous tangerine flamenco dress Mum bought from Madrid and the time Dad got picked to go up on stage with a Spanish dancer and she announced to the audience that he had more hair on his legs than his head. The anecdotes we'd told over and over through the years, they'd glued us together.

I'd tell them how I'd progressed with my career and the

satisfaction I got from one of my tattoos making a difference to a client who'd been bereaved or suffered a romantic let-down. What a good person Ash was and how they'd love his mum's cooking. I asked about their lives too, imagining the beach walks and cream teas they must have enjoyed since moving to Devon.

I'd researched the different things people did with ashes. Some had them painted into artistic paper weights or made into jewellery. They could be used to stuff teddies or produce a late loved one's portrait.

Of course I could have them put into tattoo ink – but that would have felt like an act of vengeance.

They were still at the flat, on top of a wardrobe.

I'd jokingly asked my parents one day, whether they would want to be cremated or buried – I teased them about approaching retirement age. Dad snapped that it wasn't a laughing matter and that my humour was in bad taste. He made me apologise. Mum left the room. She always took great pride in her looks – my comment must have been an unwelcome reminder that they were getting older.

'It's hard to imagine feeling frightened here. I've never felt anything but welcome and safe.'

'Well, Frederick upped and left suddenly one October evening – he'd talked about how the place was evil and stopped him from sleeping.' She snorted.

Gently I ran the base of my foot to and fro across the tiled floor as if hoping to erase the insult.

'Thanks, Jill, this is so useful. Finding out all these secrets, it gives me hope that Mum and Dad did have something to tell me about this place that might give our argument some sort of sense.'

'I'm sorry to hear you didn't get on in the end.' Her voice sounded full. 'I really feel for you.'

Jill had her own story to tell.

'How about a fresh cup of tea?' I asked.

'Yes. Yes please.' She held Taz until her drink was ready. Afraid of spilling the hot liquid on him she put him back in his bed. When she sat back down, she banged her chair against the table. Quickly she picked up the mug to avoid a spillage but hadn't got a proper grip. It slipped and boiling liquid tipped down her chest and onto the chair's seat, in between her legs.

She slammed the mug back onto the table.

'Take your t-shirt off quickly. Come over to the sink, we need to get cold water on your skin.'

Tears in her eyes, Jill hesitated for a moment before tearing it off. I already had the cold tap running. She splashed water down herself and eventually she dried off with a clean tea towel. I fetched a t-shirt of mine to wear and couldn't help gawping as I returned to the kitchen and for the first time got a proper look at her underwear. She was wearing a silky leopard print bra with a diamante stud in the cleavage. Her dress sense was normally so... plain – almost mumsy in comparison. Blushing she slipped my top over her head and sat down.

'And now you've seen my leopard print,' she mumbled and gave an awkward smile. I went to make her another drink when she caught my arm. 'I just wanted to say, I wish I'd been more like you, over the years – dressing exactly how I wanted.'

'What's held you back?' I asked.

'People can be judgemental.'

'True but that applies to everything, doesn't it? Where you live, what your job is. Would you give up working at the garden centre if someone disapproved?'

'No, but appearance matters, especially if you're pregnant at fifteen...' Her hand fell away. 'I got called names – names no young girl should ever get called – because of the way I dressed. People sneered at me as if I had no morals. I was determined no one would ever have reason to use those words in front of my child so I toned *me* right down.'

'How did you used to look?'

'I dyed my hair dark red at fourteen. Mum and Dad went mad. Then I went through a Gothic stage, with lacy black clothes and eyeliner as thick as lipstick to match. When I got pregnant, I was made to feel as if somehow, my appearance was to blame. I know I should have been more careful but I was in love. Andy didn't care what I wore. We got together because of a similar sense of humour and mutual love of rock music. I- I didn't really understand what was happening until it was too late. His parents blamed me and said he was a decent young man and that I was a bad influence.'

'How did your Mum and Dad react?'

She bit her lip.

I got out a bar of chocolate I hadn't finished and offered her a chunk. Jill talked to Taz. Smudge's glamorous pink diamante collar now made more sense. Our chat eventually turned back to the cottage.

'Have you any idea who owned this place before my parents?'

'I moved here to live with my aunt when I got pregnant. It's about ten miles from where I grew up. She had lots of room and lived on her own. My mum and dad had two other children to look after.' Jill spoke of how the first year or two, when Ben had been a baby, were a bit of a blur. 'The tenants who left mysteriously in the ambulance are the first people I knew connected to that place and I only remember them because of Ben's relationship with their children. My aunt would know but passed over five years ago.'

Jill suggested asking the neighbours, although she pointed out that several of the elderly ones had died in recent years and many of the new owners hadn't been here long.

'It might be more productive to have a chat with Neve, she's a keen member of the local history society.'

'Great idea, thanks.'

'Frederick told her about the so-called haunting one night in The Tipsy Duck. I was there. Alan called him a nutter. Frederick ended up shouting and poor Neve was so embarrassed. Oh, and I forgot.' She leant forwards. 'Trish dated the author for a while.'

'Really? What happened?'

'No one seems to know. Trish seemed so happy at first but the longer she saw him the more miserable she became. I thought she was finally getting over it but at my party on Friday she was stuck in the old gloom. It happened to her once before, years ago.'

'What, the depression?'

'Yes, just after her divorce, around the time your parents would have bought this place, from what you say.'

'When she mentioned her husband in the teashop last week, I got the impression that the break-up of her marriage had been a relief.'

'You'd have thought so, but no, she was devastated. Her low mood lasted for months. I'd invite her around for coffee but she just wouldn't come.' Jill spoke of how Trish used to be so cheerful, involved in charity events and pub quizzes, always involved with the school and happy to help fellow mums out with childcare. 'She looked after Ben more than once. Slowly, as years passed, she got back to being her old self. In fact she became friends with those tenants, Carrie and Tyler – they introduced her to Buddhism.' Jill shrugged. 'But something happened with Frederick to bring back the sadness. The cheerful, jolly Trish has disappeared to leave a different person altogether.'

14

Now

Many tattoo inks are made out of the soot ashes from burnt animal bones hence the recent emergence of vegan tattoo parlours

Thursday, four days on and Taz and I had achieved something of a routine. We played after breakfast and then he'd nap whilst I continued to fix up the cottage and do my online research into Leafton. His eyes had almost completely cleared and his appetite grew. He didn't limp anymore. Taz would nap again in the afternoon which was when I'd go out. In the evening I'd let him sit on my lap, in the lounge, whilst I watched television. The day would end with me leaving him in the kitchen meowing.

I slept well; the cottage spoke reassuring words at night – a window might gently rattle or a pipe gurgle. Although my dreams were more vivid of late and the last few nights Mum and Dad had appeared in them, looking younger and less stressed. And last night me and my friend Jimmy Jammy had jumped, screaming, into a river. If the dream had been real there'd have been no danger. As a child Mum and Dad had made me religiously attend swimming lessons, even if it meant missing a party.

Ben dropped by yesterday afternoon. He'd come around to take me up on my offer of letting him photograph the back garden and stream and he ended up staying until ten.

Part of me had wanted him to stay longer.

Silences were comfortable but we also chatted a lot and talked again about how never stopping learning was so important with art. His enthusiasm made me realise how much I missed my work – not so much the buzz and warmth of the tattoo parlour, now, apart from Katya, and that surprised me, but the deep satisfaction and thrill I felt when a design came together and a customer's face told me I'd met all their expectations. Ben wanted to start photographing people more, something he only really did at family celebrations or on holidays. Tentatively he asked if I'd sit on the grass by the stream and let him take a few shots.

'Now try to look natural… just gaze ahead across the water… relax your brow. No… don't smile, not unless that's your natural resting face…'

My eyebrows shot up as I tried to master the natural look.

'Is this okay?' I asked.

He'd laughed. 'Lizzie, you shouldn't even be thinking about what you look like. How about… let your mind wander… what are you having for dinner tonight? That's better…' He'd taken a few snaps. 'You look so serene… content…'

'Sticky pork ribs. Spring rolls… I'm in my happy place, right now.'

We'd both laughed. And later we did get a Chinese takeaway and shared stories about our childhoods and over sweet and sour chicken Ben opened up about his ex-fiancée.

'I think that was the problem with my ex – she believed I'd change. I was never ambitious enough for her.' He'd stopped chewing for a moment. 'It would have been kinder, in the end, to tell her I wasn't bothered about a fancy house or big salary.'

I thought back to Ash and me. At the end our story wasn't so different.

As I'd waved Ben off, I'd had more thoughts, like when Jill visited, about what it would be like to live permanently here. Perhaps Jill, Tim, Neve, even Trish, perhaps they'd all become my good friends. And Leafton could do with a tattoo parlour. I couldn't help grinning at that thought. It excited me, though, the idea of setting up my own business, and appearances were deceptive – I knew that from all my customers over the years. Just because Leafton looked conservative didn't mean there weren't locals who'd love to be inked.

And if, in this imaginary world, I became a local myself would Ben and I…?

But this was all a fantasy.

My life was in London. When the month was up, I'd be going back.

And then it struck me – for some reason I never called the capital *home* and already felt a stronger sense of belonging to this village cottage than my London flat, with its lush lawn, the stream, the weeping willow with the odd carving, with Ben and the kitten.

'Today I'm meeting Neve for lunch in The Tipsy Duck,' I said to Taz. 'I called by the supermarket on Monday and she agreed to tell me everything she knows about Leafton and this place.'

Having enjoyed half a sachet of chicken-flavoured food, Taz padded over to the corner of the kitchen. I'd tried to make that area more comfortable for him by putting an old tartan blanket underneath the bed. Day by day he became more alert and often sat by the French patio doors. This morning he'd meowed at a sparrow using its beak as a pickaxe on the other side of the glass.

Jill said the best way to trap mice and birds, that cats brought in, was to throw a tea towel on top and scoop them up. That idea would have frightened me a week ago but now I realised the line between humans and animals wasn't as wide as I'd been brought up to believe. I'd based Taz in the room where I prepared food and I'd eaten after handling him without washing my hands. I'd emptied the litter tray and if he peed on the floor, I'd cleared it up. Yet I hadn't fallen ill.

And he was proving to be a brilliant sounding board. He didn't offer advice but provided cuddles on tap.

As I headed into town, I even stroked a neighbour's cat. With care I'd applied sun cream to my skin as tattoos faded under strong rays. Clients needed to look after their art work. People often asked me if I was worried how they'd look as I aged, with the changing texture of skin and body shape. For me a tattoo was like a photograph – a snapshot of time that told a tale. Each one meant something important when it was taken but that meaning might alter or diminish over time. And likewise, I didn't expect the tattoo to stay the same. A photo might brown or curl, like my waist might fill out or my face line. Joints could swell, hair would grey and tattoos would wear as well and in doing so would match the whole.

I turned into the high street and crossed the road. Neve was talking to Tim who stood outside his café. She came over to me. He gave me a quick wave and Neve and I walked the rest of the way together, facing the blinding sun. We entered the pub and sat down after buying our drinks, near the front window. Today the roses in the vases were a lovely terracotta colour. I took a swig from my cider bottle. The same men were playing dominoes who'd been here on the night of Jill's party. They both looked up and gave me a smile of recognition before returning to their tiles. I must have looked surprised as Neve grinned.

'We may seem out of touch here but Leafton always welcomes new blood.'

'That sounds as if I'm going to be served up as part of some sacrificial ritual,' I replied.

Neve gave a tinkling laugh. 'The elders have clearly decided you're here to stay.'

Her eyes twinkled and for some reason I felt a warm glow inside.

'Thanks for agreeing to meet. I've searched online myself but haven't come up with much concrete about Streamside Cottage.'

'What have you learnt?'

'Ben's told me about the bombings during the war and how Streamside cottage was the only one in the road left standing. As I told you on Monday, Jill filled me in on the past residents, including the author who believes in ghosts, but on the internet all I could find out was more general, about Leafton. I found it awfully fascinating.'

Awfully. Sometimes Ash teased me about the way I spoke. A private education left a mark as permanent as an inking.

'It's like people – everyone has a story, and it's just as true of places,' said Neve. 'That's why I wanted to study history. Some say it's irrelevant but it helps you understand why the world is like it is and that's a comfort. It gives a sense of order to confusing times.'

Neve went on to explain about Leafton's farming background that made it even more difficult to understand why my cosmopolitan parents had ever bought a property here. Their other two investments were far more sophisticated – the luxury townhouse in Bournemouth, overlooking the sea, and with its terrace and orange tree garden, a modern villa outside Seville. A friend at junior school once holidayed in a remote Yorkshire village. Her parents loved hiking and birdwatching and she even slept outside one night and watched the stars. I'd asked if we could go there for our next break. Vigorously Mum shook her head and Dad told me off; said I should be more grateful for our five-star trips abroad and that the countryside was made up of nothing but dangers and filth.

Our food arrived and I ordered more drinks whilst Neve asked me about my time at university.

'Opal's such a beautiful stone,' I said later, over coffee, admiring Neve's ring finger.

'Alan wanted a diamond as it's traditional but I managed to talk him around. This is my birthstone and in Ancient

Roman times Opal symbolised love and hope.' She took it off and showed me the inner rim of the gold band. *Alan 4 Neve* was inscribed inside. 'He's quite a romantic on the quiet.'

'Will you still further your education? I believe you took a gap year because your dad lost his job and you wanted to help out.'

'That's a generous version. The truth is, money was tight because Dad got sent to prison for six months. I was a bit of a mess to be honest. He got sentenced just as I was to leave for Freshers' week. Me taking a gap year eased a difficult situation.'

'Sorry, I didn't mean to pry.'

'Don't worry. Sooner or later Leafton finds a way of passing secrets on. Dad was done for careless driving. He's an HGV driver and was running late. Overtired, he didn't attach both the supporting legs of a crane properly. One of them swung out and seriously injured a cyclist.'

'How terrible.'

'No one felt more sorry than Dad, even though the cyclist made a full recovery. Dad works as a hospital porter now. Alan came into my life at a time when nothing seemed certain. I don't mind working at the supermarket.' She twisted her ring. 'The history society satisfies my cravings for knowledge.'

'But why does being with Alan rule out getting a degree? You could easily commute to London from here or—'

'He's ready to settle down and has started jogging. Turning thirty has – prematurely, some might say – made him aware of his mortality, and we do both want kids...'

'It would only mean waiting a few more years.'

'Yes, but I see Alan's point. Why rack up a huge student loan when he's almost saved enough to put a deposit down on our own place? Financially we're in a good position to really start planning for our future. Alan's right, with the current state of the job market I could end up with no better position than I've got at the moment. He's always being sent CVs from newly graduated students for cashier positions and—'

'But the loan gets written off after a certain number of years and who's to say you won't get some amazing position curating a museum or—'

Her cheeks pinked up. 'I don't want to lose him. I really feel as if I'm beginning to know who I am. He's sent me on training courses and my job has given me such confidence for dealing with confrontation and troubleshooting… I feel as if I've grown up…. as if I'm on a trajectory now. Before him life didn't make as much sense.'

'Did it need to at eighteen?'

'Didn't yours?'

I hesitated. 'No. But it did soon after. And I met someone too, who helped me feel more grounded – but he encouraged me to follow my passion, not give it up.'

'Are you still together?'

'We split up about six months ago.' I'd often heard clients talk about losing loved ones and how it had unexpected knock-on effects. When I found out Mum and Dad had died, the last thing I'd expected was it would cause real problems between me and Ash.

'Sorry,' I said as the barman took our empty plates. 'I didn't mean to push, it's just that I came so close to never following the career of my dreams. It's great that you and

Alan are so happy together. Life often has a way of taking us down a path we'd never anticipated.'

'Like living in a haunted cottage?'

I smiled. 'So this author, Frederick, you said you didn't blame him for leaving Streamside Cottage so quickly. Do you believe he had real grounds for his ghostly belief?'

'Let's just say I can see how someone of a sensitive disposition might be convinced. We need to go back to the early seventeenth century. There was something of a witch-hunt hysteria across England – in fact the whole of Europe. Hundreds of trials took place. Women especially were found guilty and executed.' Neve's eyes shone. 'The course I'd wanted to study at university had a module in witchcraft… Anyway, Leafton was largely farmland. New workers came from further north. Two of them were a mother and son. He had a large port wine stain birthmark on his face which immediately aroused suspicion. Witchcraft was believed to run in families so the mother would have also been suspected.' Neve hardly noticed our coffees arrive. 'She fell in love with one of the farm workers who caught her sketching one evening, with her finger in the dust. The woman confided that she saw dead people – ghostly manifestations. She drew a man with a beard and told her beau it was his granddad.'

'How did he react?'

'You have to remember there were no cameras back then and peasants couldn't afford painted portraits of their relatives. They had to rely on memories that became hazier over the years. Her drawing wouldn't have had to be detailed. It wouldn't have taken much for him to believe it was his grandfather. Despite their relationship he was a

God-fearing man and reported her. The son's birthmark was called the mark of the devil, plus that summer the cows' yield of milk had been low and crops had failed – this was blamed all on him and his mother. They were both ducked in the deep part of the stream alongside your back garden.'

'They drowned?'

'Of course. Their right thumb was tied to their left big toe. Drowning proved their innocence. If they'd lived it was seen as proof of guilt. They probably suffered the better option. The water was seen as baptismal and related to God, so their survival would have been seen as a holy rejection of their bodies, and therefore evidence that they were doing the work of the devil.' Neve's ears reddened. 'Sorry, I'm going on a bit.'

'Please, don't stop, it's so interesting... so Frederick believed the cottage has always been haunted by this so-called witch and her son?'

'Yes. That might be one reason the property remained on its own – no one wanted to build near it. On the other side of the river, opposite the weeping willow, there's a big boulder with an apotropaic symbol etched on to it. Frederick walked around, through the forest, to find it.'

'A what?'

'A protective symbol, to keep witches at bay. No doubt it deterred builders as well. That patch of land and the cottage were deemed cursed and dangerous for children and anyone with artistic leanings.' Neve smiled. 'I hope, as a tattoo artist, you aren't superstitious. That's the bit that got writer Frederick really worried.'

'My dad drilled into me at an early age that ghosts and witches were make-believe and nothing to be scared of.'

And I was glad. It meant I could enjoy trick-or-treating at Halloween with him. Mum never got involved. She didn't like horror films, preferring to keep things cheerful. I outgrew enjoying her favourite musical DVDs. If I wanted to watch scary movies when I was finally allowed in the Sixth Form, she made sure she was in a different room away from the suspenseful sounds.

'The curse was specific in another way. Before being ducked, another form of torture was tried – sleep deprivation. It didn't extract a confession from the woman or her child. The first owner of Streamside Cottage had a friend to stay – a poet who faced hard times and couldn't afford a place of his own. He complained he couldn't sleep at night; that thudding noises, like footsteps, kept him awake. People said it was the vengeful spirits of the mother and her son. One day he said he couldn't stand the effects of his insomnia anymore and threw himself out of the top window.'

We sat in silence for a moment. 'Well, I've slept like a log, apart from odd dreams. Sure there are creaks and unexplained noises but it's an old cottage.'

'And these days we can see the whole story in context. The accused parent and child died because their lungs filled with water. That poet who ended his own life was probably suffering from mental illness... Frederick – he was quite a dramatic character. Mind you, he did like a drink.' Neve drained her cup and put on a bright smile. 'We all know how the world seems like a different place if you've had too much wine.'

'How did you find out so much detail about what happened?' I asked and leant forwards.

'Frederick told me about the book he'd used to choose

where to stay whilst writing his novel. It's brilliant.' Her eyes shone. 'I read the whole thing in three hours. That gave me the specifics of the case, and over the years, since doing History at GCSE level, I've collated a list of really useful websites, like one that logs newspaper articles from sixteen hundred. I could chat to you all day about the witchfinders.'

'Does the name Earl mean anything to you?' I asked as we left the pub. 'It's carved into a weeping willow by the stream, in the cottage's garden, with a number by the side of it.'

'No. Aristocracy haven't lived in this vicinity and I've never heard of a local called that.'

My forehead relaxed as sun rays hit. Neve said goodbye. I made a note to buy her a small thank you gift.

'Oh, I almost forgot... I found an old photo in one of the bedrooms...' I pulled it out of my rucksack. 'It was taken in the seventies by the looks of people's clothing. I searched online for any information. Apparently, The Best Inn restaurant chain was really popular until the end of the eighties when more cosmopolitan food took over. It went bankrupt. I can't find anything at all about the building next to it, owned by G & B – those letters are written on the gold plaque by the door. It's a long shot but does the picture mean anything to you? I don't even know if it's local.'

Neve studied the photo. 'No... can't say it does.' Her face lit up. 'But I love a challenge. Do you mind if I take this home and see what I can find out? Maybe one of these buildings was haunted too.' She grinned.

'So Frederick is the only one who believes in the witch haunting?'

'I think so, we're a pretty down-to-earth bunch around

here! Although... Trish... it's all a bit odd... she's one of the most sensible people I know. She babysat for my parents often enough and told me once that Disney happy-ever-afters didn't really exist. Mum and Dad were quite cross and just said she was probably cynical because of what happened to her marriage. But she sells stationery, she's a practical woman. Even with her beliefs in Buddhism – she's always saying that's more of a way of life than a religion revering some mythical god. So when Frederick left suddenly, with all this talk of a strange goings-on at the cottage, when I saw the change in her, how scared and unsure about everything she became... Well...' Neve shrugged. 'It seemed most out of character.'

We parted company and I walked up the high street. Worried about Taz, I glanced at my watch. For one second, I questioned whether he was safe, alone, at the cottage.

This was new, being responsible for something other than myself. I stepped up my speed and smelt joss sticks as I almost bumped into Trish who was coming out of The Pen Pusher.

15

Early tattoo removal methods included scrubbing the skin with a sandpaper-like tool

I stood on the doorstep of our South Kensington terraced home, in between white Roman columns. Ash gawped at the building. I wore tight leather trousers and Doc Marten boots. October had felt more like winter than autumn. I huddled in my grey duffle coat. Underneath was a snakeskin print long-sleeved top I'd bought especially for tonight. A healing crystal necklace hung around my neck.

'You look beautiful, Lizzie,' said Ash, once he'd stopped talking about how, one day, he'd love to live in a street like this.

We'd just walked twenty minutes from the underground station. Old time dance music escaped out of an open window. A three-storey house worked well for parties. Guests walked along the hallway mat before dumping their coats and grabbing a first drink from the downstairs kitchen. Mum always felt that gave their shoes time to discard any mud and germs before making their way upstairs to the lounge where we spent most of our evenings. As soon as I was old enough to carry a tray, I used to feel very grown up going up and down the stairs, supplying guests with drinks and canapés.

Dad had offered to collect us from the station but I knew how stressed Mum got in the run-up to hosting a party. She'd need him there to assist with any last-minute changes to the furniture positions or lighting – or her outfit. And it was just as well as the train ran forty minutes late. It was the first time I'd been home this term, even though South Kensington was only ten underground stops and one line change away from my student accommodation. I couldn't believe I was already in the second year.

'I wonder what they'll say to my hair?' I said and took off my rucksack.

'Don't worry, they won't even notice the blue once my charisma has blown them away.'

'Idiot.' I stood on tiptoe and kissed him firmly on the lips, my body automatically pressing itself close. Reluctantly I pulled away. I couldn't wait for my parents to meet Ash. He was polite, funny, a family man who worked hard and had ambition. I hadn't wanted to introduce them until we felt things were getting serious. I learnt from a girlfriend who'd taken her boyfriend home after three months. Her parents adored him but then they split up. I wouldn't want to hurt Mum and Dad like that.

'Once I've made your mum my special toasties for lunch tomorrow she'll be begging us to get married, and I'll bamboozle your Dad with my sporting knowledge.'

I thumped him gently in the ribs before putting my key

in the lock. He ran a hand over one of the Roman pillars. I dreamt of owning a smaller house away from the fumes and engine sounds of a busy road. We went in, put our rucksacks by the door and removed our jackets. I hung them on the coat stand.

'Elizabeth? What on earth have you done to your hair?'

'Aunt Fiona. Hello.' I leant forward and kissed her cheek. 'This is Ash.'

'Pleased to meet you,' he said and smiled broadly, extending his hand.

She stared for a moment and then limply returned the gesture before turning away from him.

'Have you got some pretty shoes to change into, Elizabeth? If not, I've got a pair you could borrow.'

'No thanks. How's life in Devon? You're staying the weekend?'

'For a week. Your mother and I are going to the theatre. Jack and your dad said something about golf. Perhaps you could come across for dinner one night?' She didn't look at Ash.

I gazed past her shoulder and took his hand as my parents came into view. Mum dashed forward and gave me a big hug. As always, her hair was neatly scooped up into a chignon. Her shoes were shiny enough to offer a reflection. She stood back and held me by the shoulders.

'Goodness. What *have* you done to your hair? Have you accidentally dyed the lot this time?'

'There must be an echo in here. Aunt Fiona asked exactly the same.'

'Never mind, I'll make an appointment at A Cut Above. They'll sort that out in no time.'

'It's meant to look like this, thanks anyway, Mum. I love your outfit.' She wore a dress with a military style short, gold-buttoned jacket.

She exchanged looks with her sister. I gave Dad a hug. He wore slacks and a starched shirt done up to the top.

'And happy birthday. I want you to meet someone very special,' I said.

'This is the Ash we have been hearing about over the last year?' said Dad stiffly.

Ash held out his hand again. Mum and Dad both shook it. Their eyes dropped to the black outline of a paintbrush on his wrist. Ash wasn't much of a tattoo fan but loved mine and wanted a smaller version.

'Can I offer you a soft drink, Ash?' said Dad. 'I assume you don't drink. Where does your family come from?'

'I was born in Leicester. We moved to London from there.'

'I mean originally, where in India?'

I cringed.

'My grandparents were born in Pakistan, and I do drink as a matter of fact. A beer would be great. Thanks, Mr Lockhart.'

Dad gave an abrupt nod of the head and Ash and Aunt Fiona followed him into the kitchen.

'What do you think?' I asked Mum excitedly.

'How long have you been dating?'

'About six months.' Officially, that was, although we'd kissed on and off before that. 'I didn't see the point in introducing him until our relationship was solid.'

'Is that what this is all about?' She ran her hand up and down the air between us. 'The hair, the clothes...'

'Of course not.' I squeezed her hand. 'Let's have a

proper catch up tomorrow. Now, when do you want your present?'

Chatting we joined everyone else in the kitchen. Mum and Dad asked me about my studies. I waffled and said I preferred macro to microeconomics and had just started a module about corporate social responsibility. We headed upstairs to join other guests. Ash and I mingled with old and new neighbours and my parents' colleagues. He was good like that, with a knack for putting people at ease and genuine interest in other people's stories. The room was tastefully decorated with a few gold balloons. Thanks to body heat the walnut and black granite fireplace didn't need to be turned on. I'd brought sixtieth birthday table glitter and scattered it across every surface.

'Your Ash is a real dish,' murmured Miriam from next door. 'Eyelashes to die for. Does he have an older brother?'

'Yes, but he's married.'

'Pity, I don't want to be single for my eightieth birthday next March.'

We both laughed. Ash charmed friends of my parents who also had children at university. I heard him reassure them about the loans by telling them his older brother managed fine with the monthly deductions from his salary. We danced to a Frank Sinatra number. I caught Mum and Dad watching and waved. I hoped they might have joined us but they were too busy talking to Aunt Fiona.

I'd notice, over the years, how when they hosted get-togethers their time was spent mingling, networking for work perhaps or keeping up with the neighbours. But often, after everyone had gone, and I'd supposedly gone to bed, I'd secretly creep down and watch them in the lounge.

They'd put the music on again and dance more wildly than I'd ever see them do in public, twirling each other around and laughing so hard.

Dad gave a speech and guests raised their glasses. Mum thanked everyone for coming but her usual sparkle was lacking and her demeanour reminded me of those summer days when she'd become sad and less chatty. It was heading toward midnight and we'd run out of glasses so I followed her down to the kitchen and offered to wash up as the dish-washer was mid-cycle.

Mum had always enjoyed cooking, preferring basic dishes to the elegant meals Dad grew up eating. She had lots of clever tricks, like getting me to eat broccoli and sprouts by slathering them in the tastiest vegetarian gravy. Eat up your greens and brown, she'd say, and then you can have pink. It was a silly family joke to call foods by their colour. Pink was always exciting because it usually meant ice cream.

'Everything okay?' I asked and rubbed her back with my hand. 'It's a fantastic party and your make-up is amazing; I bet no one can believe you're sixty.'

Her face softened. 'Thanks for the lovely card you painted, and the cut-glass rose. That red running through the bloom is absolutely stunning.' For a second she looked sad again and then pointed to the window sill. 'I've put it there until I decide on the best place.'

'I'm glad you like it. Ash's uncle owns a gift shop and as soon as I saw it, I knew it was perfect.'

Her body became rigid.

'You do like him, don't you?'

'I can see the attraction. At your age I had a crush on

a music student. He had long hair and was in a band, his bohemian style seemed so thrilling.'

'This is no crush, Mum.' I rolled up my sleeves and went to turn on the taps. 'I've met his mum. You'll love her as much as I know he's going to love you and—'

'What the hell is that?' Her eyes bulged.

I followed her gaze.

'Elizabeth Lockhart, what have you done?'

Mum never raised her voice like that. The Lockharts didn't lose their temper. I glanced down at the big, bold paintbrush tattoo that stood out against my pale skin. She grabbed my arm and dragged me under the fluorescent light.

'Anne, what's going on?' Dad appeared, followed by Ash and Aunt Fiona.

16

Now

A new trend is parents getting tattoos of their children's doodles

I continued in the direction of the stream as I heard Trish lock up her shop.

I replayed the thought: *I was worried about Taz.*

An indefinable, uncomfortable sensation shifted in my gut.

Increasingly, as each day passed, the kitten dominated my mind. Was he putting on the right amount of weight? Sleeping well? Did he get lonely at night? Was he bored during the day? What would happen to him once I left? Would another foster or adoptive owner love him enough?

It was as if a door had opened, just a chink, to give me a peek into the world of parenting.

Like a dark, clammy fog a chilling realisation rolled across my back. The parental instinct bypassed character flaws and fed on the best parts of us like our unselfishness, empathy, our willingness to care. Even if it magnified the latter, I could now see that the intent came from a good place.

It also resulted in a twenty-four-hour sense of concern.

It had never struck me before that parenting had a downside for Mum and Dad. I'd always seen them as setting the rules for the way I lived from a position of authority.

But now I recognised the possibility that they'd had little control over their desire to give me the best and safest life they could.

17

*When heavily tattooed Geoff Ostling dies, his skin
will be donated to the National Museum
of Australia to be displayed as art*

'Look at this.' Mum showed my arm to Dad and Aunt Fiona.

The room filled with an uncomfortable silence. I swallowed and lifted my head. It was my life, I had to follow my own heart.

Dad shook his head. 'Oh Elizabeth…You'll never get a job with that.'

'Tattoos are mainstream these days,' I said and pulled away my arm. 'It's just another form of art.'

'Did he put you up to this?' asked Mum, glaring at Ash.

'Lizzie is her own woman,' said Ash calmly.

Is that what they really thought, that I'd get something this bold just to please someone else?

'But why a paintbrush?' asked Aunt Fiona. 'I know you've always liked art but—'

'Yes. I wanted to study it at A level and university and—'

'We went through that. There's no future in that sort of degree.' Dad exhaled loudly and leant against one of the distressed wood kitchen units. 'It's a great hobby to have. Your mother and I love the cards you make and we enjoyed watching you move on from sketching to watercolours, but...' He rubbed his forehead. 'It's so naive to think you could forge any kind of career from drawing and as for maiming yourself like that...'

'With all due respect,' said Ash, 'I'm doing a degree in art and the career prospects are—'

'I should have known.' Mum folded her arms. 'Elizabeth was fine until she met you. Now she's embraced all these indulgent ideas about her appearance and lifestyle, but blue hair won't get her a serious job in the city.'

She didn't approve of my boyfriend?

'Don't you trust me to make an informed decision? I've considered this for months.'

Dad rolled his eyes. Uncle Jack appeared and Aunt Fiona filled him in on what was happening. He shot all of us sympathetic looks.

'Surely it's personality and work ethic that counts?' said Ash.

'What would you know about ethics?' fired back Dad. 'You drink alcohol. Your parents must be so ashamed.'

'Steady on, Lawrence,' said Uncle Jack.

I gasped. Hurt etched Ash's face before he tried to disguise it.

'Look, let's discuss this tomorrow when we've all had

a good night's sleep.' I was sure they'd come around and realise it wasn't as bad as they thought.

'It's too late for talk,' said Mum. 'Now we'll have to fork out for laser removal.'

'There's no point,' I said focusing hard on keeping my voice steady. 'I'm sorry but this won't be my last tattoo.'

'Don't act like a spoilt child.' Mum looked at Dad. 'Honestly, Elizabeth, the last year or so… What's got into you?'

'Your parents haven't spent the best years of their life giving you top opportunities just for you to squander them,' said Aunt Fiona.

'Maybe we should leave Anne and Lawrence to deal with this,' said Uncle Jack quietly.

Feeling sick, I turned to go and tugged at Ash's arm – the man I loved and was so proud of.

'I've made up separate rooms,' said Mum. 'It might remind you of the standards you were brought up with, Elizabeth, regardless of your friends' lifestyles.'

My patience evaporated. It was fine them not wanting Ash and me to share a bed under their roof but I wouldn't accept her implying Ash had led me astray. 'For your information, yes, I am having sex. It's my conscious decision in accordance with my own beliefs and the way *I* want to live *my* life.'

'Elizabeth!' Dad's cheeks flushed.

'What's the matter? Does that ruin your image of me as your little girl?'

'That's enough,' said Aunt Fiona.

'What has this got to do with you?'

'Everything. Your parents have given you a perfect life

on a plate and I won't just sit back and watch you throw it back in their face. It's not easy, bringing up children.'

'What would you know about that?' Shit. She'd always said that she and Uncle Jack never wanted kids – but what if they had. 'Look, I'm sorry, let's just—'

'Why don't I put on the kettle?' said Ash. 'My mum swears there's nothing a good cup of tea can't—'

'Go home, son,' Dad interrupted. 'This is our family and our business only.'

'If he's not welcome then I'm not staying either.'

'What do you want me to do, Lizzie?' murmured Ash. 'Name it, I'll do whatever you think is best.'

'Can't you see what a bad influence he is?' Mum threw her hands in the air. 'Just look in the mirror. Where's our lovely, easy-going daughter gone? And her name's Elizabeth, by the way.'

'I've grown up, Mum. Ever thought about that? I decide what people call me – to university friends it's Lizzie.'

Mum looked at me in exasperation. She came over and put an arm around my back. Like watery tattoo ink, mascara ran down her cheeks. 'You're so intelligent. You've got everything going for you. Don't let a love affair knock you off course. You're capable of getting a first-class business degree if you put your mind to it, and enjoying a financially stable life. Move back home for a while. Your father and I will sort it all out.'

'That's been the whole problem. I know you've both meant well but try to understand… I need to forge my own life and make my own mistakes. The business degree won't be happening.'

Her arm fell to her side. 'What do you mean?'

'I didn't want to tell you until tomorrow – I didn't want to risk ruining your birthday but—'

'I think it's too late for that,' said Aunt Fiona in a measured voice.

'Business studies – it's not for me, never has been. I only agreed to it to please you and Dad, but day in day out, I just can't hack it any longer.'

Dad moved forwards. 'You're swapping courses?'

I held Ash's hand. 'I'm going to train to become a tattoo artist.'

Even Uncle Jack frowned.

I explained about how I'd increased my hours in the clothes shop. How I'd secured the flat above Kismet Tattoos and could move in, in a couple of months. How I'd talked about the apprenticeship with Katya. I explained what a superb artist she was and how she'd introduced me to meditation and healing crystals. It was exciting – empowering – to realise that I'd taken control and sorted myself out a new career path and home. I was determined to prove my commitment to them and, in time, my professionalism.

'You don't need to worry, I've done the maths and will be able to pay my bills.' I clasped my hands together. 'I'm so excited, it's always been about creativity for me. I've kept practising my drawing over the years. In fact, I met Ash at the art society.'

He nodded. 'She's far more talented than many of the people on my course.'

My parents, aunt and uncle listened in silence.

I explained how everything made sense once I'd had this, my first tattoo. I knew then exactly how I wanted to use all the artistic knowledge and skills I'd acquired over time.

I told them how I should be good enough to do paid work in a couple of years and how much, potentially, I could earn. I described the equipment I'd need to buy eventually and what exactly I'd be doing for the first year in terms of helping to run the parlour and shadowing Katya and how the career possibilities were far-ranging. I could specialise in cosmetic or medical tattooing, or laser removal.

'So… that's it,' I finally finished.

Mum burst out laughing. 'Is this a joke?'

My mouth went dry. No, no, it wasn't, I'd spent so long thinking it all through.

'Is it some sort of weird birthday entertainment?' she continued, 'because no one in their right mind, contemplating such a job, would expect the support of parents who'd put them through the best private schooling; who'd ferried them to enriching hobby clubs; who'd taught them everything they'd need to know about manners and society to fit in…'

'I've never heard anything so ridiculous in my life.' Dad paced up and down. 'This just doesn't make sense. Tattooing a career?' He studied me for a moment. 'Are you on drugs, Elizabeth? Is that it? Because if you are, look love, we're here to help…'

They weren't impressed with the business, the life-plan I'd spent hours refining?

'Of course it's not going to happen,' said Dad. 'We won't allow it. You'll move back home for the rest of this academic year and it goes without saying you can stop seeing this young man. You'll thank us when you're older and look back with embarrassment.'

'*Thank* you?'

'I'd keep quiet if I was you,' Aunt Fiona said, the tension

in my chest building as she spoke. 'All that extra tuition and the educational holidays… Your mum sacrificed getting ahead quicker at work to be here when you got in from school and—'

'I never begrudged that,' said Mum and for a second I got a glimpse of the woman I used to feel so close to.

'So why was I so totally unprepared for life at university?'

'What do you mean?' Mum asked and folded her arms around herself.

I wanted them to understand but could already see distress on their faces.

'Nothing. Ash and I are going. Let's speak during the week.'

'No, I want to know. No one could have been more prepared than you. We made sure of it.'

'Maybe on paper. I got three As so academically I qualified to live as a student.'

My parents looked confused. It was all too much. I went into the hallway, the discussion was getting nowhere. The others followed.

'What else did you need?' asked Dad.

'Just leave her, Lawrence. I don't think even Elizabeth knows what she's saying,' said Aunt Fiona. 'She's just attention-seeking. What a disappointment.'

I spun around. Aunt Fiona had never really liked me; I'd sensed it over the years. I'd tried to ignore it but it had never been clearer than at this minute.

'You really want to know what I was lacking? Life experience, independence, an ability to do things for myself. I wasn't used to alcohol or staying out late or handling myself in clubs. I didn't have a taxi or takeout app like all my friends. I struggled to plan my study because you'd always insisted on doing it for me. The girl in the room next to me could rewire a plug and on the other side Heidi put up shelves. The majority had already had Saturday jobs and were used to managing money and dealing with strangers and adults of all ages. I hadn't got a clue.'

'Come on, let's go Lizzie, I think it's best that we leave,' said Ash. 'We – or you – can come back tomorrow. Let the dust settle.'

'No, they need to hear me out. They've insulted you and are still treating me like a small child. Isn't the whole point of parenting to produce independent offspring? Yet even now, in my second year, you are trying to control my life and make decisions for me. How do you ever expect me to stand on my own two feet?'

'We wanted, *we want*, what's best for you,' said Mum and looked at Dad.

'But did it never occur to you that what you thought was best for me was only your opinion and not necessarily the truth? Doesn't being happy count for anything? Is it all about mortgages and pensions and fitting in? Or is it about following your passion and talent, whatever that might be? I didn't even like sleeping on my own, for fuck's sake. You'd never once left me in the house on my own.'

'There's no need to swear,' Dad snapped.

'Why? Don't you ever? I was eighteen, Dad. Why couldn't I get drunk in the Sixth Form and have boyfriends or get a bad perm, or clothes I'd one day look back at and laugh over?'

'But you had a great childhood, didn't you?' Mum's voice faltered. Guests had come down and clearly wanted to leave but were stuck with their coats in an awkward place between us and the kitchen.

'I did, Mum.' My voice softened. '*Child* being the operative word, but once I started going through high school, I became a young woman yet you and Dad never acknowledged that. Why not? Why haven't you ever trusted me to... to do things on my own?'

'It wasn't like that,' she mumbled.

'I wish I'd had a mother like yours, you don't know how lucky you are,' said Aunt Fiona. 'You owe your parents an apology.'

'Everything I've said is true.' I slipped an arm around Ash's waist as my eyes filled. 'You imply Ash isn't a good man, Dad, but what sort of man orders his twenty-year-old daughter to move back home and drop her boyfriend? Does that really seem normal? And Mum, a young woman experimenting with her hair and fashion, isn't that to be expected – encouraged even? To find her own identity? What sort of mother wants to take charge of that?'

'I can't believe how ungrateful you're being.' Her fingers flew to her mouth.

Dad rushed to Mum's side. She looked unsteady and her face drained of colour.

'I'm not. Mum... Dad... I love you both so much and you've always been so caring, I don't want to upset you, it's just—'

'*You're* the failure, not us,' she spat. Mum reached for the cut-glass rose and thrust it towards me. 'Take this back. Leave now.'

'Please, I know you don't mean that.' Mum's party had

been going so well and then all of a sudden... I didn't understand...

'Anne, don't upset yourself,' said Dad, 'we can—'

She pushed it into my hands but I wasn't ready. It fell and smashed.

A look of desperation crossed Dad's face. Quickly Ash slipped his arm around my shoulders and steered me into the hallway and out of the front door.

18

Now

In recent years the Met Police have relaxed their policy on officers being banned from having visible tattoos on their hands or face

'Lizzie, Lizzie wait!'

I stopped and turned. 'Trish?'

'I can see you're in a hurry, so I won't—'

'I've left Taz, the kitten I'm fostering, longer than usual.' And I was keen to get changed into shorts. Wearing jeans had been a mistake today.

A tapestry handbag slid down her shoulder. 'I- I wanted to say sorry.' She plunged her hands deep into her dungaree pockets and stared at her feet.

'What for?'

'I must have seemed a little unfriendly at the party.'

I hesitated. 'It's okay. I know you've had a difficult time.'

She looked up and gave a wry smile. 'It's as if the buildings can speak to each other in this village. Personal news just seems to spread like fire during... well, I wouldn't exactly call it The Plague...'

I looked at my watch. 'Sorry, but I really need to get going.'

She hovered.

'Trish... how about... do you fancy a coffee?'

'What, now?'

I shrugged.

'At Streamside Cottage?'

'Or we could meet tomorrow.'

'Yes. Yes, we could. Although...' She took a deep breath and pulled up her bag. 'Thank you. I could do with a caffeine hit. It's been a busy afternoon for me what with the school exam season upon us.'

We walked at a quick pace, chatting about the residents I'd got to know. She said what a lovely boy Ben had been, polite and helpful like now, a child who told the funniest jokes and was always happy to chat to adults. My stomach fluttered as I thought about him and how he just seemed to be there at the moments it counted. But more than that, Ben made me feel at ease with myself and my new surroundings, and it was becoming increasingly hard to ignore the way his mouth tilted when he smiled and how that made me want to kiss him. I never thought I'd feel like that about another man but somehow Ben made me look forward to the time we spent together. Also we'd friended each other on Facebook and I'd been struck by how real his feed was. There were no selfies showing off about his latest meal or night out, he wasn't posting to impress – instead I saw countryside views, occasionally one of his photos, heart-warming videos about acts of charity and group photos of him and his colleagues celebrating someone's birthday or retirement.

As we approached the cottage her conversation dried up. I took out my keys and the familiar scrunch of gravel welcomed me as I strode up the drive. Yet the noise appeared to act as an alarm to Trish who stopped dead whilst the hanging basket swung to and fro and would need watering once the sun had gone down. I turned around. Trish had moved back onto the pavement.

'We can do this another day, if you prefer,' I said. Perhaps she was still in love with the author. Ghosts didn't exist, at least not the scary type with wide eyes and sheet-like bodies that moved through walls. But memories, did they count because they could certainly haunt us? Like every time, over recent years, I'd passed a woman on the street who looked like Mum from behind. For one brief moment I'd kid myself it was her and hurry to overtake and turn around to check. The sight of an unrecognisable face would always cause a crushing ache inside my chest.

Trish straightened her posture. 'Now's fine.'

I put my key in the lock and a shiver ran down my spine. For a moment I thought the door was already open. Slowly we entered the hallway and I swung the door closed behind us. Trish looked over her shoulder as if uneasy that I'd closed the way out. A meowing came from the kitchen and my relief that the kitten sounded okay cut through the sense of eeriness that had momentarily gripped both of us.

I pulled a face and went over to the litter tray. 'If you want to wait in the lounge, Trish… the kitchen needs fumigating.'

'It's not a problem, I'm a mum. The smell is no worse than any nappy.'

I wrapped the dirty litter in a fragranced plastic bag, dropped it in the bin and sprayed air freshener. Trish stood by the glass doors and gazed out at the stream and was still standing there after I came back from changing into shorts.

'You must be hungry,' I said to Taz and picked him up. He batted my nose with his paw narrowly missing my nose ring.

'Would you like me to hold him?' Trish ran a hand over the curved side of the pine dresser before holding out both palms. I squeezed half a sachet of salmon-flavoured food into Taz's bowl and refreshed the water whilst she hugged him to her chest. Trish pointed to the weeping willow, its leaves dangling like a beaded curtain. 'I'll tell you a secret, little man. When it's wet or the sun's rays are too fierce push your way through to discover the perfect cover. On really hot days, you can feel the breeze nearer to the stream and if you peer through the wired fence you'll spot the smallest of fish darting beneath its surface.'

There was no point talking to Taz like that. He wouldn't be here long enough to go outside. And yet I couldn't help thinking how joyful it would be to watch him explore such a diverse garden, with hidden secrets such as discarded real feathers to play with.

How wonderful it would be to live so close to nature. There wasn't so much as a backyard at the tattoo parlour.

As soon as Taz smelt the fish that had already been caught

and cooked for his lunch, his paws pedalled violently and Trish put him down by his bowl. After looking around the room she sat at the table and fiddled with her watch strap. The kettle boiled and I poured two coffees and put out a plate of biscuits.

'The cottage looks nice,' she said as I sat down.

We chatted and it would seem that some bits of news didn't spread across the village. Trish hadn't heard about my dad's letter. The more I talked about witches and drownings, the more intently she listened. Her drink went cold and her biscuit was left half-eaten.

'Neve's just told me what she knows about this place. That's how I found out about you and Frederick. I'm sorry it didn't work out.'

'Your parents never lived here?' she asked, playing with her teaspoon.

'No. I just don't understand why they didn't tell me about this property.'

Trish nodded and stared at me.

'But maybe there was a good reason and if you do find out why, they aren't around to offer further explanations.'

'I need to know more. Something, anything that might explain the argument we had.'

'What was it about? If you don't mind me asking?'

'They... had trouble accepting that I could look after myself.'

Her face softened and she picked up the rod with a feather on the end. She held it over Taz who tried to jump up and catch it.

'I should have made more effort to put things right.' My

finger traced the rim of my mug. 'The least I can do is try to understand – and I need to for my own sanity.'

'I'm sorry.' Trish's eyes glistened.

'What for? It's nothing to do with you.'

She looked away. 'One of the hardest things in life is losing the people you love. I feel for you.'

A bird chirped outside and for a moment it was all I could hear.

'You've done well to come in here, it must hold a lot of memories,' I said.

'You've no idea,' she mumbled, dropping the rod.

'I understand. My boyfriend and I split up around Christmas and it's been a difficult six months. In many ways we were such a good match.'

'Unlike me and Fred, I can see now that we were never well suited. I sold pens – he used them. That summed us up. We were at different ends of a spectrum that never met. He went jogging and dyed his slick hair whereas I can't remember the last time I ran and have greying curls I've no inclination to hide. Yet the things that marked us apart, pulled us together as they kept things fresh, but this place… all his talk of ghosts…'

I picked up Taz and he settled on my lap.

'At first I couldn't see why Fred believed in them, even though he came from the city so the only noises he was used to at night were easily identifiable, like car engines, late night revellers or sirens.'

As time passed, I missed those familiar city noises less and less. 'I come from London but as soon as I moved here felt settled. The night-time chat of the cottage has never bothered me, in fact quite the opposite. It's as if I'm not alone – it's a comfort.'

'That's exactly why Fred didn't like it. He felt he had company, as if the witch was torturing him, trying to keep him awake and hoping the lack of sleep would make him jump out of the top window like a poet that once lived here. Neve told you about that?'

I nodded.

'He asked me to move in after a couple of months. It was early on in our relationship but I felt sorry for him. He'd have nightmares and say the witch would come to him in his dreams and accuse him of being evil, of making money out of souls that weren't at peace.' Trish's gaze moved to the ceiling and then the walls.

'That must have been frightening for you as well.' I stroked Taz. His purr sounded reassuring.

'It made me ill, Lizzie. We found wet footsteps through the hallway once, when we came downstairs in the morning. I ended up taking pills for depression. One evening I found a ragged teddy, missing one eye, covered in blood in the bathroom.'

'*Blood?*' My hand stopped and Taz opened his eyes. Surely not? There had to be some other explanation.

'Fred thought the witch must have left it there as a reminder of her son and another night I heard a scream come from down by the stream.'

'What did you do?'

'We got up and ran outside as quickly as we could. Fred took a torch. I was almost hysterical by this point and wanted to call the police, but Fred couldn't face it, said we'd be laughed out of the station and if the press heard they'd ruin his reputation as a hardened thriller writer.' She put her elbows on the table and hid her head in her hands.

'What is it?' I reached across and patted her arm.

'I've never told anyone this but... I don't know you well, so perhaps that makes it easier. One reason it's taken me a long time to... to get over it all... it was ... it was all so much worse than I'd first thought... you see what happened was...'

She looked around the room and her body shuddered.

'It's okay. You don't have to explain.'

She wiped her wet face with the back of her hand.

'You've been so brave coming here today,' I said, keeping my tone soft, but wondering what she'd been about to say.

I made us another coffee and Trish drank in silence, the subject of Frederick and the haunting now clearly closed. I put Taz in his bed and, at her request, took her to see my tattoo equipment. The needles were much smaller than she'd expected and the power pack's foot pedal reminded her of a sewing machine. Being close to my tools felt good in a way it hadn't for a while. Trish flicked through my portfolio then the darkening skies outside made us realise how quickly the afternoon had passed and prompted her to leave.

'I'm sorry for everything that man put you through. I'm surprised you've stayed in Leafton.'

'It's a lovely place to live, Lizzie, the residents are accepting and friendly. People have come and gone, over the years, but whilst here the village has embraced them into its heart.'

She opened the front door and went out. A woman

approached who, despite the fading light, wore a huge floppy sunhat and bug eyeglasses and even though it wasn't raining, a long mackintosh.

'Hello, Caroline,' said Trish as she passed.

'It's not Caroline,' snapped the woman who walked straight past me and into the cottage.

19

6 years ago – the holidays

Tattoo inks can cause allergic reactions
that may surface years later

I went down into the hallway in my new leggings and t-shirt. Scones and coffee? I couldn't wait for this.

Mum tutted. 'You dress in such drab colours these days and in this humid weather it's important to keep ventilated. If you aren't careful you'll come out in a heat rash. Why not wear one of your smart dresses from the Sixth Form? I thought we'd have afternoon tea in Harrods for a treat.'

'Mum, these clothes are comfortable and they're new.'

'Then at least change those dreadful boots. You've hardly taken them off since you came home two weeks ago and are you sure about that purple streak in your hair?'

'It's just a phase, she'll grow out of it,' I'd heard Dad say last night, as if the dye were a new toy.

'We've discussed this, Mum. Please respect that I have my own style.' My voice had trembled the first time I faced their disapproval of my choppy short cut. But each time I defended my point of view it strengthened my resolve, like when faced with their shock that I was no longer vegetarian. Dad lectured me about the level of fat in burgers and horror stories about where takeaways sourced their meat and said I was setting myself up for cancer or heart disease.

My parents seemed to have forgotten their diet hadn't always been restricted. When forging their careers in their twenties, Dad had proposed to Mum during one lunch hour. They often told the story of how they met for lunch near work and Dad ordered her favourite Beef Wellington and tightly rolled up a paper serviette so that the diamond-studded gold band could act as a surprise napkin ring.

I followed Mum towards the front door.

'I'm surprised that you're up in time,' she said. 'Getting back at two a.m., it's no wonder you've got dark shadows under your eyes after your first year at university.'

'I told you not to wait up. I'm perfectly fine in a taxi.'

'Not on your own.'

I'd tried to compromise so that she and Dad wouldn't worry. At university I'd often not be back before four.

Last night my school mates Phoebe and Amelia couldn't believe the change in me. We drank cocktails together and I showed them photos of Ash. It was good to feel like an equal when, finally, I could participate in chat about relationships.

'What are we celebrating, anyway?' I asked brightly as Mum picked up her handbag.

'I'll tell you when we're there,' she said and took out her car keys.

'Mum! Don't do that.' I turned her around and wrapped my arms around her waist. 'You know how much I love you but this is really mean. Come on, spill the beans.' I pulled puppy dog eyes and for a few seconds we laughed together like we used to before I left for university.

'Patience is a virtue, Elizabeth.'

'Pretty please?'

'Oh for goodness sake, okay, if you insist…' Her eyes shone. 'It's not been easy but finally my boss said yes. I've arranged work experience for you in the office. You start the day after tomorrow and it runs until the end of the summer.' Gently she pushed me away and grasped my hands, the biggest smile on her face that I'd seen for ages. 'It's going to be so much fun, you and me working together.'

I didn't blink.

'A wonderful surprise, isn't it? The pay's decent and Greg said he'll put you to work with a wide range of colleagues to teach you as much as possible about the basics of the insurance industry. It'll look so good on your CV and who knows, you might decide it's the area of finance you're most interested in. We can lunch together and you'll meet my friends.' She looked at her watch. 'So we need to get moving. I'll buy you a new wardrobe, you'll need shoes, blouses, a trouser suit perhaps and—'

'Hold on. Mum. I really appreciate what you've done, thanks so much, but…' I let go of her hands, '… there's no way I can accept.'

A confused expression crossed her face as I told her I'd got my job in the clothes shop and they'd kindly increased my hours for the next three months. I'd only just found out and felt so excited. Yet my stomach twisted. I hated to see Mum hurt.

'I love working there and am so lucky Ash pointed out

the advert. The pay's not bad and it's the perfect flexible job for during term time.'

'But Dad and I have told you countless times to ask us if you're short.' She shrugged. 'Just hand in your notice.'

'I'm not doing that. It's about time I earned my own money.' I clenched my fists. I had to stick up for myself. 'I'm sure you'll agree it would be wrong to let my boss down at the last minute. I'm really grateful, Mum, but it's time I started sorting things out for myself.'

We still went for afternoon tea and chatted about anything but my job. I complimented the new lipstick she was wearing. She normally loved it when I noticed things like that but hardly smiled. We didn't have our usual jokey argument about which should go on the scones first, cream or jam and we had a small glass of champagne but it didn't feel as if there was anything to celebrate.

20

Now

Tattoo is one of the most misspelled English words,
often being spelled as tatoo

I stood in the hallway and stared. The woman removed her
floppy hat, the sunglasses and passed me her mackintosh
as if she were some fawned-over fifties film star.

'Caroline?' Trish was right. I should have guessed from
the pungent perfume that almost eliminated the whiff of
tobacco.

'Sorry for barging in but the height of discretion was
necessary.'

I willed myself not to say the obvious.

She closed the front door and brushed down her trouser
suit, not that it needed fluff removing. In the tattoo parlour
I often saw people's behavioural ticks that surfaced when
they felt uncomfortable. Like talking fast, twirling hair,
stroking their phone or rubbing their nose.

'About the cottage,' I said, 'I'm still not exactly sure when I'll be leaving but—'

'I haven't come about that.'

'Oh. Right. May I ask... why the disguise?'

'It's not a disguise. I just don't want everyone knowing my business.'

'Coffee?'

'Something stronger?' she asked hopefully. Tentatively she went into the lounge and surveyed the room, shoulders hunched as if she expected the roof to collapse. Eventually they relaxed. 'There's a lot of room for improvement but you've definitely smartened up the place.'

'Are you here because you've heard about the kitten and want to adopt it?'

'Good lord, no.' She pressed her fingers on the sofa before sitting down.

I came back armed with two glasses and a bottle of wine. Caroline poured whilst I fetched Taz to sit on the sofa with us. She eyed him suspiciously and put one of the cushions between them. With her immaculate executive lines, the professional no-nonsense demeanour, she reminded me of Mum, until she spoke her next, barely audible sentence.

'I want a tattoo.'

'Pardon?'

She looked at the door leading to the hallway as if worried someone might hear.

'I'm not sure what to say. I thought you didn't approve.'

'I don't. Not completely. Ink work everywhere, on show – it's not appealing, but something simple, classy, discreet... you see I've got this new boyfriend.'

Caroline got divorced five years ago. Her husband had

an affair. She threw herself into her career to get over it and then two years ago started dating again – mostly with men half her age, according to Jill.

'We've been dating for just under six months. He's… a little younger than me.' She cleared her throat. 'Twenty-one years to be exact, he's just turned thirty.' She hugged her knees and a helpless smile crossed her face, the telltale sign that told me what she was going to say next. 'I want his name tattooed on my body, across my lower back. We're going on a beach holiday together in four weeks' time. It'll be a surprise.'

'That's a bit… permanent. What if you split up?'

'We won't,' she said quickly and sipped her wine.

'Why all the cloak and daggers?'

'My boss Julie, she wouldn't approve and I'm pushing for a promotion. It's hard on my own and I can't miss out again, so I'm doing everything I can to look polished and bring in business. I know the tattoo won't be on display but even so… I think it would taint her view of me.' Caroline gave a sheepish smile. 'You met her at the party.'

'I'm sorry but I don't think it's a good idea. People usually regret such personal tattoos and have you thought… is there the smallest possibility that he might not welcome it?'

'He'll feel flattered.'

'Six months isn't that long. There's no reason he shouldn't be as serious about the relationship as you but I wouldn't be doing my job properly if I didn't make you consider all the possibilities. What if he isn't and finds the tattoo a bit overwhelming.'

'He is serious,' she said sharply and topped up her glass. Tentatively she tickled Taz's ears. 'We had an argument recently and split up for a few days, but we're back together. This will be a symbol of my commitment to him and it'll make me seem younger; show him that whatever his family think, the age difference isn't a problem.'

Oh crap – the fixer tattoo. I'd seen it many times before, the hope that a tattoo will repair a broken relationship. I've inked couples who've been through a rough patch and just got back together, but the sniping in the treatment room made it obvious they'll soon regret their matching designs. One irritable couple each had the half of a heart inked onto their wrists – they were both back within a month for laser removal.

'I'm sorry, Caroline, I just don't feel comfortable about it.' And I thought back to the tattoo I'd nearly coloured in the wrong colour and Katya's face when she'd come into the room to give me a message and, having overheard me chat about the details of the design earlier, pointed out that I'd selected the wrong ink. I'd let her down and let down myself too. What if I made another error?

And yet... My stomach fluttered.

'I'm a paying customer.' She folded her arms. 'Don't you have to do what I ask?'

'No, because I care and a client being happy with my art, forever, is more important than what I might earn.' I sighed. 'Look, Caroline, find another tattoo artist. I- I'm not right for this.'

Her arms dropped to her sides. 'Look, I've thought this through. Designs on backs are sexy. Please, I'd rather go to a tattoo artist I've got to know a little. It's a dangerous business, I've Googled it. I could end up with a misspelt name.' She leant forward. 'Or catch some awful disease.'

'Not if you go to a reputable parlour and in any case, I haven't got any sterilising equipment here. I'd have to send off for disposable needles and they could take a week to arrive.'

'Will that still leave enough healing time?'

'Yes, all being well you only need two weeks. It's not the easiest place to have a tattoo, though. You'd have to try to sleep on your side for the first couple of nights and—'

'Whatever it takes.'

I remembered the initial period of officially dating Ash, that all-encompassing excitement, the belief that nothing nor no one could ever break our bond. I didn't date with my head *or* heart those first few months. We'd made do with just kissing in the beginning. Ash sensed I was only just finding myself. But once I felt more solid in terms of who I was, Ash and me, we had sex – a lot.

'What else symbolises your relationship, say... the place you first met or got close?' I'd missed talking to clients, helping them to dig deep and come up with the perfect design for them. 'I once tattooed a man who got to know his girlfriend whilst backpacking around Asia. He had a map of Thailand across his back with a heart marking the town where they met.' I shrugged. 'Or has he ever given you a particular flower? Or—'

'We did have our first kiss under one of the oak trees in Leafton Forest. He picked some acorns off the ground afterwards and we shared them to remember the moment. I still have them in a bowl at home. He's soppy like that.' Caroline stopped stroking Taz. 'He makes me feel good, Lizzie. There's nothing wrong with celebrating that, is there?'

I put down my glass and smiled. 'What about a sprig of oak leaves, then, with a few acorns?' My stomach fluttered again, like it used to when I worked. I hadn't felt like this for such a long time. Perhaps Katya was right, being away from London was just the tonic I needed. 'You could get it done in black or add shades of brown and green.' It was such a popular tattoo to have and would also have meaning if they ever split up. Acorns are symbolic of something new growing into something strong, so it would symbolise Caroline moving on from her divorce. I showed her my portfolio to give her ideas and she pointed to a design someone had on their foot. Hungry, I made us cheese sandwiches and then sketched out a wider version to go across the bottom of her back. It was as if I'd never had a break from my art.

She scrutinised the drawing and the lines on her brow disappeared. 'I love it. Can you book me in?'

I swallowed, still hesitant, still doubting myself. 'Feel free to take this sketch to another artist.'

'Please,' she said. 'I won't trust anyone else.'

I took a deep breath. I couldn't help but feel excited.

We decided on her next day off in the middle of next week and then enjoyed general chit-chat whilst we finished eating. I helped her back into the mackintosh and she put on the hat and glasses even though it was dark outside now. Taking out her cigarettes she hurried off. I locked up the house, realised how tired I was, and Taz swiped me as I put him into his bed. Angrily he meowed as I yawned and turned off the kitchen light. It immediately went silent and stayed quiet as I shut the door. I stood outside in the hallway just waiting for one meow before I went upstairs. Nothing. I opened the door to check he was all right.

Something furry touched my foot. I turned on the light and gazed down. Blue eyes stared up.

'No,' I said.

Taz pawed at my toes.

'Oh, for goodness sake!' I picked him up in one arm and the litter tray in the other. He settled on my bed whilst I checked for hazards like loose wires. Firmly I closed the bedroom door. Because I didn't have many belongings or furniture it was easy to kitten-proof the area. I washed and brushed my teeth and by the time I got back, Taz had snuggled up to one of the pillows. I climbed in between the sheets with my phone and Taz nestled into my neck. I pulled him off and settled him further down the bed but clumsily he made his way back and once again collapsed under my chin. For the first time since sleeping here I was glad for the company, after hearing Trish's story about the teddy bear and how she'd hinted that she hadn't yet told me the full story. What if she was withholding even more disturbing details?

Yet the building itself still felt kind. There had to be a logical reason for the teddy bear and blood.

Eventually the kitten's breathing slowed and with another yawn I went on my phone and ordered a batch of disposable tattoo needles, a small part of me still wondering if I was doing the right thing, tattooing again. An advert caught my eye about a parlour in London. I did miss aspects of the capital like my favourite fried chicken takeaway, the impressive skyline and the shopping. Perhaps it was no surprise that a glamorous author like Frederick found it hard to settle here. Yet Ben's face came into my mind, along with friendly Neve, the free iced bun from Tim, the beautiful forest and the cottage's postcard pretty garden.

As each day passed, I sensed my grip on London life slowly loosening and amiable Leafton's grasp becoming tighter.

21

Now

The 2018 Melbourne Literary Festival featured a pop-up tattoo parlour inking literary memorials

I opened my eyes as a wet nose bumped the end of mine. For a brief moment reality merged with my dream. I'd been rubbing noses with my reflected friend. Mum had told me Eskimos did that. I'd run into my bedroom and stood in front of the mirror, touching it with my nose and turning my head from side to side. Then Jimmy Jammy appeared and told us it was yukky. The last moments of it got stranger as my reflection jumped out of the mirror and the two of us chased him downstairs and into the garden, threatening to do it to him.

I yawned and stared at the ceiling, letting the room come into focus. Taz butted my chin. I recalled yesterday – Trish and everything she'd said about Frederick. I picked up my phone from the pillow and out of curiosity I went onto Amazon to read the blurb for his new book. Nothing caught my eye until the end.

I re-read the last sentence.

It was a very tenuous link.

Probably nothing.

When Sal moves to Riverside Cottage she has dreams
of starting again. Her marriage to Brad is on the rocks
after his one-night stand. He wants out. She wants in.
Sal find out she is pregnant so reluctantly he finds them
a new place to live.
A new beginning.
However, her dreams of idyllic countryside living soon
turn into nightmares when she and Brad get to know
Charlotte and Martin.
Sal questions her own sanity. And fears for her life.
Why would he take an expectant mother to live in a
place that would be best hidden from a child?

The novel was inspired by Streamside Cottage and spoke of hiding the place from a child, just like my parents had hidden the cottage from me when growing up.

As I washed Taz's bowls, thoughts that didn't make sense whirred around in my mind. I brushed my hair, pulled on skinny jeans and my favourite t-shirt. I recalled the photo of Frederick I'd seen on his website. There was no doubt he was attractive with the thick black hair and strong jawline. Yet he wore a tight leather jacket that hinted at the extra pounds of middle age and a forced expression that said 'I want you to believe I'm a Very Important Author.'

How could I speak about Frederick again to Trish without upsetting her? Perhaps I'd drop into The Pen Pusher and judge her mood.

Taz didn't want to settle in his bed so I left him staring out of the French patio doors. I went into the garden and sat by the stream, theories about the blurb running through my mind as quickly as the water. As the sun shone down and the water babbled, as the weeping willow branches gently shimmied in the breeze I could have sat there forever. Over and over the last line repeated in my mind. I got to my feet and paced up and down but no revelation or insight arrived. Time passed quickly until lunchtime and I went indoors and sat on the sofa, alone with my frustration. Ben's car flashed past the front of the house. I ran to the front door and called down to his house, asking if he fancied a sandwich. I couldn't explain the compulsion that made Ben the person I wanted to talk to about this.

Apparently, he'd had a busy morning and been collared by his ex-girlfriend's parents.

'They are on my round, both retired but they've just set up a dog-walking business.' He sat at the kitchen table, and stared out of the window for a second. 'My ex… she's just got engaged.'

I nodded sympathetically. Finding that out must have been a shock.

'We split up because she'd met another bloke at the gym – it's not a hobby we shared. Her mum and dad didn't want me to hear from anyone else. She lives in Manchester now, having given up her job for him and is temping until a permanent position comes up.' Ben sighed. 'I wish her well, really I do, but I think she's rushed into that commitment just like she and I did. They've only known each other for six months. I can't even imagine going on a date with a stranger, not yet.'

I broke eye contact with him as my stomach squeezed. Then I tried to imagine what it would feel like if Ash met someone else soon after our break-up. Perhaps he had. Oddly, it didn't feel as bad as I'd have thought. Ben gave me a sheepish smile and I wanted to envelop him in a hug; it would have seemed so right.

I couldn't explain the familiarity I felt towards him without it being earned.

He took another bite. 'I guess whirlwind romances do exist outside of book covers. Anyway, enough about me, what did you need to discuss?'

I told him about Frederick's novel. 'I'm not sure what to do next,' I said. 'I don't want to push Trish to talk, the break-up hit her badly.' I didn't tell him she'd held something back.

Ben rubbed his hands together and sat up. 'Let's see what I can find out.' His eyes twinkled as he went on his phone and I couldn't help smiling as I made cups of tea. Ben's was almost cold by the time he looked up. 'He's doing a book signing tour kicking off with the launch next Thursday. Perhaps he's stayed true to the cottage's location and based the story in Hertfordshire because the first stop is at Chapter and Verse, the Independent Bookshop of the Year, down the road in Henchurch. Tickets cost fifteen pounds on the door which includes a copy of the book.' He shrugged. 'It's the perfect opportunity to meet him face to face and find out everything you need to about that blurb.'

'Thanks, Ben, that's a good idea.'

He glanced outside. Sunshine poured in the French patio doors.

'Fancy coming with me to the forest? It's a great afternoon

for taking photos and it's so peaceful there. Just what I need after this morning.'

I looked out and studied the weeping willow once more, the shape of the leaves, the curve of the branches. My fingers twitched as I recalled how it had felt to sketch Caroline's acorn design.

'It's no biggie if you don't,' he quickly added.

'No, I'd love to, thanks. Just let me get ready, I'll be five minutes.'

He beamed. 'Meet you outside. I'll just change and grab my camera.'

We stopped at Blossom's Bakes on the way and Ben grabbed a bag of cookies. Once we arrived at the bench, in the forest, I applied more sun cream, even though there was more shade. Ben offered me a cookie and we sat eating.

'However often I come here, it always looks different,' he said and wiped crumbs from his mouth. 'That's one thing I love about living in England – the distinct four seasons. There's always a new berry or flower to admire and I love capturing the changing weather.' He swigged from his water bottle, got up and took out his camera.

I watched him for a while, crouching down to snap mushrooms and looking skywards to photograph chinks of sunlight forging their way through the tree canopies. An oak caught my eye and I thought of Caroline. Tentatively I took out my sketch pad and a pencil. I opened it and stared at the blank page before drawing a sprig of the oak leaves. Then I turned my attention to a cluster of dandelions on the ground. Quicker and quicker my hand moved. I drew peeling bark, a pile of soggy leaves, spider webs and spongy moss. I turned the page and sketched the fanned-out appearance of ferns. A bush caught my eye punctuated by bright tangerine berries. Within minutes I'd transferred their image to the page.

My pulse raced. This felt good. It felt right. My eyes tingled… it had been so long since I'd dived into the moment creatively, like this. I'd forgotten how drawing really made me feel… like me.

Ben came over and hovered by my shoulder. 'Do you mind if I look?'

I paused for a second and then turned the sketch book his way. He sat down and studied my work for a few moments. 'These are really good, Lizzie. I love how you've caught the light on that bark. That's one of the things that excites me most about taking photos – how light can be so transformative. And also, how I capture a moment in time that will never be repeated.'

'I feel like that about my tattoos,' I said and nodded. 'They represent a moment in time for whatever the client wants, or needs.'

We looked at each other and smiled, a moment in time where we both felt exactly the same. Then we sat in a comfortable silence for a while. With my permission Ben took a couple of shots of me as I sat on the bench, gazing at nature. He talked about how he'd recently snapped Jill gardening and how her face lost years as she lost herself in her passion.

As the sun began to set, reluctantly I packed away my sketch pad. We headed back, Ben making me laugh as he talked about the times he'd borrow his mum's camera as a small boy, and never failed to take a photo that didn't have his finger across the lens.

We came to the cottage.

'How about I make us something to eat?' I said, not wanting to call it a day. 'I know Taz would appreciate a guest.'

22

*The Koi fish symbolises perseverance
in the face of adversity*

I stood in front of my easel, in the white-washed art room that smelt of floor cleaner. My fingers twitched as if they knew what was about to happen. The stick of charcoal felt smooth in my hand. It looked so unremarkable yet, given the right inspiration, could produce magic. I was three weeks into my first year at university. The theme for this first term in the art society was Impressionist portraiture.

Sitting on a table the society's third year president, Tom, took off his jumper revealing a beautiful orange Koi fish tattooed onto the front of his arm. I'd admired the lines and depth of its colour the week previously. He'd had it done on his return from visiting Japan in the summer, just before coming back to re-sit all his exams after stress had caused him to fail.

'Right guys, the Impressionists painted what they felt

about a subject, rather than trying to create an accurate depiction. They focused on visual impression, according to how the colour and light shifted. Let's take that a step further and simply focus on the personality that we feel shining out from our partner.'

I'd had a full morning of lectures and almost hadn't come but didn't want to let Ash down. We'd partnered up out of necessity. Everyone else seemed to have joined with a friend. Several from Ash's art course attended but he hadn't got to know them well yet. My hand moved across the paper, conjuring up the strong nose, the eyes lit by humour and thin lips that always looked as if they were on the verge of laughing. Full lips were the modern trend. I'd never got it. Ash's represented his quick-witted observational comments and added angularity and strength to his face.

I focused completely on the drawing, grateful to escape my worries – like how I'd shown myself up last night not knowing how to drink a Jagerbomb. Earlier my flatmates had teased me about having never travelled on a bus. Heidi gave me a hug and said it was sweet. She did the same when I washed my red t-shirt with white underwear and my bras and knickers came out pink. I'd tried to make Mum let me help out more at home but she always said it was her job. Mine was to study hard.

Standing out was no bad thing, but only when it was your decision.

The rub of charcoal against paper filled the silence along with the wall clock's ticking. Ash attempted to chat about the foam party the students' union was running at the weekend. Perhaps he regretted teaming up with me; I wasn't as entertaining as Megan who impersonated celebrities or Jay who'd share his Red Bull. Yet we'd inadvertently found ourselves shopping together after the first lesson and last week we'd gone for coffee after the meeting which always took place on a Wednesday when we had the afternoon free – apart from Ash's football practice but that wasn't until six. I'd ordered my usual decaffeinated black Americano but he persuaded me to try something Mum would have said was bad for my nervous system and teeth. A caffeinated hazelnut syrup latte quickly became my favourite.

I'd also bumped into him at a club and we'd danced together briefly. I was in a t-shirt and jeans. My parents had reassured me that was all students wore. Maybe back in the seventies but everything was different now. For a night in town the girls in my flat wore tight dresses and high sandals. They used eyebrow pencils and applied highlighters.

Their make-up bags sounded more like stationery cupboards.

Heidi had insisted on curling my brown hair. It was so long I only ever tied it back in a ponytail, like Mum and her smart chignon. According to her, busy people didn't have time to think about styling when they got up in the morning.

I took down my sheet from the easel as we swapped over. Ash started to draw but after five minutes he stopped.

'What's wrong today, Lizzie?'

'I'm just tired.' Uninvited tears arrived in my eyes.

Ash packed away both our sheets into his folder and made our excuses to Tom who gave a knowing look. I felt better thinking it was nothing unusual for First Years to break down. Ash placed an arm around my shoulder and guided me down to the student canteen. He had a rakish elegance – an unassuming air that I often found myself thinking about.

We snagged a table in the corner. 'Hot chocolate, whipped cream, marshmallows, all the trimmings, no arguments,' he said, making a drink sound more like a dish from a Michelin starred restaurant. He disappeared to the counter and came back with the two steaming mugs plus burgers. I took a mouthful of the rich brown liquid and immediately felt cheered.

'How much do I owe you?' I said, enjoying the light-hearted ambiance of cutlery on plates, of coffee machines grinding beans and frothing milk, of students chatting earnestly or larking around.

'I got it on my canteen card. You can treat me next week.' Something apart from the hot chocolate warmed my insides. For the first time in days a sense of home infused me.

'So what's going on?' asked Ash. He'd already eaten half his burger. His dark eyes pierced through my evasiveness. 'Is there someone back home? Are you missing them? One of my flat mates is on the phone twenty-four seven to his girlfriend.'

'No, nothing like that.' My cheeks flushed. 'I've never had a boyfriend.'

Ash laughed. 'Yeah, right.'

I stared at my drink.

'Wow, you're not joking? Sorry, I'm just surprised.'

I took another sip of hot chocolate. 'I wanted to go out with a boy at school once, called Jake. We got to know each other in Year Eleven. He worked hard and was polite, we studied together. I thought my parents would be impressed.'

'What happened?'

'They found out that his older brother was in prison for dealing. Even though his parents ran a successful business and he volunteered in a charity shop, they refused to believe Jake and his family wouldn't mean trouble.'

He tilted his head. 'No one's perfect. What sort of man were they waiting for?'

Good question.

'They… they were just being protective.'

'So, why the tears today?'

'This morning, I got an essay back.' My voice wavered. 'A fail.'

'Bad luck.' He took off his suede jacket. 'Stinks, doesn't it? But that's what the first year is all about.'

'What do you mean?'

'A levels were different from GCSEs and a degree is new again. I don't think it's realistic to expect that everyone will do great straight off. I mean, the first year of Sixth Form college was hard enough, wasn't it?'

'I stayed in the school Sixth Form… but I dunno, it seemed okay to me. Truth is I've never failed at anything.'

Ash stopped chewing. 'How's that even possible?'

Another good question.

'Mum and Dad always helped me plan my study timetables. They'd go over my homework, help me revise and check I'd done everything I needed to every night.'

'But that was just when you started high school, right?'

'No, up until the end of the Sixth Form.'

His eyebrows shot into his hairline. 'That's pretty hands on.'

It was? It had never really struck me that other parents didn't get involved with homework. 'I did fail a biology test in Year Seven once. Dad went mad.'

'Ground you, did he? Mum used to take my gadgets away for a whole week if I failed a test she thought I should have passed.'

'No, he wasn't mad with *me*. He went into the school and told them he and Mum didn't pay their extortionate fees for me to get marked down. They changed the grade and it didn't happen again.'

Ash let out a low whistle. 'The benefits of private schooling.'

Heat crept up my neck. 'I guess so, but as high school progressed, I got tutors, worked hard. It was rare for me to ever get less than an A.'

'So what went wrong this time?'

'I've been trying to stick to the timetable Mum and Dad helped me with. They spent ages and I'm really grateful but—'

'Whoa, tell me you're joking. They are still doing that stuff? And you're still letting them?' Ash pushed away his plate. 'Lizzie, come on, you're one of the most sensible people I've met here. You can do that for yourself.'

I squirmed in my seat. I could?

'So why do you think their plan didn't work?'

'They meant well but it just doesn't fit with student life. The plan sets aside evenings for study, but I'm often out or cooking with flatmates. And they always drilled into me never to study much after eleven, so that only left early mornings and lunchtimes plus a couple of hours after lectures. I just didn't have enough time to put into the essay as I wanted.'

'I'm not surprised. Lizzie. Working late into the night is a bona fide part of university life. I'm talking coffee, caffeine tablets, whatever it takes.'

I looked at my burger. How was Ash to know I was vegetarian? Not that I'd ever decided that for myself. Mum and Dad just said it was healthier but I'd always loved the smell of frying bacon if we passed a café in town.

'I reckon you'll feel your way into a study plan that suits you best, as the term progresses – and only you can do that. Your parents aren't here to see how you live, so how can they possibly know what's best? I've already realised going to the library suits me as there are too many distractions in the flat.'

'I hadn't thought about it like that. You must think me pretty lame.'

His hand covered mine. 'You're kind, generous, intelligent, funny, even if you don't mean to be. Last week in art soc you gave your water bottle to that guy who was suffering a hangover. When I bumped into you clubbing the other night, once you chilled, I couldn't keep up with your *freakish* dance moves.'

I laughed.

'It's okay to get a fail sometimes, Lizzie. You've got everything going for you. I just think you've never been used to taking risks.'

'All risks are dangerous. My parents work in insurance and have always told me that.'

'Really? Take… Bill Gates. He dropped out of college to found Microsoft. That could have backfired. And think of Neil Armstrong, setting the first human foot on the moon. He didn't know what would happen and when the rocket took off there was every chance the mission could have failed or even worse, but nevertheless he followed his heart.'

I took in every word.

'You just need a bit of self-belief. You can do this, like the thousands of other students who muddle through. Don't be so hard on yourself. Half the time none of us really know what we're doing, but we're learning.'

I lifted the burger roll and took a bite. My taste buds clung to the smoked flavours and juices. Heaven. Already one risk had paid off.

'Not even you?'

'You're talking to the person who a couple of years ago dabbled with online dating. I lied about my birth date to register. A woman asked me to send her a dirty picture.' He covered his eyes with his hands. 'I sent her a photo of me in my muddy cricket kit.'

I managed to stop giggling a few minutes later and we went outside. The October sun had found space to shine despite being stalked by a large cloud. My hair had come loose and I took out the bobble and re-tied it tight.

'Nice hair,' said Ash.

'I'd love to get it all cut off.'

'What's stopping you?'

I met his gaze.

'There's only one opinion that matters, Lizzie, that's if you want a life where you're happy inside. I've learnt a lot the last year or two about being true to myself.'

As we walked towards the library, he told me about the conversations he'd had with his parents since he was sixteen – about not wanting an arranged marriage; about wanting to go out drinking with his friends. His grandparents had moved over from Pakistan, along with a great-uncle. His mum and her brother were born here and he didn't embrace all the Pakistani traditions, so Ash's mum understood how her son felt; said it would take some getting used to but she loved him and knew he had to find his own way just like her brother had.

'Getting my hair cut hardly compares to that.'

'It does if it's the start of something big, like you finally embracing the real you.'

I looked at those thin lips and despite what Dad would have said about bad language thought *fuck it*. I reached up and kissed him full on the mouth. It was a shock when his lips parted but then everything felt warm and soft and he pulled me closer. When I eventually broke away whooping came from across the road as I caught my breath. Heidi was jumping up and down with her thumbs up. I laughed and waved back.

'Just, you know, following your advice about taking risks. I hope you don't mind.' Shyly I met his eyes.

He was laughing too and shook his head. Ash was right, instead of moping I needed to get control of my life. Mum and Dad couldn't supervise the way I lived forever – it wasn't right for me or them. They were busy people and surely me leaving home heralded a new beginning for the three of us? My parents would have less to worry about and could now focus on themselves after all these years of looking after their daughter. They deserved that.

I loved them to bits. They thought of my every need but shouldn't have to any longer.

They'd no doubt consider me taking control a huge relief.

23

Now

"As an oak cometh of a litel spyr" – Chaucer 1374

I opened the front door as rain spat down onto a woman who collapsed her golf umbrella, and with her cap and jaunty black curls pushed past me, without invitation. Indoors she removed the hat and false hair.

'Luckily my sister is into amateur dramatics,' she said, holding her props.

'I've prepared the lounge, you can lie down on the sofa and I've set up my machine.' My inks and cleaning materials were on the coffee table and I'd placed a fresh bed sheet on the sofa. I'd texted her during the week and she'd dropped in to approve the final design. She'd decided against shading so it was a simple black outline of two acorns on the left with oak leaves stretching across to the right.

My stomach twisted, partly with pleasure, partly with… fear. I felt excited to watch my creation come to life yet I still doubted myself after Katya asking me to take a break.

I checked the ink and needle and then checked them again. I gritted my teeth. I could do this.

I could do this because Leafton was recharging my passion for nature, for sketching, for following my calling.

'Let's get started; if you could lie on your front. I'll pull up your blouse and will have to tug down your trousers a bit if that's okay.'

'Why don't I just take off my top?'

Before I knew it, she was lying on her chest, head to the side, in her dusky pink lace bra. I didn't need to pull down the top of her trousers to know that her underwear would match. You can tell a lot about people's knickers. Coordination told me that Caroline wanted to impress; that she was organised and valued her appearance, and confirmed what I already knew – that her choice of tattoo would be conservative. Boy shorts and thongs were favoured by sporty, practical, go-getting types who would never admit to any pain. As for those who went commando – they didn't care about image or people-pleasing and had the most unusual tattoos. The same could be said of their antithesis – the woman who wore big grannie pants or man in white Y-fronts. They felt comfortable in their skin and felt equally at ease with whatever was inked onto it.

I put on latex gloves and cleaned Caroline's back with kitchen roll and Dettol. Then I pressed down the stencil and removed it after a few moments.

'Let's double-check you are happy with the position.'

I'd brought down the long mirror from my bedroom and leant it against the wall. Caroline got up and went over.

'Is the design low enough?'

'It's perfect.'

She lay on the sofa again. I pressed on the machine's foot pedal and as I predicted, Caroline hardly winced. Nevertheless, I always considered distraction important.

'Where are you going on holiday?' I asked.

'Italy. Just the two of us for a whole week.'

She didn't sound very excited. 'Are you sure this isn't hurting? Caroline?'

'It's fine and no worse than if you were pulling off a waxing strip.'

I carried on with the outline of the first acorn, concentrating hard on every millimetre of the design. My heart thumped a little less noisily and my breathing calmed as the tattoo started to take shape just as I'd imagined. I was doing okay.

'I've done a lot of thinking since our initial chat about this tattoo last week. I can't believe I almost had Dale's name inscribed on me, forever. You were right.'

'Don't be too hard on yourself. It's one of my most popular requests. We're wired to believe a love interest will last.'

'But I'm fifty-one, I should know better. I've also mulled over the design and exactly what it means.'

I wiped down the patch I'd just inked and pressed the power pedal again.

'My divorce... I never thought I'd get over it; never thought anyone would find me attractive again so I focused even more on my job, offering to work every weekend. The money came in handy, now I'd bought Chris out and was paying the mortgage on my own but it was more than that. I- I felt like a failure and knocked back a couple of men of my age who asked me out. I didn't want to risk getting that hurt again.'

'What changed your mind?'

'One day a builder helped me pick up shopping I'd dropped. He was only in his twenties. He juggled a couple of loose potatoes before putting them in my bag. He said I smelt great and made me laugh; made me feel good about myself. For the first time I understood the attraction of younger men and then I met Dale in a bar. He came in for a coke after working out and we got talking. Turned out he was a personal trainer. I asked for a few tips and he questioned whether I needed any, said I looked in great shape. I felt ten feet tall.'

I carried on with my work, letting Caroline talk about how they'd got together. Clients would open up about all kinds of stuff – how they hated their boss, that their partner didn't understand them, that they were suffering problems with their health.

'I've been addicted to that feeling, that high, ever since,' said Caroline. 'The thrill when a young man looks at me in a certain way and I realise finds me desirable, despite the age spots and lines I try to hide. But this tattoo has really made me face what I want from a relationship and I realise that's something more permanent.'

'Not with Dale?'

'He won't even be fifty by the time I'm eighty, and the way he talks about his nephews and nieces, I know he wants kids. It just wouldn't work after the initial lust wore off.' I stopped as she wriggled to get comfortable. 'After the holiday I'm going to try to be brave and call things off, join a dating site and start looking for someone nearer to where I am in my life.'

'This acorn's a great tattoo for you then.'

'From little acorns mighty oaks grow? Yes, exactly, that's what I thought and decided I'd have the design done anyway. Who knows where my life will go from here?'

I wiped down the skin again.

'Do you get asked to tattoo family members for free?' she asked.

'No. There was only my mum and dad and they were never fans of my art work.'

'Have you any idea why they didn't want to take phone calls from my office? Did they talk about Streamside Cottage?'

I told her about how I'd known nothing of this place, about Mum's sixtieth party and Dad's letter and briefly filled her in on what I'd learned about Leafton so far. And I made it clear I didn't want Aunt Fiona to know I was here. 'Have you ever heard of people called the Strachans?'

'No, and by the sounds of it, Jill has told you all the gossip from over the years. Not a bad amount, considering the place hasn't had a steady run of tenants. At the agency we couldn't get over those who'd been growing weed and ever since then I've been more conscientious about checking the property, so like to think I would have picked up anything out of the ordinary.'

'What about… I don't know… the thatched roof fire you mentioned? Could it have been started on purpose?'

'The cause was definitely lightning.'

Our chat moved onto the village and how it was usually impossible to keep any secret.

'Like young Neve, she got caught shoplifting when she started High School. It's ironic that she now works in retail.'

'But she seems so… straight.'

'She always had a wild side. Before Alan she had a boyfriend who'd annoy her neighbours by revving his motorbike. And then there was Ryan, Tim's son. Did you know he once dated a pole dancer? And…'

I learnt a lot about Leafton's inhabitants as the inking progressed. I could see how knowing stories about each other bound them together; the embroidery of life in the village was colourful but reliable.

'How about Ben?' I said in a bright voice. 'He's always lived here, hasn't he?'

Caroline's voice couldn't hide a smile. 'Why are you asking? Has anything happened?'

'Not at all,' I replied hurriedly as a flush of heat made my cheeks burn. 'It's just that he's a good neighbour.'

'Yes, he's a good guy. When my husband first left, I realised how much I'd depended on him for the practical stuff around the house. My dishwasher flooded and I'm embarrassed to say I hardly knew how to turn off the water supply. Ben happened to be there, delivering mail. He rolled up his sleeves and helped me clean up and promised to mention me to a plumber friend of his. True enough he did and my dishwasher was sorted that evening and Ben gave me his number and said to call if I ever needed any help.'

'All done,' I said, swiftly changing the subject. I leant back and a lump formed in my throat. I'd done it. The tattoo looked perfect.

I couldn't stop thinking about the cottage's downstairs study, currently home to my tattoo equipment. It would make the perfect treatment room. I could set up my own business. How amazing it would be to carry out my job with such a beautiful view out of the window.

I shook myself. But that would never happen. This beautiful place belonged to Aunt Fiona and in any case, I was going back to London... right?

Caroline was still smiling. She stretched and went over to the mirror and swivelled her body from side to side. There's nothing quite like seeing a client's face when they see their tattoo for the first time. I covered it in cling film and taped that down, then gave her a sheet of paper with aftercare instructions and a sachet of cream.

'Any problems just come and see me,' I said as she put on her top and paid. 'Try not to sleep on your back for a couple of days, especially in this weather as you will sweat and that's the perfect background for bacteria to grow. And tonight, use freshly cleaned sheets and change them regularly. Remember to put sun cream on in Italy otherwise it will fade.'

'Thanks, Lizzie, for taking the time and for not just doing anything I asked.' She put on the wig. 'Oh, and I almost forgot, there is one incident that stands out about this place. I wasn't sure whether to mention it as it's probably nothing. It was nine years ago, just after the pot-growing tenants left.' Caroline reached for her hat. 'A young couple with a baby moved in. They were only here for six months. Quite rightly they freaked out one day because a woman turned up and let herself into the back garden. She just stood there for a few minutes. They asked her what she was doing and told her to leave but she wouldn't explain and stayed glued to the spot. They threatened to call the police, worried about the safety of their baby. She threw a red rose into the stream. By the time the police arrived she'd disappeared.'

24

Now

Breast cancer survivors can get 3D nipple tattoos

Since my last visit with Ben my creative juices were back in full force, and I'd been keen to pay the forest another visit so headed out after lunch. Tomorrow I'd be too busy going to Frederick's book signing. I walked along the high street and noticed a bunch of red roses in the hairdresser's window.

I felt a pang in my chest as I thought of Mum. I never really understood why I loved roses so much, growing up, but when I gave her yet another drawing or gift with one on, I always felt something indefinable hang in the air between us. It didn't make sense. She never grew them or didn't use rose water and I only recall her mentioning the word as a name once. She and Dad were talking over breakfast, one Saturday morning. She'd popped in to wake me up for my swimming lesson and I'd moaned that I didn't want to go, tired from a busy week at school.

As I came into the kitchen the conversation hushed. I'd raised an eyebrow and Mum's face looked blotchy and she muttered something about problems with a staff member at work.

I passed the church and the cemetery yet a strange sensation swept over me as I approached the car park. I passed a large white van and turned around. The pavement was empty yet I could have sworn someone was following. Perhaps the gravestones had unnerved me. I hurried straight towards the clearing with its diffused sunlight and woody fragrances. As I strolled amongst the trees the differences made me impatient to get out my pencil. Some trunks were smooth and white with patches of ivy or moss, others were rust-coloured and corrugated, boasting hideouts for animals. However another instinct told me to go back to the cottage and leave this deserted area. A noise like heavy breathing had crept over my shoulder but when I dared to look, again no one was there.

A tiny bird flew past like last time with a bluish head and orange chest, except now I knew what it was, a Nuthatch, as I'd gone on the internet after my last trip. I pushed forwards into the forest and the trees thinned. I'd almost reached the clearing but then a twig snapped and bushes rustled. I quickened my pace as a bird gave the alarm call and my foot got caught. I looked down to see a horizontal tree root. My chin slammed onto the ground and I tasted blood. I lay for a few moments, taking in what had just happened then my heart pounded louder as footsteps sounded, crushing leaves as they neared me. The breathing became heavier. I scrabbled to get up.

'Trish?'

She came into view, eyes red with hay fever and wearing matching scarlet shorts and a fringed blouse.

'Lizzie, I'm so sorry, I didn't mean to scare you.' She guided my face to the sun and took off purple-rimmed sunglasses to get a better look at my chin. 'I think you'll be okay. Sorry again. I feel terrible.'

Trish held my elbow and steered me over to the log. She sat down next to me. My lip stung where I'd bitten it.

'I spotted you in the village and wanted to talk, privately. Yet every time I caught you up, I changed my mind.' She gave an apologetic smile. 'I should have thought that you might hear and feel spooked.'

'It's okay, you didn't know this would happen,' I said and took a mouthful of bottled water, swilled it around and spat into a bush. Trish passed me a tissue and I wiped my mouth.

'Quiet here isn't it?' She picked up a fallen leaf and twisted its stalk between her fingers. 'It gives you time to think, which isn't always a good thing.'

'I was thinking about people I've lost,' I said, rubbing my chin.

We sat in silence for a while.

'I lost my sister three years ago. The cancer took her quickly. We used to get together every Christmas and I'd moan that she cooked everything in goose fat. I'd do anything for one of her greasy roast potatoes now.'

'I'm sorry to hear that,' I said and paused. 'My parents left me a long time before they died.'

'Loss comes in different shapes – a malignant cell, an angry mouth, a broken heart. Sometimes I still think about

Frederick and how badly things ended and how he's gone from my life for good.'

Trish closed her eyes and leant back, her face catching sun rays that had found a way through the thick tree canopies. My lip hurting less, now, I retrieved my sketch book from my rucksack, intrigued by the different shaped leaves carpeting the ground. Had Mum and Dad become fans of nature whilst living in Devon or did they miss the hard-hitting architectural lines and energy of the city? I thought I'd find it hard to live without the dining choices, the entertainment, the people-watching, yet was beginning to appreciate the simplicity of rural living.

They and I could have been happy in a place like Leafton, me going to the local school, the three of us enjoying cake in Tim's shop, the fresh air and tranquillity of the garden. Without the dangers of London life, perhaps they would have trusted me to be more independent. Perhaps they wouldn't have done the *terrible thing* Dad had talked about in his letter. Sometimes, at night, I'd try to imagine what that could have been, sweating under the covers, stomach churning. Neither parent was a violent person. Both put spiders outside instead of squashing them. They didn't want pets but always contributed to animal protection charities if collectors came around. They paid their tax and carefully respected speed limits, never driving after drinking alcohol. Mum left a shop one day and accidentally forgot to pay for a magazine. The next day she went back to confess.

How could they have ever done something really bad?

Trish opened her eyes, glanced at me and then went to get up.

'Sorry. You wanted to talk? It's hard to stop drawing once I start.'

'Why not use your talent on canvas where it can be displayed in galleries?'

'Because it's not living… It's not personal enough. My tattoos will stay with someone for their entire life.'

She relaxed onto the bench again, shoulders slumped as if the trees had bent over to rest their boughs on them.

'Everything okay?' I asked and put down my pad. She didn't reply. I tilted my head and examined her skin – the age spots and nose to mouth lines, the mole in the middle of her left cheek. 'If you're not in a hurry could I sketch you?' I said. 'I haven't done a portrait for months. It won't take long.'

'Me?'

'Why not?'

I'd been longing to sketch Ben's face for a while now. Those freckles and soft lips, the way his mouth looked crooked when he felt shy, the eyes that crinkled in the corners if he was making a joke. But for some reason, asking him, it would feel so intimate.

I faced her and started with the eyes that were slightly hooded with folds at the corner and heavily shaded underneath. The nose had a slight curve half-way down and small nostrils. I studied her straight teeth sitting like rows of matching chair backs. My fingers ached as I finished drawing the curls in her hair. Finally, I flexed my hand and showed her the drawing.

'Good lord. I'm the spit of my mum, that's her nose exactly – although she always appeared happy with her lot. I look a right misery guts.'

'That's not what I see. To me the drawing portrays a strong-featured person who's got through tough times.'

Her face brightened.

'That's the exciting thing about art, everyone's got their own interpretation.'

'Fred used to say that about his writing.' She threw down the leaf. 'I wish I didn't still think about him. The other day… what I said about the haunting being so much worse than I first thought… I feel you should know what I wanted to tell you then… Fred… he was laughing behind my back about being frightened.'

'What? So he wasn't really scared? Not even about the teddy bear covered in blood?'

'It wasn't real, Lizzie. He made it all up.' Eyes glistening she went on to explain.

Frederick's paranoia had been an act. He'd used Trish as inspiration for the main character of his new book who falsely believed she shared her house with a ghost. Fred had got up early and walked through the house in wet shoes. He'd screamed to wake her up and swore the noise came from the stream and Fred bought an old teddy bear from a charity shop. Plus he'd talked incessantly about the area's witchcraft history and his supposed fears, to build up a picture of an author who believed in what they wrote about.

'What a bastard. How did you find out about his lies?'

'I became suspicious. That blood-covered teddy bear was like a prop out of a horror film. He's an egotist so I flattered him, said I understood if he'd made it all up; told him he'd been so clever to pull it off. Fred couldn't help bragging. He said his new novel was going to make waves in the literary world and was glad I realised, for that any sacrifice was necessary.

'I was emotionally vulnerable at the time. That's the worst thing. I think Fred realised I would be susceptible to his deceit. I was the perfect victim and he was desperate for inspiration. His publisher was losing patience because the delivery deadline had already passed.' Trish wiped her eyes. 'He said he was truly fond of me but he didn't even stop when he knew the doctor had put me on tablets. He was that obsessed about having another bestselling book...' She sat up straight. 'I think he honestly thought I'd be honoured that he chose me to help with his research. You see his new novel is a gaslighting story about a cheating husband. He tries to convince his wife she was mad and needs to be sectioned as she's refusing to divorce him. Fred wrote it so that the reader wouldn't know whether the witch was real or not, until right at the end.' Her cheeks flushed. 'The perfect twist from a twisted mind.'

'Did you report him to the police?'

'No. He couldn't understand my angry reaction, said I took it too seriously and that it would be his word against mine. He called things off between us and said people would just think I still loved him and wanted revenge...'

Out of nowhere a Labrador bounded up. Trish jumped up to avoid its wet tongue. The owner followed in its tracks full of apologies but emboldened by living with Taz, I bent over to pet the dog. When I stood up, Trish had gone.

I made my way back to the cottage. When I got there, Ben was chatting to Jill whilst she dug in the front garden.

He waved and walked onto the pavement, coming my way.

At that moment a car drew up – red and sporty-looking.

I gasped as the driver got out of his car.

'Ash? What are you doing here?'

25

Sanskrit is an ancient Indian language and popular in the tattooing world

I hugged Amelia and Phoebe. 'Okay. I'll ask Mum and Dad tonight.'

'I'm so excited,' said Phoebe and pulled down her bobble hat. 'Thinking about this is going to get me through next year's exams.'

'And hopefully divert your thoughts from your decidedly uncool crush,' said Amelia and pulled a face.

'It's those hands and the way Mr Hargreaves holds the baton – imagine how he'd conduct himself in bed.'

I forced a laugh, relieved to see Mum's white Range Rover pull up. I sensed this was going to lead into one of those conversations to which I'd have nothing to contribute. Phoebe lost her virginity last year, on her sixteenth birthday, under a tree. It sounded so romantic – she said it wasn't. Amelia hadn't slept with Callum yet but they'd done lots of stuff I didn't know about. I'd had to Google words she and Phoebe had mentioned over the year so as not to appear too dumb.

'How was orchestra practice?' said Mum as I got in. She turned on the windscreen wipers as sleet began to fall.

'We've started a new piece.'

'Great, let me take a look when we get home.' She pulled up at traffic lights. 'Did you get your marks back for that maths homework we worked late on, last week?'

'Eighty-one per cent.'

'Fantastic, well done, darling.'

My chest glowed.

'Grandpa and Grandma will be so proud. We'll Skype them this weekend.'

Mum missed them since they'd moved to France.

The lights turned green. 'How about a slice of the carrot cake I made when we get back? Dad's finishing work early and seeing as it's Friday we could watch a movie.'

I looked at my phone and my classmates' chat about their Friday night. Those who'd already turned eighteen this term, like me, were off out clubbing with colleagues from their Saturday jobs or younger school friends willing to risk using forged ID. I'd been invited to a party but it was easier to say no. It was worse being the only one to have to leave early than not going at all. And I felt guilty if I turned down my parents' suggestions of spending time together. They'd already started saying how empty the house was going to feel when I went to university.

The car stopped outside our house and I walked past the Roman pillars. Mum let me in. I took off my shoes, hung up my coat, glad that the timed central heating was on.

I went up two flights of stairs to my bedroom and changed into comfortable jogging trousers. A deep voice sounded in the distance. I looked in the mirror and crossed my fingers. When I got downstairs three slices of carrot cake were waiting. As I sipped my decaffeinated coffee my stomach knotted.

'How was your day, Dad?'

'Not bad, Peter was retiring so we went out for an Italian at lunchtime.' He smiled at Mum. 'Remember that weekend in Rome we took, to celebrate you saying yes after I finally managed to get you on a lunch date so that I could propose? I'll have to take you and Elizabeth to this place. The tortellini was just as good.'

'I'm really lucky with all the holidays we've been on,' I said. 'None of my friends have seen so much of Europe and that's one reason why Phoebe and Amelia are going inter-railing around Europe next summer before we go to university. They've asked me along. We've done the research, I've drawn up a list of how much the tickets will cost and—'

'I'm sorry, love,' said Dad and he looked at Mum. 'It's out of the question. You are far too young.'

'Dad, I can get married now if I like. Soldiers travel the world from the age of sixteen. And you and mum have taken all sorts of trips in the past – trekking through the rainforest in Peru... didn't you even hitch-hike around the States one summer, when you first got together?'

Mum looked at Dad. 'That was a long time ago. Times change. Age brings you a wisdom you don't have when you're younger. The answer's no, Elizabeth. How many times do we hear on the news about a young English woman getting murdered abroad, whilst travelling? It's not worth the risk.'

I wished I could just stand up to my parents and say I was going inter-railing whatever they thought but I'd never done anything without their support. What if I messed up? I'd just turned eighteen but had never smoked, nor had sex. I'd never even walked alone in the dark.

Mum and Dad were only looking out for me.

26

Now

*Ivy is an evergreen plant that continues to grow in the
toughest environments*

'Lizzie, it's been a while,' said Ash and he gave me a
warm smile.

I studied the fitted shirt, the crisply ironed jeans. We were
both a world away from the people we'd been in the first
year, that very first term, when we met.

'How…? But why…?'

Ben's voice interrupted. He looked awkwardly between
me and Ash.

'Hi, Lizzie. I won't keep you. About tomorrow afternoon's
book signing – how about I drive you there? I could pick
you up straight after my round. We could grab lunch out
beforehand.'

Ash smiled and held out his hand. 'Ash Kharal. Pleased
to meet you.'

Ben hesitated before returning the gesture.

'Do you want me to give you a lift anywhere, Lizzie?' asked Ash. 'I'm happy to help. I thought we could spend a couple of days together.' His phone bleeped and he took it out of his pocket.

I still couldn't find any words. What was Ash doing in Leafton? Ben filled the silence after glancing at the car.

'No problem if you've made other arrangements, I didn't know you had a visitor,' he said. 'Nice to meet you Ash. Right, I'd better get back – weeding calls.'

'No, Ben, it's not…'

But he'd gone. Ash swiped a message off the front of his phone and put it back into his pocket. He looked up at me.

'Aren't you going to invite me in?' His eyes twinkled.

I'd forgotten how they did that.

He followed me indoors and into the lounge. We sat on the sofa. The bottom of my denim shorts was frayed and they revealed the green climbing ivy tattoo I'd had done after Ash and I split. It crept from my knee to the top of my thigh.

'Nice,' he said, looking at it. 'Love that shade of green.'

'Thanks.' I met his gaze. 'Ash, what are you doing here? You couldn't even ring first?'

'I- I called by the tattoo studio. I wanted to tell you something but then Katya explained about you taking unpaid leave.' He took my hand and I remembered how soft his fingers felt. 'I'm worried about you, Lizzie. I know we're not together now, but all those years… they meant something. Just because we're not a couple doesn't mean I don't care.'

'I just needed a break from work.'

'Why here?'

'I... look, you don't want to hear all of this Ash. We're not together. It's all a bit of a mess, to be honest.'

'Lizzie, of course I'm interested. You were a big part of my life.'

My eyes tingled and I gave a small smile before it all came tumbling out. I showed him Dad's letter. I also mentioned Frederick's book.

A couple of hours passed as we talked it all through. Like I'd done a hundred times, Ash tried fruitlessly to work out the reasons Mum and Dad had kept this place secret.

He frowned. 'What's that noise?'

I listened. An indignant meow.

I jumped to my feet. 'Oh, poor Taz, I completely forgot about him.' Ash followed me as I hurried into the kitchen. He stared as I emptied the litter tray, as I hugged Taz and poured biscuits into his bowl.

'Wow, Lizzie, you owning a cat?'

I couldn't help laughing. 'I don't own him. It's a long story. But yes, guess I've really overcome my fear of germs.'

I made us both juice and sandwiches whilst Ash played with Taz. During the first years of our relationship I'd often pictured us older, in a house a bit like this, with a family.

'So your parents had three properties, along with their home in Devon?' he said, in between mouthfuls. 'That was quite a portfolio.'

I shuffled in my chair.

'Lizzie, no, I wasn't making a point. Sorry, that was tactless. I completely understand, now, why you didn't want to touch your parents' money when we were together. It was wrong of me to ask.'

I put down my glass. 'It wasn't, Ash. I've had time to think too.'

His cheeks coloured up.

Taz jumped onto Ash's lap again and he picked up the stick with a feather on it. I stood up to make us coffee, my mind drifting back to the moment Ash found out I had thousands of pounds in the bank, as I filled the kettle…

'How much?' Ash had said nine months ago. 'Is this a joke?' We'd been picnicking in the most scenic local park, even though the autumn blew cold. I thought it might be romantic, us huddled up together under a rug – I'd try anything to cheer up our flagging relationship. We couldn't afford to do anything expensive at weekends. My earnings paid most of the bills and anything spare was siphoned off into a meagre savings account for our future. Ash earned the minimum wage as a barista and contributed what he could, frustrated that interviews in art therapy had been thin on the ground. He had plans, big plans for the future and was raring to go.

'It's the final total after cashing in my parents' financial policies and selling their home in Devon and the investment properties in Spain and Bournemouth. A large part of the estate also went to charity. They'd bought wisely.'

Ash had put down his sandwich and sat up. 'I didn't know they had a property portfolio, let alone had left anything worth that much to you. Why didn't you tell me before?'

'It didn't seem important. I don't consider it mine. Mum and Dad didn't want contact and I'm sure they wouldn't have wanted me to have their money. I've no doubt, at some point they would have changed their will so that it was all left to Aunt Fiona or good causes.'

'But that's mad. We've been under so much stress. Just a bit of that would really take the pressure off and give us a good start, helping us buy a home and move on with our lives.' He'd spoken with such excited tones.

'I'm not touching a single penny. I just can't.'

'See it as a loan,' Ash had implored. 'We'll pay it back. Lizzie, you can't be serious about us staying in that crappy little flat now.'

'Leave it,' I'd snapped. 'It's my decision not yours.'

He'd packed up the picnic and virtually pulled the rug away from my legs. 'Remember when my great-uncle's money paid for the insurance on your first car? Okay, so it was a small amount but I thought we were a team, Lizzie. We share. This is the break we've been waiting for. You deserve it after everything your parents have put you through. I can't remember the last time either of us had dinner out or bought a new pair of shoes.' He shook his head. 'You know it's not about the money per se – I love the bones of you whatever your bank account says, but with an amount that big, we can fulfil all our dreams.'

Could we? Increasingly I'd felt my heart wasn't in his plans for fancy cars and mansions. I'd longed for a simpler life, after growing up with my high-falutin' parents, whereas Ash had plans for a luxury life – not at the expense of a personal one, or a fulfilling job, helping others, but working hard and reaping the benefits inspired him.

'Ash, I'd do anything to take the strain away – to help you get the job I know you'd love, but can't you understand? I've forged my way in life with no help from my parents. They always said tattooing would never earn me enough money for a decent life. I was adamant that they were wrong and prejudiced. If I use their money to get the life I want, it's as if they've been right all along and me standing up for myself was all for *nothing*.' I'd squeezed his arm. 'We don't need their help. We *can* do this, Ash.'

But the argument had continued all afternoon. The next day we hardly talked and he'd gone to his parents for dinner. As time passed, and he hated his barista job more, resentments on both sides meant the sex and then communication completely stopped.

But then three months later, he'd asked me to marry him...

'He's a feisty little chap,' said Ash, bringing me back to the present. Taz had jumped onto the floor and was playing with Ash's shoelaces.

I sat down opposite him. 'It must have hurt you, me not wanting to use Mum and Dad's money. I'm so sorry. Please forgive me.'

We stared at each other and his brow relaxed. 'There's nothing to forgive, Lizzie.'

'But I should have supported you in the way you'd always supported me.'

'It's okay. Honestly. Recent months have given me perspective too. Grief skews logic, it was a tumultuous time for you.'

'But what I said... when you proposed... it was cruel... I hope you know I didn't mean it.'

'About me only being after you for your money?' He sucked in his cheeks. 'I can't lie, I felt blindsided, but time helped me see that wasn't really you talking.'

'It was a self-defensive mechanism, my way of rejecting the proposal and keeping myself safe, because you asking for my hand in marriage made me realise until I understood my parents' rejection, I'd never be able to settle down. The three of us had been so close yet they'd broken all contact and, illogically I feared being married and then being cut off by a husband and having to go through that sense of loss again.'

That was why I needed to find answers in Leafton.

'I never knew. I wish we'd been able to talk about it,' he said.

'Me too. I should have explained.'

'And I should have been more understanding.'

We held hands for a moment.

Also I worried there was something really wrong with me. There had to be for Mum and Dad to have let go. I'd hurt them and I didn't want to hurt Ash. That's why it had been so important to visit Streamside Cottage. To find out something – anything – that would help me quash those fears.

'Looking back that proposal was just my way of trying to fix us, but we were too broken by then. I can see that now.'

I smiled. It was the same old Ash. Fair, calm, caring.

'I just want you to know,' I blurted out, 'you were the best boyfriend ever. How you made me realise I had the power to control my own destiny, you helped shape me as a person. A corner of my heart has your name on it, and always will.'

'Oh Lizzie…'

'Strong and dependable, you steered me through stormy waters. I'll be eternally grateful.' I squeezed his fingers.

He paused. 'Grateful enough to have a tattoo of my name?'

'Never.'

We smiled at each other in an easy way and for a second, I felt how I used to with Ash – as if everything was going to be okay. Without thinking I leant forwards and was about to place my lips on his. Ash leant forwards too. But for some reason I thought about Ben and just couldn't.

I drew away. 'Sorry… I don't know…'

'I'm sorry too, I got caught up in the moment.' He gave a lopsided smile and took away his hands. 'Look, I'll go.'

'No, look, stay the evening. Why not head off first thing tomorrow? We can have a catch up. Come on, let's go out the back, I'll show you the garden, it's beautiful.'

We spent the rest of the day sharing news from the months we'd been apart. His brother's wife was pregnant with their second child and his little niece and his mother couldn't have been more excited. We got takeaway and talked about how we'd both, secretly, had thoughts, on and off, about how maybe, just maybe, we weren't the perfect match after all.

'Call it shallow,' he said and smiled, 'but I like nice clothes and dream of owning a big house. I've always sensed that's not how you feel.'

I'd nodded. 'I sensed that difference between us too. I can't think of anything worse than wearing a pair of designer stilettos and having more than one bathroom to clean.'

It felt so good to talk honestly with each other, as if we were both closing a door on our past together that had been left just a little bit open.

I made up the spare room for him. He got up at the crack of dawn to avoid the rush hour back to London.

'It was great seeing you, Ash,' I said as I stood on the doorstep. I was still wearing my pyjamas. 'Thanks for stopping by. I- I'm going to be okay, if I can just find some answers here.'

'Keep me posted?'

I nodded. We hugged.

'Oh, what did you want to tell me, when you popped into the tattoo studio?' I asked.

'Oh yes, I forgot that.' He gave a sheepish grin. 'It was really just to thank you for the job I told you about last night, that I've landed at the hospital. Being an art therapist on an eating disorders ward is going to be so satisfying. It's everything I've ever wanted and will give me the experience I need to one day set up on my own. You always encouraged me, Lizzie. What you said about me yesterday... well you too... you were the best girlfriend ever.'

'It's everything you deserve,' I said. 'Really. I'm so proud of you. I wondered how you landed that car.'

He grinned. 'Not mine, I'm afraid. My cousin owed me a favour so I asked if I could take it out on a trip. It drives like a dream. But who knows?' He shrugged. 'Maybe I'll have my own one day.'

A car drove past as we hugged again. Ben. I pulled away from Ash and waved but he can't have seen me.

Ash glanced after the hatchback. 'That... Ben was he called? Seems like a decent bloke.'

'He's been really helpful.'

We looked at each other. Smiled. I waved him off, feeling an uncomfortable knot in my chest, that had been there since we broke up, unfurl.

27

Now

*In 1999 Mattel created the Butterfly Art Barbie doll that
had a butterfly tattoo on its stomach*

I walked down the high street the next morning, heart
thumping. I'd just passed by the estate agency and Caroline
had come outside to catch me. Apparently, sprucing up the
cottage had attracted the attention of potential buyers, with
its clean windows and hanging basket. Indeed I had tidied
up the front garden and washed the front curtains, putting
a vase of flowers from the back on the window sill. She
wanted to thank me for brightening the place up – said
she felt unexpectedly confident that, at the end of my
month's stay, the cottage could be quickly sold; that the
owner, Aunt Fiona, had finally agreed it was for the best
seeing as Caroline didn't think it would be a long process.
In fact, Caroline was sure one interested party would ring
back any minute to ask to view it and wanted to warn me
she might be contacting me to arrange it.

What if I still hadn't got the answers I'd wanted? At the back of my mind I'd been thinking that maybe, just maybe, I could stay on an extra week or two if I still needed time. Now it looked as if that might not be possible.

In fact… I swallowed. The thought had crossed my mind, more and more frequently, that living in Leafton, not leaving at all… it felt appealing. The rural setting, the beauty of the garden and the forest, I found it so inspiring. I was making friends and slowly felt wounds from recent years beginning to heal. My artistic passion had returned and I could see myself happily working from the cottage.

I sighed and entered the supermarket and past people queuing at the post office area. I was hoping to catch Neve going on a morning break. She might have news about the photo I'd found. It made no sense to me. Why would anyone want a permanent reminder of two buildings that weren't picturesque or historical, that didn't have a friend or family member standing outside them? Neve had just come off the till. Keen for some relief from the cool air con, she collected the photo and her purse from her locker and bought a packet of two muffins. We went out the back of the shop, into the sunshine. A worn bench crouched near the delivery entrance. Gratefully we sat down and drank bottled juices as the breeze nudged a discarded vape canister across the ground. She'd had a busy morning with one staff member ill and Alan confined to the office, a load of preparatory guidelines having come in for Christmas stock.

So much of modern-day life demanded forward planning – as if wishing your life away was the construct for good organisation.

Perhaps dreams existed to take us back into the past and redress the balance.

Last night, once again, I'd been taken back to my childhood. I was playing with my best friend Jimmy Jammy. I didn't see a clear face, just felt him force my fingers flat so that a centipede on his arm could switch terrains and move from his hairy skin to my smooth palm. Eventually I passed it back and he started to laugh, said it tickled. We returned the tiny creature to the grass, saying how cool it would be if we had multiple pairs of legs, then all of a sudden I was sitting on a carpet in front of a mirror. My reflection actually stroked my fringe and asked if we could play hairdressers. The dream had felt like everything my life wasn't at the moment – stable, carefree – with a sense that the girl in the mirror was looking out for me, until Mum and Dad suddenly appeared in it, looking upset. Their distraught expressions made me feel sick for a few seconds, as I woke up with a jolt.

I took a muffin and the photo from Neve.

'I was going to ring you tonight,' she said. 'I searched online like you and sure enough couldn't find out anything about a company called G & B. Of course, the photo was taken twenty or so years before we had the internet.' She ate a chunk of muffin. 'But the fact that there is no mention of the company at all online makes me think it went bankrupt or closed down for some other reason. Notes for live registered businesses are kept at a place called Companies House, but after twenty years are either destroyed or moved to The National Archives. Tonight I was going to access the latter's website, on the off chance records might be held there.'

'*But...?*'

She smiled. 'Granddad dropped in early this morning. His washing machine has leaked and he wanted Dad to take a look before work. I'd already asked some older neighbours about The Best Inn and one mentioned visiting a branch in Luton forty minutes away. That was going to be another line of enquiry – driving out there at the weekend to see if any of the buildings in the town centre matched.'

'I really appreciate this,' I said and stared at the black and white image on my lap.

'However, Granddad recognised it immediately. The restaurant from this picture was located nearer, in St Albans. He'd visited often because Grandma had a bar job there before she got pregnant with Dad. He's sure that's the one because he's never forgotten the large brass pine cone door knocker on the outside of the building next door. The employers, all financial whizzes, used to have lunch where Gran worked. She asked them about the knocker once.'

'Pine cones represent the Third Eye, don't they?' I asked, thinking back to one of my clients.

'Yes, but any supposed foresight didn't help the business. An employer was embezzling money and even though he was brought to justice and jailed, the company went bust in the eighties. That's why there's no trace of it on the internet.' Neve looked at her watch. 'I haven't helped much, have I? None of this explains why your parents bought a cottage in Leafton to rent out.'

'You've been brilliant. I really must take you out for lunch again as a thank you. Do you know if G & B stands for anything?'

'Just surnames, of the chairmen, I presume. Green & Brown.'

We stood up.

'I'd almost forgotten, there was just one thing that's odd. If you look really closely where the two buildings join, halfway down the photo someone has drawn a symbol in biro.'

Squinting I stared at the photo and saw a sideways eight like the one on the trunk of the weeping willow. Of course. How could I have been so stupid? Neve was right to use the word symbol. That was no horizontal number. It was the infinity symbol. What could it mean?

Deep in thought I went back to the cottage, to grab something to eat before heading off for the book signing. As I reached my drive Ben's car pulled up outside his house. He got out.

'Ben, wait!' I called and hurried down to his driveway. He stood in his baggy black shorts and red top. Perspiration had made his spiky hair curl.

'Do you still want to get lunch in Henchurch? I could do with the company.'

'What about your friend? That was your ex, right? I saw you and him, on the doorstep this morning.'

'He decided to get off, before the rush hour, you see—'

'Right, well, I'm not sure, Lizzie. It's been an exhausting morning at work. I had more promotional leaflets than ever in with my letters and parcels today.'

'Oh. Never mind. I understand. I'd better get back and work out the route. I'm not known for my navigational skills, it's a miracle that I made it to Leafton at all.' I smiled and turned around, a twinge of discomfort in my chest.

'Wait a minute.'

I turned back.

He shrugged. 'I suppose I could do with shopping. If we scrub lunch that will give me time to relax. If you like I'll pick you up in a couple of hours. You can head off straight to the signing and I'll meet you afterwards.'

My chest twinged again. Had I got the signals wrong between me and Ben? I thought there had been some sort of... chemistry. I couldn't think of a better word.

True to his word, Ben drove outside around two and hooted. We didn't talk much on the way, with the radio on. We parked up and walked down Henchurch high street. The town was bigger than Leafton, with rows of fancy bistros either side, plus branded stores and idiosyncratic gift shops.

I studied his face. 'Ben, have you really never lived in London? I could have sworn we'd met before I arrived in the village.'

'Nope, I'm a Leafton lad through and through, with one of those indistinct faces you could mistake for any other, even though it's covered in freckles. That's what Mum says. She means it as a compliment. Apparently being a postman is the perfect job for me as she reckons I've got the gift of the gab that puts people at ease. Apparently my dad was like that.'

'Have you ever met him? Andy, isn't he called? Your mum told me his name.'

'Yes, we're in touch.'

Silence fell between us again. I didn't understand. He was usually so open.

'Did you see him as a little boy?' I ventured.

'I first met him when I was three.' He paused. 'His parents

hadn't approved so he waited until he was eighteen to make contact, but by then he'd fallen in love with someone else and is still married to her.'

'That must have been hard for Jill.'

His face softened as we continued walking. 'Yes, it broke her heart. He had to move right down south with his job but sent money when he could and as a child I saw him a couple of times a year. Mum was good like that – she never let her own feelings get in the way.'

'Do you see him now?'

'Yes, and I've got a step-brother who's just started Juniors. It's his ninth birthday next month, I'm shopping for his present. In fact, I'd better get off. Text me when you are ready to meet,' he said in a matter-of-fact voice.

'Okay, thanks again for the lift.'

'Good luck,' he said and went off in the opposite direction. I stood and watched him for a while.

Then I continued down the high street, rehearsing what I was going to say to Frederick, keeping everything crossed that he'd have something enlightening to share before Caroline sold the cottage.

28

Now

*One of the most common reasons for tattoo
removal is mistranslation*

I arrived at Chapter and Verse bookshop and people
were filing out, women mainly. I looked at the poster in
the window. Frederick was handsome but it was as if he'd gone
from B to A list since I'd seen his website photo. He'd lost
weight, along with the arrogant expression and the hair dye
wasn't so harsh, and he'd acquired a tan. I went in and
squeezed past readers excitedly chatting and admiring the
inscriptions inside their copies of Unspeakable Truths. It was
a decent-sized shop with a small but welcoming café at the
back, ochre table covers matching the shop's walls. Above
its glass counter a blackboard listed literary-themed treats
such as Rainbow Fish Rocky Road. A narrow staircase on
the left wound upstairs to fantasy and horror fiction like
a spiral galaxy leading to another world. Colourful book

spines jammed the shelves. Frederick sat behind a table next to the till. I went up to the pay desk and took a copy of his book from a tower of paperbacks.

'I'm sorry but the event's over,' said Ian. That's what his name badge said. He wore a bow tie printed with quills.

'Do you think he'd just sign this for me? I'd be ever so grateful.'

Ian caught Frederick's eye. The author consulted his watch and nodded.

'Thanks,' I mouthed to Ian and took my copy over to be greeted by an overpowering whiff of aftershave.

'Cool tattoos,' said Frederick, 'especially that paintbrush. Many years ago, I had an artist girlfriend who had a palette tattooed across her back.' He opened the book. 'What would you like me to write inside?'

'Oh, just your name. That's fine. Thanks.'

With a flourish he signed, handed the book back to me and put the lid on his pen.

I hovered. 'I come from Leafton.'

He stood up and stretched.

'You based the story there, didn't you?'

Frederick put down his pen. 'Yes.'

'I'm currently staying in Streamside Cottage. It used to belong to my parents,' I said quickly. 'Lizzie Lockhart. Pleased to meet you.'

He hesitated before reaching out a hand. 'Then I owe your family a thank you for the inspiration. I've lived in lots of different locations to write my novels – a prison cell overnight, a five-star hotel for a month, a council flat tower... can I just say that your cottage was one of the prettiest.'

'Would you mind a quick chat about your time there? I won't keep you long. You see—'

His face flushed. 'Do you know Trish?'

'Yes, but that's not why—'

'How about one of our famous hot chocolates, Frederick?' called over Ian. 'I think you've earned it.'

'Cheers, that'd be great.' He ran a hand through his movie star hair. 'Want to join me?'

Ian let us use the staff room and whilst waiting for our drinks we chatted. It was a relaxing space with pastel walls but Frederick sat on his chair as if the upholstery were made of nettles. He asked about my tattoos again and I told him how I'd dropped out of university. He talked about Leafton and the view from the cottage. Ian brought in two mugs and the sweet-smelling cocoa soothed my nerves.

'How is she?'

'Okay.'

'My behaviour was… unconscionable.' He loosened the collar of his black shirt. 'I only came out of rehab two months ago. I never fully admitted to Trish that I was an alcoholic and I've spent the last few weeks making amends to everyone I upset during that period, but when it comes to her, I don't know what to do – whether to make contact or simply let her forget all the hurt.' He shot me a direct look. 'She's told you everything?'

'Yes. I think her overwhelming memory is feeling like an absolute idiot.'

Frederick perched on the edge of his chair. 'I was cruel to fool her about the haunting. I boasted about it to my agent, laughed about how a grown adult could believe in ghosts, and despite all the money I've earned her – and could in the future – she dropped me; said she couldn't work alongside an author with so little integrity. That was the wake-up call I needed. I went to see my doctor the following day.' He stood up and went to the window. 'I often think about how selfish and brutal I was. I didn't even stop when she told me about the tragedy she was involved in, at the cottage, twenty odd years ago. You must think I'm a right bastard.'

'What tragedy?'

He spun around. 'Bugger. Trish trusted me. I shouldn't… I mean…' Frederick sat down again and rolled up his shirt sleeves. A black tattoo of the AA symbol stood out on his wrist. I'd inked a few of those over the years. He caught me looking at it. 'I also got a couple of tattoos done when I was a drinker. Bloody stupid I was. One was kanji for *eternal happiness*… at least that's what I thought. A few days later someone told me it actually said *foot fungus*…' He gave a wry smile. 'Look, what's this all about?'

'Your blurb.' I explained about the fall-out with my parents and their deaths. He concentrated hard. Perhaps my story would end up in one of his novels.

'Dad left me an unfinished letter talking about a secret. Your blurb… especially the last line…' I opened my copy and read it out loud.

Why would he take an expectant mother to live in a place that would be best hidden from a child?

I put the book down. 'I know it's a long shot, but the wording really resonated. My parents never told me about the property in Leafton. Effectively they kept it hidden. I haven't been able to find much about your book's plot as the novel's not been released until today, but I know from Trish it's a gaslighting story. Is that all there is to it? The expectant mother feels the place should be hidden because a boy was drowned there once, and her husband's convinced her that the vengeful ghosts of him and his mother haunt the building?'

'So you know about the history of your cottage?'

'Yes, I got details from a local historian, Neve. I think you met her.'

'The witch and her son who got ducked, they are Charlotte and Martin.'

Their names sounded so ordinary.

'In answer to your question, yes, I'm afraid it really is that simple.'

I leant back in my chair, disappointment prickling.

Frederick sipped his hot chocolate. 'But can I give you a piece of advice? Secrets, hidden information, scandal, intrigue – that's what my writing is all about. Voraciously I read the tabloids, I watch historical and crime documentaries and there is one thing that has always stood out.'

I raised an eyebrow.

'People lie, change their stories, disappear, but buildings are reliable, loyal things. They'll withhold evidence and information in walls, secret rooms, under patio slabs… secrets are always there waiting to be discovered and however hard they try buildings can't deter a determined investigator.'

Was Streamside Cottage holding onto evidence about what Mum and Dad did?

'Like that sculptor accused of murdering his actress lover – it was in the papers last week. There was no evidence that they'd had an affair despite her sister's insistence. Almost fifty years later, when he was dead, new owners of his house renovated the basement. They found a false wall behind which were a bundle of love letters.'

'This is going to sound stupid,' I said, 'but I've always felt close to the cottage as if it's... it's a friend who's got some kind of story to tell, just for me. But I don't even know what I'm looking for.'

'Did you do a good clear-out of the cottage when you moved in?'

'Not really. I searched a bit before cleaning and found an old photo at the back of a cupboard. But then I just tidied before moving in some of my things.'

'It's like the old cliché of people being like an onion – buildings are the same. What you've done is just put on another layer. You need to take it off and then strip the cottage back as far as you can. Perhaps remove old wallpaper and lift up floorboards even if they aren't squeaking.'

I stood up. 'Thanks for your time. Good luck with your book and recovery.'

Frederick got to his feet. 'I've mentioned Trish in the acknowledgements... could you pass her a copy? I'd like to write in it how sorry I am, will you give me a minute?' We went through to the shop. He wrote into one of the hardbacks and then walked me to the door. 'I'm sorry I couldn't be of more help and that you didn't find anything useful in my or the Strachans' story.'

'Strachans?' I said and my shoulders stiffened. That was the name Dad mentioned in his letter.

'That's the surname of Charlotte and Martin mentioned in the blurb – the ghosts… the witch and her son. They were Scottish.'

29

At the turn of the century tattooed ladies were a popular attraction in freak shows

I stood outside the gates and chewed the side of my index finger. It was my first day at high school. Mum and Dad stood with me, having both taken the day off work. Dad's hand rested on my shoulder. Other students walked to school on their own or were in groups and laughing. My parents said I couldn't get myself here on my own as it would soon be getting dark in the mornings and afternoons.

Perhaps they were right. Mum was always talking about stranger danger. So we'd driven here in Dad's new Mercedes, Mum talking non-stop. She said not to worry if I found myself on my own in the playground at break times – the first week at any new place was always challenging. She suggested I went to the library instead or joined a club. The thing was, half the time I didn't worry about the things Mum mentioned. It hadn't crossed my mind that I might not make any friends at all, although it would have been easier if I'd been allowed to go to the local state school like my junior school friends. Berkley High was private. In the summer I'd have to wear a straw hat.

It was a very important day for my parents – their child's first day at high school. I knew this because Miriam next door told me so. But it's made Mum's eyes look red and for some reason she's been quiet the last few days, like that time every summer when she spent days in bed. And she got very cross and slammed a door last night when I forgot where I'd put my new pencil case. Today she's avoided looking at other children and parents, and Dad has kept squeezing her arm.

The same unspoken feeling that told me Brussels sprouts would make me sick, told me not to ask Mum about this. Instead I'd eaten all my breakfast, even though first day nerves had already filled my tummy and I didn't complain about the boring talk show playing in the car as it was her favourite. I just wanted Mum to be happy.

'You look lovely, darling,' said Dad and winked.

Did I? My skirt was a good two inches longer than everyone else's but Mum said that made me look professional and smart. A group of girls looking at their phones and chatting walked past and giggled. I mustn't think they are laughing at me. Perhaps after a few weeks my parents would let me travel to school on my own as it was only three underground stops away. Last year we'd gone on holiday to Kyoto. After touring temples, each night I'd scribble furiously in my sketch book. Children as young as seven travelled alone on the subway. At first my parents were horrified but the longer we stayed in Japan they appreciated the low rate of crime, the lack of graffiti and litter…

'In you go,' said Mum and kissed me on the cheek.

My stomach lurched as Dad did the same. Suddenly I didn't want to do things on my own. My parents were like protective armour against anything that could go wrong or hurt, Dad being the breastplate and Mum the sword.

Without them I was bound to fail.

As I headed into the playground, I focused on my after-school first day treat – they were taking me out for cookies and milkshake. I was so lucky.

'Any problems just text us, love,' said Mum quietly.

Relief flushed through my limbs. Of course, I could contact them if I was worried and I knew they'd text me at lunch. Messaging them back would give me something to do if Mum was right and I ended up standing alone. I loved my parents so much.

30

Now

*Daisies are often seen in Christian art and symbolise
purity and innocence*

Stuck in the rush hour with Ben on the way back, I told
him what Frederick had said, leaving out anything to do
with Trish. He pulled up outside his house and turned off
the engine and I glanced at his arms resting on the steering
wheel for a second, aware of a longing to brush my hand
over them. If I tried to replicate the pattern of his freckles
with ink, the client might not be happy with so many gaps
but Mother Nature's artwork was more forgiving and the
spaces enhanced each brown spot's individuality.

'Thanks again for taking me,' I said.

He nodded without looking at me. 'No problem, Lizzie.'

I opened the car door and swung one leg outside. 'Oh, the
joys of domestic life – the washing machine isn't draining
properly and I need to work out why. Thank goodness for
the internet.'

'I guess…' Ben paused. 'I could take a look if you want. It happened to me and Mum recently. Turned out the drainage pipe was blocked.'

My heart lifted. 'Well, if you're sure, Ben? It might save me some time.'

How had things become so formal between us? I didn't understand. It made me realise how special the friendship we'd been building had been. We made our way up the street and entered the hallway. I pushed open the kitchen door, looking forward to the joyful reunion with Taz. Never in my life has someone been so consistently pleased to see me but he wasn't in his bed or on the chairs. I went over to the French patio doors but he wasn't hiding behind the curtains. A draught lifted my hair.

'Oh no! Look at that gap,' I held on to the open door to steady myself. 'It must have happened when I hung out my clothes, I was running late. What if a bigger cat or fox attacks him or he wanders off and gets lost? He's so tiny.' My hand flew to my mouth. I felt as if I was going to be sick.

Ben looked outside, and then caught my eye. The frown lines on his forehead that had been there most of the way home softened. 'Don't worry,' he said, 'he's a clever little sod, Taz will be okay. He's probably sleeping in the sun or doing his best to stalk birds. Our cats have disappeared lots of times over the years. We'll find him.'

I slid the doors open and shouted the kitten's name, running down to the water's edge. I almost slid on the bank as I stopped. Despite the shakiness in my legs I stepped over the fence and crouched down. Mud-flecked hands frantically moved clumps of algae.

'Do you think he could have swum over to the forest?' I asked when Ben caught up.

'Lizzie, there's no way he could have got under or over that wired fence. Try not to think the worst.' Ben spoke some more in a reassuring tone, warmer than it had been all morning, before he hurried home to fetch Jill. The three of us looked under plant after plant, parting bulrushes and reeds. I peered through the weeping willow's hanging branches. All that was there was the carved word Earl. A squawk caught my attention and I looked up, blinded by the sun. What if a bird of prey had carried him off?

Eventually I sat down on the grass, breathing in the smell from the soil, or rather its bacteria. We learnt that at school. What if Taz caught an infection? This was my fault, he'd trusted me to look after him and I'd let him down.

If Taz ever turned up I'd make it up to him in the future. I'd never leave the cottage for so long and when I did go out, I'd check every window and door. Ben and Jill sat down next to me as I plucked a buttercup. Mum used to hold it under my chin and even though it reflected yellow against my skin she said it showed I *didn't* like butter, explaining how margarine was much healthier. She also used to tell me the ice cream van playing music meant it had run out. Years later this made us laugh. She said certain lies didn't count if they were for someone's own good.

'Ben's right, he'll turn up,' said Jill. 'Cats are known for wandering off, it's in their instincts, he's just exploring. Taz will come back when the sun sets and his stomach demands to be fed.'

'It's such a responsibility, caring for a pet, I can't imagine what it must be like to bring up a child.' I'd thought this several times since living with Taz; thought about me and Mum and Dad.

'It's not easy,' said Jill. 'You have to work it out for yourself. Your heart tells you to wrap your offspring up in cotton wool, but your head reminds you that in the long run, that won't do them any good. It's an impossible balance to strike.' She shot an apologetic glance at Ben. 'And even when they are grown up, you can't help thinking you still know what's best.'

I stared at her and bit my lip. I'd always thought Mum and Dad's parenting style was unique but maybe it was just a magnified version of everyone else's.

I tried to imagine bringing a baby home from hospital and having to look out for it twenty-four seven from then onwards – see it suffer with colic, watch your child struggle at school, be unable to put things right when your teenager had its heart broken…

I threw away the buttercup and picked a daisy instead. I used to make chains out of them when I was little, with Mum, not knowing that years later I'd be creating permanent versions on skin.

'Have you got any fish?' asked Ben.

'A cod fillet.'

'Steam it with the patio doors open. That's always done the trick for our cats. In fact, let me do it. He'll come back, Lizzie, don't you worry, and if he takes his time I'll stay here and wait with you, however late it gets tonight.'

The tightness across my forehead eased a little and Ben gave me a thumbs up before getting up, more like his old self.

'I'll quickly make up a leaflet with Taz's description and

your address,' said Jill. 'It won't take me long to push them through neighbours' doors.'

'Okay, I'll look around the front, just on the off-chance.'

We got up and Jill headed inside. She stopped dead in her tracks and beckoned for me to go over.

'Did you hear that?' She put a finger to her lips.

A small meow that came from ground level. One of the doors of the Welsh dresser was just a couple of inches open. Ben crouched down, I could hardly breathe. There was Taz curled up in a saucepan. Eyes tingling, I reached in and lifted him out. Ben squeezed my shoulder as I stroked Taz's.

'You had us so worried,' I said, voice thick, and I buried my face in his fur, in my head thanking the cottage for looking after him. A lump formed in my throat and I looked at Ben and Jill. 'I'd never let him out if he was my cat, it's just too risky.'

'That's a knee-jerk reaction,' said Jill. 'Taz loves looking out of the window and is clearly a cat that wants to get its paws dirty. You couldn't turn his home into a prison.'

Her words almost took my breath away. That's how I'd felt about my home sometimes, growing up.

I insisted on buying the three of us fish and chips for tea. Ben left to collect the takeaway.

'Now that he's gone,' said Jill in a low voice, as Taz and I played with his feather, 'I've got a favour to ask. I've been thinking about it for a while.'

'Shoot.'

'It's just, I'd like a tattoo done. Of course, I'll pay.'

I stopped playing with Taz. 'What's brought this on?'

'Talking the other day with you – about my pregnancy and how I used to be different…'

'But have you thought through a design in detail?'

'I've spent ages searching online and printed one out.'

'Why not think about it a while longer?' I said. 'There's no rush, Jill.'

'To be honest I've been thinking about it ever since Ben was born.'

What did she mean?

'Well if you're certain…' Caroline's tattoo had gone fine, in fact more than that, she'd loved the final look. And I'd felt such a high afterwards, a high that had been absent from my work for so long.

Truth was, I felt excited at the prospect of inking a design again, the desire to get out my tattoo machine pumping through my veins.

I took a deep breath. 'Okay, I'm free all weekend. How about tomorrow? Are you working this Saturday?'

'Only until one. I could pop around after that.' She beamed. 'I want it on my inside wrist.'

'And what—'

The door went and Jill broke eye contact. Ben brought in the haddock and chips. Taz had his cod. They finally left about ten. As Ben walked away, he glanced over his shoulder and gave a small smile as I waved. I could have jumped up and down. I locked the front door, brought Taz into the lounge and turned off the lights. We sat on the sofa lit only by street lamps.

The purring eventually disappeared to be replaced by the cottage's familiar night time noises. My mind drifted to Charlotte and Martin Strachan and how talk about a haunting could have affected sensible Mum. Then there was Trish's tragedy, whatever that was, linked to this cottage that Frederick had accidentally mentioned. I also wanted to read Unspeakable Truths.

But as I sat in the dark, all I could think of was the past and how it had just been illuminated – as if what had happened with Taz had lit a lamp. I ruffled his head and placed him on a cushion next to me. I bent my knees up and hugged them tight.

When Taz disappeared, I swore I'd never let him out of my sight again. This wasn't because I thought him especially incapable or weak. It was because a powerful protective instinct had kicked in. I gulped. This could have been how it was for Mum and Dad because they were always telling me how clever I was, celebrating each good grade and every time I excelled at music or sport. Yet when I wanted to go inter-railing it was my safety that my parents feared for. At parties it was potential bad batches of drugs that got them worried.

Could it be that they were focused on keeping me safe from other people's weaknesses, not mine?

The room span for a second. My whole view of the past was now under question. I needed to think but it was all too much as I flipped back through the pages of my childhood, examining it with a different perspective.

Hours later I finally turned into bed, still struggling to take it all in. I gave Taz one last stroke before warm tears ran backwards past my ears and onto the pillow. However old Taz was, whether he was an adult or a kitten, if he was mine I knew my feelings would always push me to care and look out for him. Protect him. If I'd felt so distressed over a lost animal I'd only known a couple of weeks, it was hard to imagine the level of anxiety associated with being a parent of a child you'd nurtured for years.

I stared at the crack in between the curtains until the night turned to day.

Mum and Dad were logical people, they assessed risk for a living. I always thought that made them paranoid, but Taz's disappearance had made me realise that it was possible a one-off traumatic event might have intensified that inclination. They wouldn't have done so well in their jobs if their view of risk was also skewed for everything else.

It was only when it came to me.

I couldn't imagine it had been triggered by our life in London. The capital had more crime but our life there was more transparent, busy, dynamic, without enough space to conceal a secret for decades, whereas remote Leafton could easily shroud a mystery within the forest, within its buildings, the garden, within the heads of its residents…

'If you're hiding something, there's no need, I'm strong, I can deal with it,' I said to the cottage. 'Whatever Mum and Dad feared me finding out, please, now's the time to reveal it…'

31

Now

*In medieval times cats were associated with witches
and evil and often burnt or beaten to death*

I opened the front door and Jill came in. Taz was snoozing in front of the French patio doors so I'd decided to tattoo her in the kitchen. She wouldn't need to lie down seeing as it was on her wrist. We sat down and she took a piece of paper out of her pocket – a printed out copy of a design she'd seen on the internet.

'A cat? No surprises there. Any reason it is black? Just so you know, I can do all sorts of colours – tabby, ginger, Calico...'

It was solid black, not just an outline, and sitting up majestically.

'I want it just like that, please.'

I made the stencil using my tracing and carbon paper realising how much I'd missed the smell of ink and the focus on detail as I drew. I missed Steve's bad jokes and dinner with Katya when she turned up with a Tupperware box of her favourite meatballs. However, bit by bit, I missed certain aspects of London less, like buses braking outside the parlour and lack of birdsong.

I put on my gloves and sterilised her wrist, feeling the rush of adrenalin I always used to experience at the start of bringing a new design to fruition, before Mum and Dad passed, before Ash and my relationship fell apart. When I peeled off the tracing paper, I made her double-check the print it left behind, confirming the cat was the right size and in the correct position. The ink and my machine were already set up and I pressed my foot pedal and looked at Taz. He hardly noticed the noise, awake now and watching a blackbird outside tug a worm out of the lawn. I started with the cat's head. As the needle vibrated, I felt alive.

'Okay?'

'The feeling reminds me of when I got sunburnt, once, in Margate.'

'Why a black cat? Have you owned a particular favourite over the years?'

'No.'

We chatted about the ongoing humid weather and I told her about the meeting with Frederick Fitzgerald. She mentioned how Ben had talked about a flash visitor I'd had. I supposed Ash must have looked like that. I'd text Ben later and ask if he could come around tomorrow to help me search the cottage. My stomach fluttered at the thought but then I had a strict word with myself. In his words or rather his mum's, Ben was a postman and by default friendly with everyone – the way he was with me wasn't special. In any case he'd backed off the last few days – clearly, as he said, he wasn't ready for a new relationship after his broken engagement.

I completed the cat's outline and started to shade it in. Some clients preferred to look away whereas others, like Jill, followed the application of every millimetre of ink.

'You're so talented, Lizzie. I wish I excelled at something creative.'

'I've seen your hanging baskets and the way you combine the plants and colours isn't so different.'

We fell into silence whilst I shaded the tail.

'My mum and dad were avid gardeners. I could have given them lots of cheap plants over the years.'

Could have?

'We don't talk either,' she said quietly. 'Just like you and your parents.'

I carried on working. In my experience the machine's noise reassured people who needed to share.

'It was tough when Ben was small. I was so proud of everything he achieved but they wouldn't see him.'

'Not even once?'

'Ben hasn't told you?'

I shook my head. As my shading moved into the cat's body, the whole story poured out about her parents' disgust when she got pregnant and insistence that she get a termination. Her dad told her she was a disappointment, that she had no morals, that the clothes she wore were slutty.

'If it wasn't for the support of my aunt, I don't know what I'd have done.'

'But it didn't happen in the fifties. Why such a harsh approach?'

'Mum and Dad never gave a reason, instead my aunt told

me when she thought me old enough to understand. So I get your frustration about not knowing why your parents never reconciled with you. I cried myself to sleep so many times when Ben was a toddler, but as I matured, he started school and I got a job, as I became more level-headed and started to look after my aunt instead of the other way around, she explained that Dad's mum had him out of wedlock. Back in those days it brought nothing but shame. At school he was called a bastard and when he turned eighteen moved away from where he grew up for a fresh start. Me getting pregnant brought it all back and he couldn't cope. My aunt said he and Mum felt they'd failed and I was a constant reminder of that.'

So they contacted Jill less and less and made it clear that unarranged visits weren't welcome.

'Cats are symbolic of independence, so this tattoo reminds me of how far I've come and I wanted it that colour because black cats are considered unlucky and outcasts. I can relate to that.'

I finished the design and wiped it down.

'For the first time in twenty-five years I- I feel like there's something about my appearance that reflects the real me again, regardless of what other people think.'

'Powerful, isn't it? As if you have taken control of your destiny. That's how my first felt for me, even though me changing came at a cost.' I stared at her. 'Everything I've told you about my parents – how overprotective they were… can you in any way understand it, as a mum yourself?'

'It does sound extreme – I'd never have taken things that far – but yes, absolutely. No one warns you, you see, when you get pregnant that from that point on you'll always put yourself second. Thoughts about safety and health will focus on your child first. It's nature's way, instinctive, it's about survival of the species, I guess, but with your parents it must have soared to another level.'

I took in every word. When I focused again Jill was studying the cat. I wrapped it in cling film that I taped together at the back. I gave her an aftercare sheet and a sachet of cream.

'Any problems, you know where I am.'

'This is the first time since I've had Ben that I've risked disapproval. I've spent so long trying to fit in and be seen as upstanding and decent,' she said, words trembling. 'But I've grown to realise I'm just as good as anyone else because we are all human and make mistakes. Thanks, Lizzie. Thanks for coming to this village and making this happen.'

'It's not down to me. I'm full of admiration for you, Jill and how you've brought Ben up and made the best of such a difficult situation. Sometimes, late at night, voices still tell me I'm selfish and that what happened was my fault,' I said. 'Yet I know it would have been impossible to live a lie. I just wish I'd gone down to Devon to try to put things right. The problem is, I thought I had all the time in the world.' I sighed. 'It is what it is. I have to accept that.'

'Yes, yes, yes. One reason I wanted to share the story of my parents was to make you realise that you mustn't regret what would probably have been a fantasy.'

'What makes you say that?'

'When Ben turned eighteen, he wanted to meet his grandparents. I said it wasn't a good idea but he's his own man and needed to follow his gut instinct. So he turned up at theirs one Sunday.'

'Out of the blue?'

'I was worried that if he rang them first, they'd say no outright.' She bit her lip.

'Ben's a real credit to you, Jill. Does he see them regularly?'

'They invited him in and spent an hour having a chat. He told them about his new job as a postman and latest girlfriend. They said they were pleased but didn't want to have contact. They've got their own lives now. I try to remember that Dad had a rough time growing up and this – me and Ben – brings it all back, and that Mum's there to support him but...' Her voice grew thick. 'I don't think I've ever been so angry at the broken look on Ben's face.'

I felt a painful tightness in my throat at the thought of Ben hurting so much.

Ben who was increasingly in my thoughts, making me laugh, making me want to get close, making me want to draw that smile, the eyes that slanted when they teased, the strong forearms I longed to feel encircle me.

I'd tried so hard to control my feelings but finally closing the door, that last chink, on me and Ash, confirmed what I felt for Ben, what I'd sensed from the very first moment we met.

'We had tears and then he got cross too and finally understood how I'd felt all these years. So what I'm saying is, don't beat yourself up with the what ifs. Don't fantasise that if your parents were still alive things would now be perfect. My parents have remained as unforgiving as ever.'

Later that evening, I stood in the front window of the lounge, Taz in my arms, both of us peering out into the street. He liked to watch passers-by drive or walk past.

The street lamps had just turned on and a bat swooped towards us, rising vertically and out of view at the last minute. The elderly neighbour over the road – Mrs Tate I now knew she was called – was peering out of her window too. On seeing me, she gave a little wave. I waved back with one of Taz's paws. She smiled and drew her curtains.

We sat on the sofa and Taz fell asleep. Hours passed and the lounge darkened. Jill had a point, who was to say my parents would ever have got close to me again? The letter was from Dad, not both of them. He might never have been able to talk Mum around.

Since their deaths, when I'd thought of them, my mind became a muddle of images – snapshots from the past and imagined scenes from the future, lining up to form a chaotic mosaic. But now it was as if the pieces were slowly reassembling themselves to form one single picture of the three of us sitting on the sofa at home, laughing and hugging, just how it had been when I was a small child. The past couldn't be changed but if possible, over time, more joyous times were the ones I'd rather recall.

I moved to the front window again and yawned as a car quietly drove past. Ash was so happy when he finally got a car and always said it felt like an extension of him – of his arms and legs; as if he wasn't sitting in something when he drove down the road. I never understood those sentiments until I lived in Streamside Cottage. When I walked around barefoot the floorboards didn't feel alien. When I brushed up against the walls it felt familiar. It gave me a sense of tranquillity I never enjoyed in my Finsbury Park flat.

And in this moment, I realised I didn't want to leave it.

I was about to go up to bed when I noticed a message on my phone from the vet. I pressed play.

'Matt here. I hope you and Taz are well. No doubt you will be pleased to hear, I've managed to find the kitten a permanent home.'

32

Now

Black is the easiest ink colour to remove during laser treatment as it absorbs all the wavelengths

I always knew when it was Ben calling. Honed by his job, the knock was firm but not aggressive. He'd replied to my text to say he'd be happy to help me search the cottage – but he hadn't added the smiley face he usually signed off with. So when I let him in I was surprised that no sooner had I shut the front door, his arms wrapped around my shoulders. He glanced at me quickly as if asking permission. I nodded and, in that moment, realised this was a person I trusted. He pressed me close just long enough for me to breathe in his aftershave. It smelt like holiday ocean – fresh, guileless, unblemished. I lost myself for a moment, electric sparks tingling across my skin where we touched.

'What was that for?' I asked as he stood back, face flushed.

'Just... you know... I wanted to say thanks for Mum's

tattoo. She's really perked up.' I led him into the kitchen. Ben picked up Taz, sat down and ruffled the small grey ears. 'We chatted late into the night. She hasn't talked about my grandparents so much for months. That's down to you.'

'Jill told me what happened when you visited them.'

'She did? Well, I'm over it – as much as I can be – and I think this tattoo is going to be the start of something significant, in terms of moving forwards from the shame her parents tried to pin onto her. It's as if she's making herself a badge of self-confidence to pin on instead. Apparently on the way back from yours she showed it to Mrs Tate across the road, risking disapproval but not caring, although as it turned out Mrs Tate called it classy.

And Mum texted me from work this morning – she offered to cover it at work if her boss wasn't happy. He said he didn't care what she looked like as long as she carried on being such a good employee. Then last night she talked about joining a dating site. It's funny...' He shook his head. 'How such a small thing can have such a big impact. Thanks, Lizzie.'

I never stopped being surprised by how a design could change a person's motivation, outlook or self-esteem. Like the client with anorexia. Her tattoo also represented the first time she'd not cared about judgements regarding her appearance.

'Does this mean you'll happily ever after be living with your mum?' I grinned.

'I didn't say tattoos could work miracles. This morning she told me off for leaving a damp towel on the floor.'

We looked at each other and I couldn't help laughing at the hard-done-by expression on his face. Proper laughing from the gut, heartfelt and spontaneous. Ben's shoulders relaxed and he joined in.

He put down the kitten.

'Last night Matt rang. A customer wants to adopt Taz.'

'Oh. That's great news – right?' He stared out of the French patio doors.

'No.'

Ben looked back at me.

'I can't believe I'm about to say this but…' I took a deep breath. 'I can't part with my little man.'

Ben's jaw dropped. 'This from the woman who declared she'd rather look after a snake? So, I guess you'll be taking him back to London?'

'No, because I can't, I just can't give up a cottage that feels like part of me, either. I'm going to see if I can rent it for longer or…' I swallowed. 'If there's any way Aunt Fiona will sell it to me.'

'*You're staying?*' Ben held onto the back of a kitchen chair before collapsing into it.

'I think I am.'

Ben shook his head. 'I never saw this coming.'

'Me neither. But for a while it's been growing, a sense within me, that Leafton feels more like home than London ever really did.'

'But what about… I mean you have a life there… Ash – you and him…'

I frowned. 'There is no me and Ash.'

'But I saw you hugging on the doorstep… he stayed the night…'

'You thought we were back together? Ben, no. Ash and I… we've got complete closure now. Nothing happened. We don't feel like that about each other anymore and certainly from my perspective, I haven't for a while.'

Ben ran his hand through his hair and his cheeks flushed. 'I... Mum will be over the moon that you're not leaving.'

We smiled at each other for what seemed like forever.

I'd got up early and written down a list of things I'd need to do if I decided not to leave. It was hard to let go of the camaraderie of Kismet Tattoos and my favourite clients, but in time I'd find another position or bring to life the thoughts I'd had about running my own tattoo business, although there was no urgent need with the money I'd inherited.

Unexpected tears welled in my eyes.

'Lizzie? You okay?'

'Sorry. I don't know what happened,' I said, quickly wiping my eyes on the back of my arm.

He'd taken hold of my hand. Gently his thumb rubbed across my knuckles.

'It's just...' I gulped. 'This last year, since Mum and Dad died, trying to get over it and then suffering a bad break-up... I never thought I'd feel remotely content again. Remembering everything is still so painful. I've felt so alone at times,' I whispered. 'Then this cottage, with all its simplicity, welcomed me in. It's as if it knew I needed to belong to someone or something, or somewhere, again.'

Tiny seedlings of hope dared to take root in my chest. Even though, for some reason, my night-time dreams here were becoming more and more disturbing. Last night I'd been running across grass again, with my friend Jimmy Jammy and the reflected girl in the mirror. The three of us held hands, me in the middle, going as fast as we could.

Scared I turned around. We were running from Mum and Dad who'd looked terrified as well.

But I hadn't woken up feeling frightened of the house. Instead I had the oddest sense that it was trying to tell me something.

'Funny isn't it,' he said, 'how the little things can mean so much? You can't put a price on, say, a beautiful sunrise; one will keep me whistling for the whole of my postal round.'

I stared at him and nodded. A transparent expression stared back. Ben didn't have a side, a hidden face, he spoke from the heart and you also couldn't put a price on that.

I stood up to get some kitchen roll and switched on the light. Dark clouds had ambushed the sun.

Ben held out his hand. 'Come on. Let's get cracking and start our search upstairs.'

I slipped my fingers into his hand. It felt right, a gesture that needed no explaining. We were just about to make our way upstairs when a knock sounded at the door. Ben lifted Taz up and held him tightly whilst I answered it.

A woman stood there behind a large bunch of flowers. At least I assumed the person was female due to the skirt and high heels. Petals were missing due to a strong breeze. From the distance came a rumble of thunder.

She checked behind her before pushing inside. After I'd shut the door, she thrust the flowers into my hands and smoothed down her hair.

'Caroline. Hello.'

'A grateful customer gave these to the agency. I–I've just taken them out for a while. They aggravate Julie's hay fever.' She peered into my face. 'Do you suffer too? Your eyes look red.'

'Um—'

'Anyway, I wondered if you could check my tattoo, I know you said it would scab but—'

Ben cleared his throat.

Caroline looked down the hallway. 'Oh. I didn't see you there. When I say tattoo what I really mean, is, is…' She shot me a desperate glance.

'Mum had one yesterday,' said Ben. 'A cat, on her wrist. It's really cute.'

'She *what*? *Jill*?' Caroline gave a nervous laugh. 'What an outlandish thing to do.'

'Is outlandish such a bad thing?' he asked.

She paused, thought for a moment and then leaned forwards. 'It's been really itchy but my niece thinks it looks fantastic. I can't wait to show it off on the beach. I guess you could have a look if you wanted,' she said to Ben. Without waiting for a reply Caroline pulled her blouse out of her skirt, hitched it up and turned around. I switched on the hallway light.

Ben got closer. 'That's pretty cool.'

'The scabbing's a bit gross,' said Caroline. 'I just wanted to check everything was as it should be.'

I studied her lower back. With a first tattoo it wasn't uncommon to worry about the healing process. 'It's fine. Remember your tattoo is effectively an open wound, then it scabs over and that hardened layer will soon start to peel and flake away. It will look perfect by the time your holiday arrives, I promise.'

Caroline tucked in her blouse. 'Thanks so much. Right, I'd better go before it starts to rain.'

I picked up the flowers. 'Do you want to take these?'

Caroline looked at me and then Ben. 'No. You keep them. And Ben, tell Jill I'd love to see her tattoo.' She stepped outside and then came back in. 'By the way, Lizzie, I was thinking about our chat, about the tenants who'd lived in this cottage and I remembered something, just a small detail, it's probably nothing.'

'I'm listening.'

'The strange woman who visited and freaked that young couple out with the baby.'

'She threw a rose into the river.'

'Yes. Well, the couple kept going on about the fact that she was extremely well dressed with shoes you could see your face in and her hair tidily swept up into a chignon.'

33

Now

The Indian Apatani tribe used to tattoo young girls to make them unappealing to rival tribes who might abduct the most beautiful women

I thanked Caroline for the information and said goodbye. I stumbled outside, collapsing onto the doorstep. Ben joined me.

'Where's Taz?' I asked, numbly.

'In his bed. Lizzie, do you know the woman she described?'

'It makes no sense. I'm one hundred per cent convinced it was Mum.'

A worm twisted its silky-smooth body across the soil and onto rough gravel. Its unsuitability to the new environment reminded me of my first days in Leafton. I transferred it back to the border and sat down once more.

'She did own the property,' he said.

'But their solicitor, George, had made it clear no one was

to ever contact them directly – so why would she visit? Why would she throw a rose into the river?'

Mum had stood on the back lawn just like I had. She'd breathed in this pollution-free air, smelt the fresh flora.

I still missed her.

I still missed Dad.

They'd have got on so well with Ash if they'd got to know him properly. The Christmases we could have had, playing board games or snooker... and he could have talked to Dad about high-spec cars and Mum about exotic holidays. What's more, they would have considered Katya a great boss – a hard taskmaster who expected nothing less than excellence.

I sat with my knees up, arms folded across them.

'Were roses a favourite flower?' asked Ben gently.

'I used to think so. It was mine and I'd always draw it for her Mother's Day card. Mum would look so pleased but as I got older, I noticed something else, just fleetingly – a faraway look.'

Perhaps giving her that cut-glass ornament for her sixtieth birthday had been a mistake. Maybe she was glad it had smashed. Ben and I talked over the possibilities. Could there have been a love story behind the rose she'd thrown? What if Mum had an affair with one of the tenants? Perhaps my parents' marriage almost broke down and that's why she and Dad never breathed a word about Leafton. Yet they were both so prim and upstanding I couldn't imagine either of them ever cheating.

Dad said the Strachans had an effect on Mum. Was the rose to remember them by? Perhaps she believed they'd had magical powers. Was that why she was so against me doing art? Did she believe in the curse that made the poet jump out of one of the top windows? Had she fretted that bad luck might follow me because they owned the cottage?

But Mum was always so level-headed. Questions whizzed around in my head.

I stood up and yanked Ben to his feet. We started searching in the biggest bedroom, opposite mine, as clouds outside formed ranks and blackened. Apart from the bed, a side cabinet and huge wardrobe the space was stark and my stomach fluttered as I imagined the colours and textures I would use to furnish it. Ben and I moved the furniture as rain beat the windows. Inch by inch we examined the interior of the cabinet and wardrobe and we pulled up the mattress. We checked all the floorboards to see if one was loose and yanked up a couple of random ones, on the off chance.

'One room down,' I said as we headed into the smallest bedroom, the other one at the back. The lack of space inside was balanced by the outside view. Ben stood at the window and I joined him. Rain drenched leaves, and gusts of wind dodged in between branches as if spreading trouble. We went through the same process as before, going over the interior of all the furniture and checking for loose floorboards. Ben went back to the window sill having noticed a small area of rotten wood. His shoulders jolted as a clap of thunder sounded in the distance.

I shivered as a ghoulish, persistent caterwauling crept up the stairs. Ben left to see to Taz. I sat on the bed and surveyed the room, my eyes returning to the sill's rotting wood. It was often people's flaws that revealed their deepest secrets, maybe it was the same for buildings. I went over and carefully jiggled the sill up and down. My fingers splayed out, pulse quickening as I felt a ridge underneath. I held it with both hands and carefully pulled.

A hidden drawer?

I jolted, let go and stood back as if the wood had burnt me. There might be something inside that would change my life forever, or it might contain nothing but dust and air. I stepped forwards and shook the drawer from side to side until, little by little, it came out. A musty smell filled my nostrils. Paper covered in mould lined the bottom. On top lay a book.

I took it out, along with a pencil and sheet of curled paper. In the corner of the drawer were three... fruit chews. I recognised the branded wrappers from my childhood.

I ran my hand across the wood.

Thank you.

I sat back down on the lumpy mattress and looked at the sheet of paper first. I should have got up to switch on the light but my legs wouldn't move. It was a child's drawing. The artist couldn't have been out of infants' school as the people sketched had circles for bodies and basic arms and legs. It was of three adults – two men and a woman – and two children, both girls, one taller than the other. They stood in front a swirl of blue – the stream? And next to either a giant's head with long green hair or what was more likely an attempt to sketch a weeping willow.

I put the drawing to one side and brushed my arm over the book. It was purple and flowery with swirling doodles across the front. Slowly I opened it. A photo album? A snap of bulrushes was stuck to the first page. It was wonky and slightly out of focus. The grown-ups must have let this girl have a go with their camera. On the next page was a ticket for the cinema – the movie 101 Dalmatians. So, this was more of a scrapbook. I flicked to the next page and a picture cut out from a magazine of a dog. On the page was a drawing of a stick girl next to a cat. I turned over again.

A flash of lightning lit up the room and my eyes fell to another photo, a much older one, this time. Her parents perhaps? It was a young couple from the seventies, wearing flares. My eyes narrowed before I quickly turned over the page. Then I went back. I studied the woman's face and the man's, their relative heights, her strong nose and thick hair… his prominent chin.

A clap of thunder punched me in the chest.

'Ben!' I shouted. 'Ben!'

He appeared within seconds. Ben was a good friend. He'd gone to the vet's with me when I first found Taz. He'd taken me to Henchurch for the book signing. He'd woven his way into my life here without me realising it. I couldn't think of anyone I'd rather have here to share this.

'I don't understand, this photo – it's of my mum and dad.'

'A scrapbook? Where did you…?'

I jerked my head towards the window sill as cascading rain collided with the glass.

'This is crazy.' He took it and flicked through. 'Are you sure?'

'It must have been taken whilst they were at Cambridge University, where they met. In fact look…' I pointed to the Gothic chapel behind with its arched stained window. 'I'd swear that's Kings College.'

Was there a connection between this and the photo I'd found of The Best Inn and Green & Brown?

'Then this book must be yours.'

My hands shook as I picked up the drawing again and glanced at the figures – Mum, Dad, me... who was the other girl?

'Why would these be hidden? It's as if we all lived here once and if that drawing is of our family, who is the second man?' I turned to another page. 'Do you think that's a sketch of a birthday cake, with five candles?'

He nodded. We looked at another drawing of a girl, and a boy with sticky-up hair.

I progressed through the scrapbook, studying tickets to parties stuck in and favourite sweet wrappers. Finally, I settled on another photo and shook my head. 'Look. That's me... me when I was little with another girl.' We were holding hands. My finger rested on the other child. She looked a bit older. Lightning illuminated her features. Shortly afterwards thunder threw another punch.

It winded me.

The reflection... the girl in the mirror who featured in my memories and recent dreams.

She had been real.

I turned to the last page, part of me not wanting to look, part of me unable to wait. It was another photo, of me and a little boy, we had our arms wrapped around each other.

'Jimmy Jammy,' I said without thinking. 'That was my best friend. I couldn't pronounce his proper name. We were always playing out.'

'What the hell?' Ben pored over the photo then straightened up. His eyes scoured my face. He got to his feet and paced up and down, running his hand through his untidy hair. He sat down, voice trembling. '*Lilibet?*'

The hairs stood up on the back of my neck.

'Jill used to say this good friend of mine, her mum thought Lilibet was a sweet nickname seeing as Elizabeth was too difficult for me to pronounce.'

I stared at his face as the room appeared to spin.

'My name's Benjamin,' his voice faltered. 'I can't believe this. The friend, it was in infants, called me Jimmy Jammy because Benjamin was too tricky. Then one day she and her family disappeared without even saying goodbye.'

'Jimmy Jammy?' I let go of the scrapbook and it fell to the floor. Instead I scrolled back through my childhood, searching for concrete evidence. Even though the images in my mind had dimmed, the feelings kept true, the pure joy of running through fields, hand in hand, without a care in the world; the stomach ache from incontrollable laughter; the yucky hot breath of in-the-ear whispers. The... the oneness.

'I... I remember missing you.'

'Missed you too,' he mumbled.

'You being disgusting kissing me on the cheek when the teacher wasn't looking...'

'You always telling me we'd be best friends forever if I gave you my last sweet... I've thought about you, now and then, especially during the teenage years and recently. You left without a word, my grandparents didn't want me, then splitting up with my long-term girlfriend last year... in dark moments I've wondered if I'm just one of those Teflon people who can't get people to stick.' He sighed. 'But then I get a bit of perspective, stop the pity party and realise – it's just life, and you leaving, that suddenly, would have been completely out of your hands.'

Teflon people? It was like me and my parents, like me and Ash.

In so many ways Ben and me were alike.

I went back to the drawing of the girl and boy.

'Look closely,' I said. 'I think it really is you. His arms and face – they are covered with dots.'

We stared into each other's eyes with confusion but an ease that time hadn't managed to steal.

'It's weird to think I must have lived here once. If I'd stayed, you and I, what a history we'd have had. We spent a lot of time together, didn't we?' I said and picked up the scrapbook.

'Mum's talked about you, over the years, and how close we were. We were in the same class at school and spent our spare time together as well. We both loved fish fingers and doing snail races. Our knees were grazed all the time from climbing trees. Apparently, you were always jealous of my freckles and I wanted the strawberry shaped birthmark behind your ear.'

Apart from my parents and Ash no one else knew about that.

It made sense now. All this time I felt I'd known Ben previously but he'd never lived in London – it had been me who'd lived near to him.

An image of a toy penguin popped into my mind. The heatable one I'd called Jimmy Jammy. Mum and Dad had made me change its name. It's like they wanted to erase this part of my history.

'Your parents didn't always get home in time to pick you up from school,' he said. 'Trish used to babysit and let me come around to play. Sometimes she'd cook – nice stuff, not the green vegetables our parents steamed.'

Green vegetables... My parents and work...

'Oh my God, of course!' My heart raced. 'I remember now... the G & B building... Green & Brown... the photo from the back of the wardrobe...'

Ben's brow knotted.

'Mum used to say *eat your greens and brown* when I was very little and about to eat vegetables and gravy. This was during our family's phase of naming foods by their colour. We'd laughed about it years later. She explained it had started because at the time they were working for a company called Green & Brown. Neve's Granddad said "financial whizzes" from the company next to where his wife worked went to the Best Inn for lunch – that would apply to insurance brokers.'

I ran into my bedroom and came back clutching the photo.

The Best Inn. That must have been where my Dad proposed to Mum during their lunch hour, before their vegetarian days, her eating Beef Wellington, him using the engagement ring to hold a napkin. That would be why they took this photo and kept it. And the infinity symbol drawn onto it... maybe that represented their love.

'And there's something else,' said Ben and he rubbed the back of his neck. He looked nervous.

The caterwauling started again. Reluctantly Ben went downstairs, muttering to himself and shaking his head. I asked him to switch off the light as he went. My head hurt.

Rain. Thunder. Lightning. I sat in the dark as the storm raged. Ben came back up and I took Taz. Frederick spoke of Trish suffering a tragedy to do with the cottage. She'd known my parents. Was there a chance that what upset her had to do with my family's time living here?

'I need to see Trish,' I said and looked at Ben through the darkness. 'I reckon she'll be able to make me make sense of all this.'

'First there's something I need to tell you, now that I know who you are.'

But I hardly heard him, thoughts swirling like windswept leaves about the scrapbook and the photo of my living reflection.

'Lizzie?' He shook me gently. 'Are you listening? You see—'

I pushed Taz into his arms and picked up the scrapbook. I pointed to the other girl. 'Who *was* she? We must have been close. Does she still live around here? Perhaps you can introduce—'

'No, she doesn't. That's what I'm trying to say.'

He released Taz onto the bed, put a hand on each of my shoulders and met my eye, steadying me.

'Lizzie, she's your older sister.'

'What?' I snorted. That was the last thing I'd expected him to say. 'Wouldn't I know if I had a sibling? I spent most of my childhood wishing I had one. Why would you say that? I don't understand.'

'Lizzie, I'm sorry but it's true. I remember her and my mum will too. My best friend came from a family of four.'

'But how could I forget something like that, someone like that?' I shook his hands off my shoulders and shuffled away from him.

'The Lilibet I played with had blonde hair,' he continued,

gently, 'so did her sister, they looked so much like one another and—'

'My parents may have kept secrets from me but that's one not even they would have hidden.'

'Perhaps they had good reason.'

'Are you serious?'

'I know it's a lot to take in – I'm still reeling from finding out who you are, but honestly, Lizzie, listen to me—'

'No. No, I'm not listening to this anymore.' I gagged and the room span for a second. I just wanted to be alone.

'But—'

'How could it be true? My parents lying to me all these years about something that big? They might keep something made out of bricks and mortar hidden, but a real flesh and blood person?'

'Okay,' he said, calmly. 'We can talk about it again tomorrow. But... what was her name... Oh, I remember... of course. It was Rose.'

'Get out!' I shouted. 'You've said enough.'

34

In 1932 many parents got their babies tattooed after the baby of famous aviator Charles Lindbergh was kidnapped

'Jimmy Jammy! Wait for me!'

I hurried out of the big glass kitchen doors. Trish made me wipe my mouth clean after eating an orange. The juice was all sticky and ran down my chin. Me and Jimmy Jammy were going to see who could count the most fish.

I skipped to the stream. Poor Will, Trish's little boy, wasn't allowed outside without his mummy because he was only three. Me and Jimmy Jammy were five and had just finished our first year at school. We had weeks and weeks of sunny holiday before we went back into Year One. Out of breath I stopped at the edge. I took Jimmy Jammy's hand and prised it open.

'Shhh!' I put a finger to my lips. Mummy didn't think I knew where the biscuit tin was. She joked that she counted them but she couldn't have because I always took a sneaky one after meals. 'They are chocolate this week,' I said and delved into my pocket. There was one for him and one for me. I pushed it into his hand.

We took big bites. I went nearer to the water and wobbled.

'Elizabeth! Step away from the edge this minute!' shouted out Trish.

She always worried because there wasn't a fence like there was at the bottom of Jimmy Jammy's garden. I did as I was told. I liked Trish. We could say silly things about bums and farts and she didn't tell us off like the teachers at school. I liked her curly red hair and the way she wiggled her hips if the radio was on. I heard Mummy and Daddy talking one night and they said she was really strong to leave her husband because he was a complete joke.

I didn't understand the way adults talked sometimes. Mr Trish sounded like good fun to me.

'Do you think the fish are hungry?'

'Don't know, don't care,' said Jimmy Jammy. He grinned before eating the rest of his biscuit.

I broke a bit off mine and threw it into the water.

'I need a pee,' he said and grabbed his trousers.

Jimmy Jammy was bonkers like that. He never seemed to have a warning and had to hurry off to the toilet at top speed.

'Don't be long. Remember we're going to build a bird's nest out of long grass.'

He jumped up and down. 'Maybe we'll get eggs in there by the end of the summer. Blackbird ones.'

I swallowed my biscuit and ran right, to the curved part of the stream.

'Watcha doing, Rose?' She was holding a long stick and

playing with it in the water. She wore her pink dress. At the moment it was her favourite colour. I wore colours more like Ben's and today I was in brown shorts.

'Looking for gold. We heard about it in class last term, cowboys used to do it, it's called panning. Mum will go mad if I use one of her silver pans so I'm trying to dig out lumps of gold with a stick.'

'It will match your pretty hair,' I said.

She stopped for a moment, dropped the stick and gave me a hug. We held hands and span around and around until we couldn't stop laughing. Sisters were special. They always knew exactly what would make you feel all light and giggly.

'Will you share your gold with me?' I asked.

'Of course, and with Mummy and Daddy. I'll buy us a big palace and they won't have to work. We can eat all the chocolate we want and I'll only wear clothes covered in glitter.'

'I'll own a hundred dogs and cats. Perhaps we'll be friends with the queen.' I leant near the edge.

'Come back, Lilibet,' said Rose in a grown-up voice and folded her arms. 'You're too young to go close, it's dangerous. Trish said the current is fast today.'

I've always wondered why the stream has currants and not my favourite squishy sultanas. I tasted the water once and was sad that it didn't taste like fruit cake.

Rose went back to playing with her stick. Will started crying. Trish said he'd had a poorly ear – perhaps it had come back. Jimmy Jammy waved to me from the kitchen doors and I ran over. He'd changed his mind about making birds' nests and wanted to play upstairs. Our favourite game at the moment was making up stories starring my plastic dogs. I bet he peeked in my bedroom and saw my new black one. I collected them by getting a special comic every week and had nine now. We'd pretend one was a teacher and the others classmates, or sometimes they were wizards or just mummies and daddies. The time always went too quickly. Best was when we were allowed sleepovers and could continue the dogs' stories by whispering in the dark.

We had a really long game. Our dogs met, fell in love – that bit was yucky – they got married and had a big family, they owned pets and ate out together as well as going on holiday. My stomach rumbled loudly and Jimmy Jammy giggled. Trish called up that it was dinner time and he had to go home. We pulled faces as our game had only just got to the good bit. Slowly we went downstairs. The front door slammed shut – Mummy and Daddy appeared, both laughing. She kicked off her high heels and Daddy took off his tie. Trish wasn't in the kitchen. She and Will must have gone to fetch Rose from panning gold.

Daddy kissed me on the cheek and started to chat to Ben. Mummy gave me the tightest hug and asked me about my day when a horrible, high wail floated in from the garden.

I clutched Jimmy Jammy's arm. Daddy rushed through to the kitchen whilst Mummy told us to go back upstairs and play for a while longer. They hurried outside and I shrugged before grinning at Ben. We rushed upstairs, excited to carry on our game.

35

Teardrop tattoos are symbolic of time spent in prison

Ben left and I heard footsteps go downstairs but they sounded very, very far away, as my mind zoomed in on one word he'd said.

Rose? The tattoo on my leg... all the Mother's Day cards to Mum that produced a faraway look in her eye... the cut-glass ornament I'd bought her...

Was this why the word Rose had always meant so much? I shivered as a memory shifted in my brain.

That Saturday morning, when I was younger, I'd gone into the kitchen to find Mum and Dad talking about someone called Rose. They'd stopped as soon as I appeared. Her face was blotchy. She'd muttered something about having problems with a staff member at work.

But what if...?

The pelting rain sounded louder and louder in my ears

and I could hardly breathe. I stood up and then bent straight over, feeling dizzy. And suddenly feeling very, very alone.

'Drink this.'

I looked up. He was back. Ben hadn't left. I took the glass of water with shaking hands. I gulped it down before handing it back and I straightened up, again, body still swaying as I focused. I pushed myself into the corner of the room and lightning flashed as I slid to the floor. However, the corner supported me, its two walls reaching out like a pair of strong arms.

Ben crouched down and took my hands, helping me back onto the mattress. Blindly I stroked Taz.

'Sorry for shooting the messenger,' I said in a strangulated voice.

'Don't worry,' he said, softly.

'It doesn't make sense,' I whispered, eventually. 'But then in some ways it does. The dreams I've been having... I always had a sense that the girl in the reflection was looking out for me... perhaps this is why.'

He nodded. 'Deep down you never forgot her, Lizzie.'

'If this is true, where is she now? What happened to her?' I thought of the *terrible* thing my father mentioned.

'Unless... look, let's have a cup of tea and—'

'Unless what?'

'I'm only guessing, Lizzie but... if... if the worst happened perhaps your mind blocked out the upset. That could explain why your parents managed to keep it from you and why you created this doppelganger in the mirror.'

The worst? Trish... the tragedy twenty years ago...

The timing fitted perfectly.

I ran to the bathroom and pulled up the toilet seat. I knelt down and my body convulsed. A hand rubbed my back as I retched. Eyes watering, I finally stopped. I washed my face with cold water and Taz in his arms, Ben led me down to the kitchen. He put the kettle on. We drank tea in silence, the battered plants outside looking as fragile as I felt.

I flicked through the scrapbook again before putting it to one side.

'Right from the off my parents never trusted me,' I croaked. 'Not even with the information that I had a sister. Why not? Did they really consider me so weak?' I looked at Ben and couldn't help giving a small smile. 'I remember you and me climbing trees... stealing apples... carrying spiders in our hands... both of us so adventurous and confident...'

'The Lilibet I recall was all of that and much more. Do you remember Luke from our class?'

I thought hard. 'Curly brown hair and a big attitude, was that him? I can't picture his face clearly but he was a right bossy boots in the playground.'

'He went through a phase of picking on me and would easily push me over and steal my packed lunch. So one day before lessons, you put soil inside my marmite sandwiches. It stuck brilliantly.'

'Did he eat it?'

'Let's just say the bullying stopped.'

'A sister, Ben, I had a sister and no one ever told me.' Tears rolled down my face. Year in year out Mum and Dad had strived to manage my life and make choices for me, right down to deciding that I had no right to know about Rose.

How dare they? She was as much a part of my life as

theirs. Indignation burnt in my chest. I wiped my eyes on my arm. We were blood-related. We loved each other.

'Let's call Mum over, she can tell us more.' Ben consulted his watch. 'It's six. She finished at five and should be home now.'

I looked into the garden and still couldn't quite believe that once I'd walked on that grass with my family and that I'd sat in this kitchen and played with Ben. Jill hurried over. She stood at the kitchen doorway.

'Lilibet, oh sweetheart, I can see it now, the bow on your top lip and those gorgeous green eyes – I should have seen it before.' Ben passed her the scrapbook and she sat down.

'Jill… did I have a sister called Rose?' I asked, voice wavering. 'Is it really true?'

'Yes, my darling, yes. These photos bring it all back – the family of four who suddenly disappeared that summer. You lived here for your first year of school and Rose was one year older. You looked very much alike although she was the quieter one, a sensible little girl who enjoyed reading, whereas you and Ben preferred running around outside or playing with toys.'

One year older, that made sense of Mum visiting here nine years ago to throw a rose into the stream – it would have been her eighteenth birthday. Perhaps Mum came on her exact birth date.

Then all those summers… Mum going to bed for a few days… it must have been because she was missing my sister, a significant date marking something.

'Did you know my parents well?'

'Not as much as you might think, considering you and Ben were best friends but they were always so busy. They both worked full time, you see, and paid Trish to babysit. She was glad for the money after her marriage broke down. Sometimes that stretched into the evening. They had business dinners to attend – quite a social life I remember. You'd be dropped off early to breakfast club.'

The parents I remembered always made sure one of them was around to take me to school and pick me up.

'And then at weekends they'd focus on you two girls. However, I remember their faces and their laughter. Both were always smiling and had a kind word for everyone. I'd often see them chatting to locals in the village at the weekend. Despite their executive jobs they were free spirits, your mum's long hair loose around her shoulders, your dad wearing flip-flops everywhere in the summer, even when it was raining. And they were so affectionate. I remember looking at them and wishing I had a relationship like that. More than once I saw them kissing in their drive and when you were out as a family the four of you held hands. It was lovely to see. They must have been pushing forty but acted as if they were the same age as twenty-year-old me.

'Do you remember their names?' I said, part of me hoping this was all a mistake; that my parents' deception hadn't been at this level. It was possible Jill and Ben had got it all wrong. This couple didn't sound much like my mum and dad.

'Anne. Anne and Lawrence. A friend of mine owned a cat that had kittens. Your parents were going to buy one as a surprise for you and Rose, but then you all left.'

'My parents were going to get a pet?'

'Anne thought it was really sweet that you stole our ginger

cat Pumpkin, once, and had him in your room all night. Anne found you both curled up together in the morning.'

The Mum from the childhood I remember would have been furious and scared of the imagined health risk.

Scared.

If something bad had happened to Rose... is that why they never trusted me to look after myself? Because they were terrified they'd lose me as well?

Jill carried on talking but noticed my wet cheeks, however I insisted she continued. She told of how Mum and Dad would give me and Rose piggy-backs into town. How they'd take us to Blossom's Bakes and often buy a slice of gateau for me to bring home for Ben.

'They were the most laid-back parents and often let you stay up late.'

Laid-back? Surely not? But as I scrolled back through time, I recalled the occasional carefree glimpses I'd seen of them, dancing wildly after guests left a party they'd hosted or getting back late from a night out and laughing loudly with the babysitter...

In the space of one afternoon I'd gained a sister and lost the parents I thought I knew.

'What happened on their last day in Leafton?'

'Ben came home after you'd been playing, a bit later than usual – and really excited because a policeman accompanied him. The officer just said there'd been an incident. An ambulance was outside the cottage. Ben didn't know anything and just kept talking about the game you two had been playing with your little plastic dogs. I went around later that night. My aunt and I were worried. No one answered the door and the next day you'd all gone.

'Ben cried for two days straight. He didn't understand why you'd left.'

I reached across the table and briefly my fingers touched his. He looked at our hands and then at me, his eyes shining.

'But what about Trish?' I said. 'Didn't you ask her?'

'I went straight around the next morning,' said Jill. 'But she'd closed the shop for two weeks – told Tim next door that she was going to stay with relatives. When she came back, I asked but she said she didn't know and I'd seen nothing in the papers. There were no arrests or court cases that I knew of. Trish wasn't the same and had gone into some sort of depression like she recently has. I think her marriage break-up was just starting to hit home and didn't like to push her for information. When the professional packers arrived to clear the cottage out, we knew you all definitely weren't coming back.'

We drank more tea and eventually Jill headed off leaving behind an order to go around to hers tomorrow for lunch on her day off. Ben wasn't working either. The two of them said we could talk things through as much and for as long as I wanted.

He sat with me and Taz in the lounge for a while. We didn't talk. With so much to say I couldn't say one word.

He gave a wide yawn.

'Sorry,' I said. 'You've been up early. Go home.' First thing tomorrow I'd be visiting Trish in the hope of finding out what she knew.

'I'm not leaving tonight, Lizzie. I'm here for you. We're friends, right?'

'Even though I snapped?' I said, a lump in my throat.

Please don't go, then. I can't think of anyone I'd rather be with, right now.

'Of course.'

He squeezed my shoulder and tingles ran down my arm. 'I'll sleep on the sofa. In case you wake up in the dark and… I'd just feel happier staying here, if you don't mind.'

'Is this some sort of nostalgia trip?' I forced a smile. 'You're hoping for a sleepover?'

We stared at each other.

Getting ready for bed, I didn't brush my teeth or rinse my face. I pulled on pyjamas, inside out. Taz snuggled down next to me. The only noise was his purring. But I couldn't sleep and eventually picked up Taz and went back downstairs. I put the kitten in his bed, in the kitchen, and sleepily he settled. I shut the kitchen door and went to the sofa. Ben was still awake too and I curled up next to him, resting my head on his chest. He stroked my hair and told me everything would be okay, that I had him and his mum, my new friends, Taz, the cottage, Leafton.

He was right. So why did I feel so empty? Robbed of a life I never knew I'd had with a sibling, a best friend and happy-go-lucky parents.

If I'd stayed in Leafton would I still have been the same Lizzie?

I lay in Ben's arms, and snuggled closer, reminding myself that I was safe, in his arms, even though everything about my life had changed.

36

Now

Tattoos were popular with royalty until they became affordable to the masses

The smell of frying bacon woke me up and I rubbed my eyes and got up, splashed cold water onto my face and changed into jeans and a t-shirt. Half-heartedly I tidied my hair. I stood by the French patio doors for a while, getting lost in the garden, imagining past scenarios. Like me, Mum and Rose sitting in the lush grass, making daisy chains... the four of us holding hands at the stream's edge, looking for fish... playing hide and seek under the weeping willow... Throat feeling thick I turned around and stared at Ben as he opened the fridge door. My recent dreams made sense now, the boy and the centipede... The cottage had been giving me clues.

'Thanks. You didn't need to...' My voice broke.

He closed the fridge door and came over. Warm arms encircled me. My body shuddered for a moment and then

I relaxed and leant against him. Eventually, I sniffed and pulled away.

'Sorry. It's still all sinking in. I must look a mess.'

'Looking back a couple of decades, I've seen you much worse, covered in mud or with jelly around your mouth.'

We smiled at each other and I sat down at the pine table.

'Drink this. You'll feel better.' He passed me a large glass of orange juice.

I did as I was told, irritated he was right. I smiled again and Ben raised his eyebrows.

'I've got a feeling you used to get on my nerves sometimes. A memory's come back about the plastic dog games we used to play that your mum talked about. Jimmy Jammy always insisted he knew which were male and female.'

'I was a bit of a know-it-all.' He grinned. 'But you'd get your own back. I turned up one day to find you'd tried to paint my favourite man dog with your mum's pink nail varnish.'

We looked at each other, lost in the past for a second. New feelings brought me back to the present, like the warmth gushing through my chest as he gave a lopsided grin. I felt the urge to kiss those crooked lips. Little Lizzie and Jimmy Jammy would have gagged at such a suggestion. Reluctantly I broke eye contact and picked at the food. After a mouthful the usual morning hunger considered a return. It was half-past eight. I wanted to catch Trish before she opened The Pen Pusher. Ben went back home and I hurried into town. The lights were on in the stationery shop but the sign said closed. Usually it opened at nine. I couldn't wait a minute longer and I put away my phone having tried to ring Aunt Fiona. I'd texted her that we needed to talk; that it was very important about my parents' past.

I rapped on the door firmly. No one appeared. I rapped again. Trish came out from the back and opened the door.

'Can I come in? It's important.'

A look of resignation crossed her face. Trish locked the door behind us and took me out the back. There was a large stockroom to the left and a staircase. We went up and into her flat that was punctuated with paintings and ornaments of wildlife, with embroidered cushions and ornamental elephants with a Buddhist twist. Joss sticks had also been burned up here. I recalled my very first day in Leafton, when I'd met Trish eating – or rather not eating – a slice of cake and she'd told me about the forest. It seemed like months ago, now, not weeks.

'Coffee?' she asked, in an unsure tone. 'It won't harm to open half-an-hour late.'

'No... no thanks.'

Trish indicated for me to sit down on a mustard coloured sofa and she joined me. I paused and then opened my rucksack.

'I hope you don't mind, but I met Frederick in Henchurch at a book signing.'

She winced.

'I've been trying to find out more about the cottage and my parents and I thought his book might give me some clues. I didn't tell you about my visit. I didn't want to upset you.'

'You've seen him?' she asked.

'Yes.'

'Right.' She clasped her hands together. 'And did it help?'

'Kind of. Not really. I'm hoping you can fill in the gaps.' I pulled out the book he'd given me for her. 'He gave me this to pass on to you. Frederick said he mentioned you in the acknowledgements and he's written a message. I haven't read it. He seemed genuinely sorry, for what it's worth. He's stopped drinking and—'

'*What?*'

'He's been to AA. He looked well and kept saying how much he regretted the way he'd treated you.'

Trish hesitated before opening the book. 'I can't believe he's admitted he had a problem, let alone got sober.' She quizzed me about my conversation with him and we discussed the haunting. 'So how can I help?' She fiddled with the corner of the front cover.

'Trish,' I stared straight into her eyes. 'I know.'

She didn't reply.

'Ben and I found an old scrapbook in the cottage yesterday. You worked it out, didn't you, that I'm *that* Elizabeth Lockhart from your past. That's why you've been avoiding me. I know I used to live there with my family, and that I knew Ben before.'

She looked down and gazed vacantly at Frederick's message. Slowly I closed the book, took it off her and placed it on the cushion behind me.

'It's okay. I just want to know what happened. Why did my parents leave? What happened to my sister Rose?'

She gasped and looked up.

'Please, please tell me.'

'The more I saw you, the clearer it became who you were.' Her voice sounded croaky. 'You look just like your mum in certain moments, like at Jill's party, smiling and chatting.

Anne had such an infectious belly laugh. I remember her doing an impression of some politicians in The Tipsy Duck once. She had us all in stitches.'

The mother I knew rarely let herself go.

'I never mentioned Rose because I figured your parents must have had a good reason for not telling you, that it wasn't my place, that it wasn't my business... it's such a massive revelation. Nevertheless, I've been expecting this moment, not just since you've turned up but for the last twenty years. It's...' Her voice wobbled. 'It's kind of a relief now that it's arrived.'

'What happened that afternoon you were babysitting, Trish? Why did my parents leave so quickly?'

'I... I've practised saying this so many times and now...'

I rested my hand softly over hers.

'Will was ill and screaming with an ear infection. I was making dinner. You and Ben were upstairs playing in your bedroom. Your sister, Rose, she...'

It really was true.

I still could hardly believe it.

I had a sister.

'She never went near the edge of the stream and always called you back if you went too near. I assumed she was playing with her skipping rope as usual or next door's cat. I should have checked. I- I finally called you all in for dinner. I didn't think Rose had heard me, so I went outside...' Trish closed her eyes.

'Rose wasn't to be seen. Then a flash of pink caught my eye in the water.' Her voice wavered. 'She'd fallen in. Mud was pressed into the soles of her feet. The police thought she must have slipped on it and lost her balance. She'd knocked her head on one of the big boulders that was in the middle at that corner part of the stream. She was lying face down. I screamed and put Will onto the grass. Your father arrived just as I was wading in.'

'But there's a wired fence along the water's edge,' I said, hardly able to get words out. I felt as if I couldn't breathe. 'Did she climb over that?' I asked, feeling detached as if another Lizzie were talking.

'The stream wasn't fenced off in those days.'

'What happened next?'

'Your mum sat in shock until the paramedics arrived, whilst your dad and I frantically did CPR. She kept saying the same thing again and again, that the cottage was cursed, that the drowned witch had lost her son to the stream and had been biding her time to make sure it happened to a future landowner. The paramedics took over whilst Lawrence tried to calm her down but she wouldn't stop, even when they got Rose's heart beating again...'

Wait... My chest started to heave in and out...

'She'd started shouting and saying she'd never live at the cottage again. That it was evil and a threat to you, that the family was to move out that evening. It was obvious your dad was going to do anything to make her feel better.'

'So Rose...'

Trish's eyes glistened. 'It didn't look good. I'm sorry, Lizzie, but I'd be amazed if she'd survived.' She dropped her head into her hands and gulped. I reached out and squeezed her arm.

Poor Rose. Poor Mum and Dad. Poor Trish. When Taz had disappeared after I'd left the patio doors open I'd been consumed by fear and guilt, an utter sense of hopelessness along with despair. If that had been a child…

And… I swallowed. I would have loved to have a big sister.

'It was all my fault and I'm so sorry,' said Trish to the carpet.

'Was Rose happy?' My eyes tingled. 'On her last day?'

Trish looked up. 'Oh yes, she really was. Rose was such a content child. You two were always dancing together. She would coordinate routines and you'd try to follow. Rose was a much-loved child as you both were and she thought the world of her little sister, that much was clear.'

'There's a chance she could still be alive, isn't there, just a small one?'

Trish's eyes filled again.

We sat and talked until lunch, her saying how Dad was a great tickler and was great with her son Will, far better than Trish's own husband had been; how Mum loved to play hide and seek in the house and always let one of us kids win.

'If they could have afforded to be full-time parents, they'd have given up their jobs in an instant, but they wanted to provide the best future possible for you both, Lizzie, and that's why they worked so hard.' She took out a tissue and dabbed her eyes. 'They really were extraordinary people and so young at heart. They'd often talk about taking a year out of their careers when you and Rosy were older, to travel the world. Anne and Lawrence wanted to show you America, the Far East – they'd both gone backpacking in their twenties. They said being parents felt like a second youth. As soon as she got in Anne would kick off her high- heeled shoes and Lawrence would take off his tie. They'd studied maths at university and loved the insurance business but I think becoming parents changed that. You and Rose were clearly their priorities.' She shook her head. 'I can't imagine what they went through. I wasn't related but it... it took me months to recognise any degree of normality again.'

'It happened near your marriage break-up, didn't it? I heard that depressed you for months afterwards.'

'My depression had nothing to do with the divorce. That was the best thing that ever happened to me. No it was about your sister and everything I'd deprived her of. I just want you to know I've never stopped thinking about her. When Will had his first girlfriend I thought about how popular lovely Rose would have been. She adored books and when Will went travelling, I could imagine her studying English literature in somewhere like Paris. I wished for so long that I could meet your parents and say sorry. It tore me apart. Their solicitor wouldn't give me their new address. I couldn't even write to them. The silence between us with so much to say – it's been unbearable.'

I understood that.

'Well you've said it to me and... it's all right, Trish, it was an accident. From what you and Jill tell me about her, Rose would never have wanted you to have suffered so much.' I picked her copy of Unspeakable Truths off the cushion and passed it back to her, feeling hollow inside.

'When Fred mocked up the haunting... I- I think I believed it because I felt like I deserved a ghost, like that of Charlotte Strachan, to be a reminder of how I'd caused a child to drown.'

I held her close, the book in between us. It was the best I could do. Should I have felt angry? By all accounts her neglect had caused the death of my sister. It had destroyed my family and changed my parents irrevocably.

Or had it? Some might say my parents should have never bought a family house near a stream and that there should have been a fence there. I was beginning to realise that a range of factors caused any tragedy.

Was making some choices for myself solely to blame for the estrangement with my parents? No. The more I found out the more I realised the past played a role in the future and life happened, stuff happened, it wasn't all perfect, life got messy for everyone. All we could do was our best to manage it.

I said goodbye and left. I stood in the breeze, cool air reviving me, realising I wasn't an only child anymore. Rose had always been with me, in my memories, in my dreams. In my sketches.

My phone buzzed and I wiped my eyes. It was a text from Aunt Fiona. She'd drive to London to meet me tomorrow.

37

Paw print tattoos can be a tribute to a pet or symbolise moving forwards with life

I walked into Kismet Tattoos and past the wicker chairs. After living with the unobtrusive decor of Streamside Cottage, with its blood red walls the vibrancy of the reception area struck me. Today's music was hip-hop and sure enough Katya stood by the appointment book. I headed over and gave her a hug.

'It's great to see you again.' Katya pushed me away and her eyes scanned my body. 'Looking good, girl. I've been so worried about you, these last months, but village life clearly suits. That's the most tanned you've ever been.'

'Thanks for being so understanding about me leaving. Without you... what you've done for me...'

'Hey, this isn't goodbye, right? We won't be that far from each other.'

'You'll have to visit.'

'Do you think the village can cope with another tattoo artist?' Her eyes twinkled.

'You'd be surprised, I've already inked a couple of the villagers.'

Her eyebrows raised. 'And how did that go?'

'It was great. Really great. I felt the old passion come back, the old focus, my confidence.'

'That's such good news, I'm so glad. You're one talented artist.'

My cheeks felt hot. 'So how's the new mentee doing that you've taken on?'

'Keen. Clean. Personable. He has all the necessary credentials.'

A man with a Mohican haircut strode up and slipped an arm around her waist. He kissed near her ear before going to tidy up the portfolio books on the glass table.

She looked at me and blushed. We headed up to my flat and I opened my rucksack.

'For you,' I said and handed over the cardboard box. 'Red velvet cake. There's an amazing teashop in Leafton.'

'It sounds delicious, thanks. And remind me when you leave that I baked Banitsa for you to take back.'

'Your pastry is amazing.'

'Not as good as my gran's used to be but it's getting better.' She gave a small sigh. 'I'll miss seeing you every day, like I miss my family, but... you're happy?'

'Visiting Leafton – it's the worst thing I ever did,' I said roughly. 'And yet, the best.'

'It's like me living in England. My life is better and I can send money home but it's not without its challenges. But then, life isn't. Our clients are proof of that.'

'Tattoos represent how resilient people are; that they can overcome the worst situations and find hope.'

'Yes, like your birdcage tattoo. We each hold the key to our own freedom. It may be hidden and hard to find but it's there if we look close enough. Then it's up to us to be brave and put the key in the lock and fly out from the constraints of the past and into a brand new future.'

We stared at each other. I reached out and tapped the end of her nose. We both smiled.

I thanked her for airing the flat before she went back down. She'd also got in fresh milk and insisted on coming up for a coffee after Aunt Fiona had gone to check I was all right. I looked at the kitchen clock. It was almost four. She'd be here any minute. I set out another box on the unit by the kettle, containing fruit cake and filled the kettle before perching on the edge of my sofa.

I missed the sound of small paws and the creak of old floorboards. Compared to Streamside Cottage the flat now seemed as sterile as the treatment rooms downstairs.

I jolted at a knock. I opened the door. Aunt Fiona stood with the same indifferent bob and rimless glasses but she'd lost weight. Loose jowls hung either side of her face and a floral blouse drowned her. I hesitated before stepping forwards but to my surprise thin arms wrapped around me first. I showed her to the sofa and busied myself with mugs and plates.

'How are you?' she asked when I sat down.

I couldn't sit and make small talk, not even for a minute, not after everything I'd found out.

'Still trying to get my head around the fact that I had a sister.'

Her hand flew to her throat and her jaw dropped open.

'Why, Aunt Fiona? Why continue to keep Rose a secret, after the funeral?'

'How did you find out?' Her voice trembled.

'I've been staying at Streamside Cottage.'

'What!' She gasped then shook her head. 'The estate agency said they very much wanted to rent it for a month. I've wanted as little to do with that cottage as possible but Jack said from a business point of view it made sense to let it now and again, until… until I was ready to sell it.' She gave a wry smile. 'He gave me the same advice I'd given your parents, years ago.'

I told her about the scrapbook and Ben. Our drinks got cold.

Eventually she dabbed her eyes. 'I'm sorry. So sorry. I wanted to tell you, Elizabeth, once your mum and dad had died, really I did.'

'But you didn't.'

'To be honest, I was so angry about their deaths. I blamed you for their move to Devon and therefore blamed you for what happened. It's ludicrous and unfair looking back.' She fiddled with the hem of her blouse. 'And I'm struggling right now. You should know everything but at the same time it's not my news to tell. What if I'm being disloyal by explaining things your parents never wanted you to know?'

I pulled Dad's letter out of my rucksack. 'Does this help? It got lost at George's office. I didn't receive it until recently.'

She read it and her eyes filled. 'He wanted you to know.'

'Did you know about the Strachans? They supposedly haunt the cottage. And this terrible thing he talks of…?'

'I'll start from the beginning.' She took a deep breath.

'Your parents, they struggled for years to get pregnant. Anne endured several rounds of IVF before they finally conceived Rose.'

'I didn't know.'

'Anne had polycystic ovary syndrome. She worried you and Rose might somehow inherit the condition and seemed almost scared to talk about it, as if that would act as a jinx and you'd struggle to have children too. That was the Anne after Rose's accident – before that, well, I'm sure she'd have been open about it when you both grew up, but after Rose, Anne changed. Both of your parents did.'

Poor Mum. And Dad.

'I just assumed they'd wanted to travel and concentrate on their careers before having kids.'

'They did go on trips but for as long as I can remember – even when she was a little girl – Anne spoke about wanting to be a mother. Your dad too – he had a very happy childhood and it had always been part of his plan to be a parent. They started trying as soon as they got married. It brought their relationship under a huge amount of strain and they agreed to separate for a while.'

'Separate?'

She nodded. 'Both half-heartedly dated a couple of people during this time. Of course, I knew they'd always get back together. They were like a lock and key – neither felt their life served a purpose without the other. Anne rarely laughed and Lawrence contacted me now and again asking how she was. But then, your mum met someone briefly.'

'What?'

'An American called Cooper.'

My upright, prim mother? 'They went out together?'

'Hardly. He was visiting from overseas and was some sort of bigwig in the insurance industry. You have to understand, your mum was in a fragile mental state at the moment, mourning the loss of yet another potential pregnancy – and the future of her marriage seemed up in the air. Anne told me it was just a one-night stand and,' Aunt Fiona took a mouthful of tea, 'Anne got pregnant. She couldn't believe it.

'She was so happy, Lizzie. Glowing, when she talked about the baby. Yet this was mixed with moments of real sadness. She didn't want to be with Cooper. She was still deeply in love with your father.'

'Was the baby Rose?'

'Yes and Cooper wanted to be a big part of her life. However, he was single and travelled the world with work. When Lawrence heard about the pregnancy, he went to see your mum straightaway. They couldn't deny that their feelings for each other, if anything, had got stronger. He wanted to bring up Rose as his own and the prospect of a child, at last, helped heal the wounds between them.'

'So what about this Cooper?'

'He wasn't happy but agreed it was the best thing for his child. He visited whenever he could. They sent him photos and Rose was told she had two dads.'

I thought back to the drawing in the scrapbook Ben and I had found – the picture, drawn by a child, of a family with two daughters, one woman and two men.

'I met Cooper once. He seemed a decent sort.'

We sat in silence for a few moments.

'Was I conceived by IVF?' I asked eventually.

'No, Anne couldn't face any more treatment and she and Lawrence were over the moon when she got pregnant again naturally. It was as if having a child took the pressure off – perhaps that helped.' She took another sip of tea, even though it was cold, looking more relaxed than when she'd come in. 'They didn't want you to grow up in the city so they bought Streamside Cottage when you were just about to start school and Rose was in Year One. They hadn't liked her old school's location, right by a main road. Leafton Primary seemed idyllic.' Aunt Fiona told me how they struggled to balance commuting and living in the village but were determined to make it work. 'They used to ask a woman called Trish to babysit.'

'I've spoken to her. She blames herself for what happened.'

'She shouldn't, Elizabeth. Trish told your parents several times they should have a fence built around the stream. Years later your dad told me they never blamed her, they blamed themselves. He and Anne had always been so busy and kept putting it off and that hot summer after your year in Reception, they didn't want it ruined by having workmen in the garden. They promised themselves they'd get the fence built in the autumn.'

'Why did they leave so quickly? No one in the village knows what happened apart from her. How come it wasn't in the local papers?'

My aunt shrugged. 'Your parents had lots of contacts in the business community – journalists and judges included. I imagine your dad must have pulled a few strings.'

We sat quietly and finished our cake but I found it increasingly difficult to swallow. I pushed away my plate. 'You sit here talking about Rose as if it's the most normal thing in the world. I only found out about her yesterday. Mum and Dad had no right to hide her from me. You and

Uncle Jack should have told me when they died – it wasn't your secret to keep.' I stood up and paced the room. 'It's not fair.' My throat hurt. 'I always wanted a sibling. You and Mum were so close. I could have had that as well.'

I stood and looked out of the window, onto the busy road. My sister never learnt to drive, had never been kissed. She never did a job she felt passionate about. Most of all, it wasn't fair for her. 'Mum and Dad should have been more careful.' The words burst out.

'Have you never made a mistake? One you spent years wishing you could take back? Because if you haven't already, believe me, it's just a matter of time.'

I turned to face my aunt.

'Whether we like it or not, that's life, isn't it?' she said. 'Making errors and learning from them.'

'Is that what her death was to Mum and Dad? Simply an error?'

Aunt Fiona frowned. 'Who said anything about Rose dying?'

38

Now

*George C Reiger Jr had to receive permission from Disney
for the tattooing of their copyrighted character images
onto his skin. He's had over 1000 done*

'She's alive?' I managed to say.

'Yes. Elizabeth, sorry.' She ran a hand through her bobbed hair, messing it up. 'Of course you would assume...'

Everything went black for a second.

Footsteps. I opened my eyes. Aunt Fiona was sitting closer with a glass of water.

'Sip this,' she said, gently. 'You've had a shock.'

My eyes watered. I couldn't ever remember her speaking to me in such a soft tone.

I glugged back the water. 'Please, go on.'

'Rose was badly injured and there was some damage to her brain,' she said, 'but she healed well and it only left her with slight memory loss and some confusion. It could have been so much worse.'

'So where is she? Why didn't Mum and Dad bring her up? Did Social Services get involved? It was an accident, surely—'

'No. Cooper... Lawrence said he'd never seen anger like it. He caught the first flight over when he heard what happened. What with Anne's fragile mental state after the accident he declared she was an unfit mother. Cooper was married by then and no longer travelled with work. He insisted Anne could never look after two children properly and was prepared to fight her in court for custody. Your mother just wasn't up for the battle, even though she and Lawrence were heartbroken at the thought of Rose moving to America.'

'Cooper must have been a stranger to her. Poor Rose must have been so frightened.'

Aunt Fiona shook her head. 'She was especially confused during the first weeks of her recovery – I think this helped her accept Cooper becoming her main carer. He and your parents agreed to weekly phone calls and he sent photos but that proved distressing for you, and Rose didn't really understand about having another family in England. In the end the adults decided it was better for both of you if such regular contact ended and Rose had more of a clean break. Just occasionally Cooper sent over pictures.'

'I'd love to see one.'

'I carry one around, along with snaps in my purse of Anne.' Her face reddened. 'It sounds silly but I- I think my sister would like that.' She reached for her bag. I sat upright and brushed hair out of my face. Aunt Fiona passed over the photograph.

'She looks just like me,' I stuttered, gazing at the bow on

her top lip and those green eyes. I studied every centimetre of the shot of a woman in her twenties, the jeans and pretty top, and the tabby cat she was holding. I thought about the reflection of the girl in the mirror I'd played with in my memories. Now she was staring back at me. Oh she was taller and older but the smile was the same, the eyes full of cheekiness, the caring side shown by the gentle way she held the cat.

'Why, why would Mum and Dad hold onto the cottage all these years?'

'Your parents knew the ghost story about the Strachans and used to laugh about it before the accident. But your mum had always been interested in the unexplained and she took an interest in astrology during the teenage years and also joined a society that debated conspiracy theories at school. Your sister's brush with death and the guilt she felt over it triggered an obsession about the witch and her son. She truly believed the house was haunted and didn't want to risk you living there. She agreed with Cooper's sentiment that she must be an unfit mother and worried your life would also come to a tragic end. It destroyed Lawrence to see her like that. He just wanted to do anything he could to make her despair stop.' She sighed. 'That's why he'd agreed immediately to never live there again. Anne ended up in a psychiatric ward. It was a chaotic time for your parents. Your dad managed to find a place to rent in London, as a temporary measure. They wanted to sell the cottage but what with everything going on, I think it was just easier for them to leave it in the hands of the agency and I persuaded them to consider letting it out. Otherwise it would have gone to rack and ruin and they'd never have been able to sell it. Your dad had to take time off work to visit your mum and you came to stay with me and Uncle Jack for a few months.'

'I did?'

'Jack loved having you to stay. It made me feel guilty because I never wanted kids. He knew that when we married and said it didn't bother him but seeing you and Jack together made me realise he lied. I guess…' She swallowed. 'I'm sorry, Elizabeth, I bore a grudge against you for that.'

That explained the lack of warmth I'd always sensed over the years. She never used to ask me about school. Birthday cards never had love or kisses. Uncle Jack would include me in conversations when we visited but my aunt kept me on the periphery.

'Seeing as we're being open about everything, was there a reason you didn't want children, if you don't mind me asking?'

'Presumably Anne told you about our dad – your grandfather?'

'Yes. My grandmother died when you were seven. My mum was four. I got the impression he managed the best he could.'

Aunt Fiona snorted. 'If that means cavorting with other women and going to the pub when we were in bed, then yes. I practically brought up my little sister; she was more like a daughter to me and I protected her from the worst of it.'

'Mum always said you were such a support when she was small. You read to her at night, made her snacks, sorted out bullies… She considered you invincible.'

Her eyes glistened. 'Anne was more delicate and I soon learnt what a burden it would be to have children. Growing up I worried about my little sister the whole time. It put me off wanting to become a mum.'

'It must have been difficult.'

'You have no idea. Dad's girlfriends could be almost as selfish as him. It was such a relief when my sister married your father. He is… was such a good man. But I still prayed she'd never get pregnant, that they'd never want children. When she did that was it, I felt helpless, I couldn't protect her from what I knew was coming… that lifelong, unconditional concern for someone you love to bits. I knew eventually she'd get hurt and then she did, firstly when Rose nearly died and then the estrangement with you. I tried to pick up the pieces but…' Her voice caught. 'Each time they never fitted back together quite like before. There were always gaps left in her that filled with sadness.'

'I'm sorry. Sorry for you too. We've all been hurt in this,' I said.

'Your Mum always meant the best for you. Both your parents did.'

'But they only ever made me feel as if they didn't believe I could be strong and capable. It feels as if they didn't trust me enough to tell me about Rose.' I reminded her about how they took over my school life, shadowing my homework and setting revision timetables. How they were so controlling over my diet and insisted I was vegetarian. How I wasn't allowed out late – they assumed I'd get drunk and lose control, and vetted any potential boyfriend, plus ignored my desire to study art instead of maths. I threw my hands in the air. 'And they never gave Ash a chance. He's a great bloke. You'd all have liked him. I know me dropping out of university was a huge thing but I was twenty – an adult capable of thinking things through logically. I told them how I'd thought about finances and worked out paying for living costs and my flat.'

'All these years I believed they just thought me weak and useless. It's only recently I've started to question this theory.'

'Oh Elizabeth. Every time we spoke on the phone, when you were younger, Anne would rave about your latest achievements or how well you handled yourself. It thrilled her to see you maturing. She spoke proudly about your kindness. She often told me stories of how you helped classmates. She and Lawrence were so very proud.' My aunt took off her glasses. 'It was never about not trusting you. It was all about protection. You meant so much, perhaps too much to them.'

'But why this exaggerated need to protect me? They must have seen something in me to cause that. What happened with Rose – it was an accident. They weren't even there.'

'You've got to remember, they lost pregnancy after pregnancy trying to conceive, and then they lost Rose. They thought you were strong, intelligent, and often spoke of how they knew you were going to achieve great things, but for as long as they could, both were determined to do everything to keep you safe.'

'It wasn't because I was a disappointment...' My throat hurt. '... and lacking in some way?'

'Quite the opposite,' she said, firmly.

We sat in silence for a moment.

'For so long with the years of unsuccessful IVF they – especially your mum – felt overwhelmed by a sense of failure, and then when Rose almost died, they felt they'd let her down too.'

I thought back to the argument at the party… the smashed cut-glass rose…

'… and then they felt they'd failed you. That's why it hit them so hard when you dropped out of university.'

Aunt Fiona talked about how they blamed *themselves* and decided they were useless parents. How they *were* angry at first about me dropping my studies but really saw breaking contact as the ultimate act of protection. I listened as my aunt explained how Mum convinced herself my life would be much better off without her and Dad in it. She said they always talked about Rose's accident as a terrible thing that they could have avoided if they were better parents; and about not telling me about a living sister as a terrible thing they should have remedied.'

Dad's letter.

I tried to speak but my throat felt choked.

My life with them began to make sense, like the last turns of a Rubik's cube aligning and matching up the jumbled squares. Like my mother's face on my first day of high school… the sadness I'd detected when she looked at other families. She must have been thinking of Rose. Then there was my parents' dislike of the countryside and how Dad would turn off any television programmes to do with rural living; how Mum got upset once when I'd jokingly asked if she wanted to be buried or cremated. Dad had got so cross. And those days during every summer, when Mum would go quiet and need time to herself – that must have been around the date of the near-drowning. And how they were so strict about me getting swimming lessons…

Aunt Fiona's words reminded me of Jill's when she talked of her parents cutting her off because they felt their daughter's pregnancy meant they had failed. I remembered what an overwhelming sense of failure I experienced when Taz went missing.

Without looking at Aunt Fiona I reached out my hand. Hers met mine. We squeezed each other's fingers tight.

39

22 years ago

In Ancient China the Weeping Willow
represented immortality

We got home from our picnic in the forest with circles of ice cream around our mouths. We'd stopped to buy some on the way home. Me and Rose had strawberry and Mummy and Daddy had mint. I didn't like that because it tasted of toothpaste. We went into the back garden and Rose, me and Mummy collapsed on the lawn. Daddy fetched a funny looking knife from the shed and said something about a surprise before disappearing through the branches of the weeping willow.

Mummy laid back on the straggly grass and closed her eyes. I picked up a long blade of grass and tickled under her nose. She jumped up to scare me, and me and Rose ran away screaming whilst she laughed. Rose taught me a new dance whilst we waited to see the surprise.

Finally, Daddy's voice boomed out: 'Come and have a look.'

We raced over, each of us grabbed one of Mummy's hands and the three of us ran his way. Holding hands, we pushed through the branches of the weeping willow. Daddy stood there with see-through pearls of sweat at the front of his head where he tells me hair used to be. It was the hottest summer ever. He had a big grin on his face as he knelt down and pointed to the tree trunk. We got on our knees too. All three of us gaped.

Daddy had carved out a... finicky symbol. It meant that things never stopped. And next to it was the word Earl in capitals, going up and down.

He didn't need to tell us why. Mummy kissed her fingers and leant forward to trace each letter.

'E for Elizabeth,' I said.

'A for Anne,' said Mummy.

'R for Rose,' said my sister and clapped her hands.

'L for Lawrence,' said Daddy, 'and an infinity symbol because we'll all love each other forever.'

'We'll never be apart, will we?' I asked.

'No,' he said firmly. 'Even when it may seem that we are.'

I wasn't sure what he meant but Mummy nodded so it must have made sense.

'We should make a pact,' said Rose and puffed out her chest. 'Whatever happens in the future – if we get cross with each other or go travelling or marry princes and go to live in castles, we'll never forget that our hearts belong here. Together, at Streamside Cottage.'

I gazed at my sister. She was so kind and fun. One day

I hoped to be just like her. She caught my eye, reached out and gently tapped the end of my nose. I loved it when she did that and we both giggled. Then Mummy and Daddy opened their arms and me and Rose threw ourselves forwards.

40

Now

A red rose symbolises a love that can withstand time and death

Ben stood in the hallway and stretched. His hair was streaked with white. He held up an empty paint can.

'I need this filling with tea, I'm parched. In this heat, painting is thirsty work.'

I grinned as I finished the skirting board I'd been glossing and straightened up. 'Not until we finish the second coat. I can't wait to start painting my designs on it once it's dried.' I'd decided to turn the downstairs study into a treatment room where I'd do tattoos. I'd contacted the local council and was in the process of registering my business with the appropriate organisations and getting the correct licenses, plus sorting out insurance. I hadn't felt so excited in a long time. I was going to paint popular tattoo motifs onto one wall, and had already ordered inks, gloves, tracing paper in bulk… everything I would need.

'You're a hard taskmaster. I can just stay at home to get bossed around like this.'

'But Jill doesn't let you use half a bottle of ketchup on your eggs like I do, and I'm frying some for lunch.'

'True.'

We smiled at each other. Last night we'd ordered a curry and talked into the early hours, reminiscing about our childhood. We'd done that a lot the last few weeks, since I'd met up with Aunt Fiona and found out about my hidden past. The comfortable easiness between us had fully returned – and something more. A depth, a trust, a sense of knowing, all built on the last few weeks but also our childhood together.

Taz dragged a catnip mouse across the hallway floor.

'You're going to have your work cut out now that this chap has been given a free run of the place.'

'Not completely free. I have to be around and know where he is but it is time his world got bigger. Yesterday he was in the lounge but hurried into the kitchen to use his litter tray – so I think things will work out.'

'He's a lucky chap, being rescued by you.' Ben bent down to stroke him.

I came out of the study and also bent down and tickled Taz's ears. Really he'd rescued me. The stray kitten and abandoned cottage, both of them making me stay... making me face the past. I'd spoken to Aunt Fiona every few days on the phone. When things settled down, she and Uncle Jack were going to visit. Aunt Fiona was going to bring all the photo albums she'd taken after Mum and Dad died and she was more than happy for me to buy the cottage from her. She said she didn't want paying but I insisted on a fair market price. She and Jack deserved an easy retirement. Aunt Fiona also offered to email Cooper but I said it was something I needed to do myself. I'd done so last week but hadn't heard back yet – maybe I never would.

I'd asked her why my parents had never, in the end, sold the cottage, and why she hadn't either. She said Mum just couldn't part with it and had wanted to keep it in the family... that even though she'd cut herself off from Leafton, the garden was the last place Rose had been happy and that was something to be treasured. Because of that Aunt Fiona didn't feel it was her place to let it go.

Ben and I both stood up at the same time and I bumped into his chest. We stared at each other, only a couple of centimetres between our faces. This man with his sticky-up hair, the freckles and irresistible smile, he'd been by my side since I'd arrived in Leafton helping me find out the secrets hiding in my old home. I looked at Taz, the hallway ceiling, I heard birdsong. I had everything I wanted here – almost. Was it greedy to ask for the last piece of the jigsaw?

I couldn't hold back any longer. I leant forwards and pressed my lips against his. Ben jolted and drew back.

'Lizzie.' His eyes widened. 'I didn't—'

'Oh God, sorry Ben.' Heat flooded into my face. 'Have I gone and messed everything up? I should have listened to my head, telling me you weren't ready for another relationship.'

'What makes you think that?'

'You said, after the break-up with your ex...'

He stepped forwards again. 'You're right, I'm not ready for anything with someone new, but you... it's always been different. Even before we knew about our past, I had a feeling that we... we were linked in some way.'

'You felt that too? And I- I've felt an attraction towards you, I have to admit, a feeling that has grown and grown, but I didn't feel it was reciprocated.'

'It's been the same for me, Lizzie, even though we were practically strangers – or thought we were – but I haven't wanted to take advantage, you've been understandably emotional… and I guess I've been confused about starting to feel things for another woman when I was still getting over what happened with my ex.'

'When Ash visited you backed off for a while. I thought that was your way of letting me know that you really only saw me as a friend.'

He put down the paint can. 'I- I suppose I was protecting my feelings, me still feeling bruised after my break-up. When I though Ash stayed over it hurt me more than I expected. The strength of that feeling scared me.' A shy look crossed his boyish face. 'But for so long, Lizzie, as each day has passed, I've wanted to get closer. It's been hard staying friends. But that was better than nothing, I didn't want to spoil what we have.'

'You really feel the same?' I said, a tremor in my voice. He leant forwards and once again our mouths met. It felt soft, warm and tender but above all it felt right. Strong arms wrapped around me and held me so tight. My stomach fizzed. I closed my eyes and lost myself in darkness with him, with kisses that embraced our past and looked forwards at the same time. My heart raced so hard I felt as if all the air had left my chest.

He took my hand and led me into the lounge, Taz under one arm. We sat on the sofa and Taz curled up at the end, looking tired. Ben brushed my hair behind my ear and cupped the side of my face in his large hand. Gently a thumb ran over my cheek.

'I've always felt as if you've been in my life all the time, if not physically then in my mind. You coming back to Leafton... this... I never got over that sense of something, someone missing from my life, but now, once again, I feel whole.' He gave a crooked smile and his face flushed. 'I know it sounds corny but I've felt that since the first moment I saw you, in the back garden.'

'You did?' I croaked. 'Me too.' We kissed once more. Eventually I extricated myself from his arms. 'Who'd have thought – Lilibet and Jimmy Jammy.'

'They'd have been horrified,' he said and laughed.

'I don't think I would have, you know. I looked through the scrapbook again yesterday and found something on the back page. It was a big heart and inside I'd written *Lil loves JJ*.'

Ben's eyes crinkled. 'Seeing as it's confession time... I've always remembered the games we played with your plastic pet dogs. You gave me two to take home once, I think, and I remember playing on my own and pretending they got married and... and that they were you and me. You forgot to ask for them back and I kept them. After you left, I was glad I had.'

A meow brought us out of the past and we both smiled. We chatted some more, held hands, kissed. Then Ben lifted up Taz and went to see how the paint was drying. I ran my hand over the sofa and surveyed my new home.

You opened your doors to me. You knew I belonged here and helped me find my sister and now I'll return you to your former glory as a thank you.

I'd gone to see Trish the day after meeting my aunt and said I knew about her requests for a fence to be built. I told her my parents never blamed her for the accident – and that Rose was still alive.

Tears had rolled down her cheeks. 'Little Rose didn't die? I didn't cause her death?'

I'd held Trish close, her body racked with sobs as she let go of twenty years of guilt. She pulled out a bottle of wine and we got a little bit drunk. She revisited the idea of her stocking my gift cards in the shop and I had an idea, about Ben making gift cards too, from his amazing photography shots. I'd mention it to him. Trish had contacted Frederick and he'd apologised once more. They wouldn't be meeting again but for the first time in a while Trish said she felt an inner calm.

'It's over, I've found some sort of peace at last,' she'd sobbed after the second glass. 'I can't believe it, Lizzie. I'm so, so happy about Rose.'

Perhaps I should have also felt a sense of ending now I knew the truth about my parents, but instead it felt like a start...

Someone knocked at the door. It was Neve. I'd never seen her hair tied back before. She looked like a Sixth Former. I'd seen her in the teashop yesterday and told her everything I'd discovered. Ben came down with Taz on his shoulder and the three of us chatted about the plastic duck race that was taking place in the stream next weekend, to raise money for Leafton Primary's new wildlife corner.

'I never knew you had a tattoo, Neve,' said Ben and moved for a better view of behind her ear.

'Me neither. Who's Kyle?' I asked, looking at the letters.

Neve blushed. 'A teenage crush. We broke up two weeks after I got this done. Alan wants me to get it removed. He hates tattoos.'

'What do *you* want to do?' I asked, whilst Ben played with Taz who had crawled down his body and was swiping the mouse tails threaded through his shoes.

'He's been on at me for ages, especially since you arrived in Leafton. I've been meaning to ask you about laser removal.'

'I'm not trained to do that but—'

'That's okay. Alan was shocked at first. He'd had our whole future planned out – marriage, kids, us both working at the supermarket and to be fair I went along with it. But if I don't follow my dreams, I might end up resenting him. Getting to know you and how you followed your heart, despite the great cost, it's inspired me. It's the wake-up call I needed to spend my life doing what I believe I was put on earth for. So I'm going to carry on with my job but go part-time and study through the Open University. Eventually I want to work as an archivist. I don't want to lose him but I need to do this.'

I smiled. 'So this tattoo...'

'I've decided not to get it removed. Could you cover it, instead, with a flower? Can I see your portfolio?'

Neve flicked through many of my designs and then went to leave to do more research on the internet, hoping to get the tattoo done in the next week or two.

'By the way,' she said as we headed to the front door. 'My cousin turns eighteen next week. He's had a really rough year and would like to get a semi-colon tattooed onto his wrist – to show how he's looking to the future now, his next chapter; that he'd not reached the end. My aunt and uncle aren't happy but I told them about you and that's put their mind at ease knowing that a trustworthy local could do the work.'

I waved to Neve. Ben shut the front door.

'See,' he said. 'It's right that you don't leave Leafton. Your work here isn't done.'

'What do you mean?'

'The village has been waiting for you to return.'

I went upstairs and sat on my bed. Yes, I was here, living in the cottage, admiring the views and slowly finding my place amongst the locals. I felt a little heady at the thought of setting up my own tattoo business and had already looked into the necessary paperwork. The cottage had brought me back to my roots and back to my artistic passion. But Rose wouldn't skip across the lawn again as a small child, hand in hand with me. We could never get that time back. And Mum and Dad wouldn't sip beer and cross-examine their day at work in the lounge.

I pulled out a nondescript wooden box from under my bed and ran my hand over it.

'I'm back home, where we were all happiest,' I said, looking at the knots in the wood. 'I've emailed Cooper. I'm going to do everything I can to get back in touch with Rose. I'm sorry about the argument and I know from Dad's letter you are both sorry too. We all followed our hearts, you protecting me, me chasing my dream. I've thought a lot about this and no one's to blame.

'It sounds silly but now I own a kitten – a cheeky little chap, I think you'd like him – it's made me realise that when love comes with responsibility, it's one of the most scary, powerful things. How strong you both were, to carry on after what happened with Rose, carving out a life for yourselves, trying to carve out a life for me.

'Last week Taz peed on my favourite cushion.' I gave a small smile. 'He does lots of annoying things but I already love him so much. That's helped me accept that you still loved me at the end.' I bent down and kissed the box before hugging it tight in my arms. I closed my eyes as memories came back of holding hands, Eskimo kisses, of tickle fights and helpless giggles.

I felt a sudden urge to sit under the weeping willow and, taking the box, headed downstairs and out into the beautiful garden. I pushed my way through the branches, and sat down on the grass with the box on my lap, lost in thought. Ben came out and passed me a lemonade. We exchanged intimate smiles and he left. I stopped drinking and looked at the tree trunk and the Earl engraving. The stream and birds coloured in a long silence. My eyes ran up and down the word. Once. Twice. Six times.

Vision blurred, heart racing, I shuffled back.

With a shaking arm, I kissed my fingers and reached out. I ran them over the letters.

'I so wanted you to be proud,' I whispered to the box, 'but as I got older, I realised the most important thing was being proud of myself.'

I looked at the letters again, as my phone buzzed. On automatic I opened the email and gasped.

Hello Lizzie. It's Rose – your big sister…

Tears tumbled down my cheeks as I read the text. Here

in the garden, under the tree, one had become four again, symmetrical and balanced. Maths had played such a big part in my parents' lives.

I took another look at the carved infinity symbol.

Of course.

I sat up straighter and wiped away the tears. One day soon I would add that symbol onto the charm bracelet tattoo around my ankle.

'I'll cherish this place and bring it back to life,' I said to Mum and Dad. 'Streamside Cottage never forgot you, never forgot us – it never gave up. It's been nudging me, all the way, to discover the truth. Now, like you, it can rest easy.'

I smiled. 'Its forever family is home.'

Read on for an excerpt from
The Summer Island Swap...

**Sometimes the best holidays are the ones
you least expect...**

After a long and turbulent year, Sarah is dreaming of
the five-star getaway her sister has booked them on.
White sands, cocktails, massages, the Caribbean is
calling to them.

But the sisters turn up to tatty beaches, basic wooden
shacks, a compost toilet and outdoor cold-water
showers. It turns out that at the last minute Amy
decided a conservation project would be much more
fun than a luxury resort.

So now Sarah's battling mosquitos, trying to stomach fish
soup and praying for a swift escape. Life on a desert island
though isn't all doom and gloom. They're at one with
nature, learning about each other and making new friends.
And Sarah is distracted by the dishy, yet incredibly moody,
island leader she's sure is hiding a secret.

I

'I still think it's madness,' I said, getting up from the faux-leather sofa to peer over Amy's shoulder. 'To come into five thousand pounds, only to blow it all on a single holiday...'

Amy turned around from the circular dining table and folded her arms. 'No. Madness would be turning down a month of luxury, all expenses paid. I've spotted a great deal. Even my winnings wouldn't normally cover four weeks at this particular destination. Our break must be written in the stars.'

'Written in platinum, more like. And who on earth goes away for that long?'

'Someone who hasn't been on holiday – not a proper one – for nine years, because she's been so busy building a home and a future for her amazing younger sister. That's me, by the way.' She smiled.

My cheeks felt hot.

'And I'll be left with a bit of my winnings. Perhaps I'll finally get to enjoy all the musicals I've been longing to see, like Hamilton.'

Over the years Amy had developed an obsession with West End musical shows. Perhaps it was an obvious outcome after being addicted to Disney films as a child. I'd never believed in the whole 'prince and princess' story. Being older, observing my parents' relationship, I always knew that grown-up life was different.

'But you could use your windfall to go one step further with your career. It would boost your finances to start studying full-on veterinary science and probably pay for the first year's accommodation. What with student loans and...' I talked for a few minutes. After years of scraping money together to keep up the payments on our modest London flat, it wouldn't feel right splashing out on private sunbeds and cocktails. It went against all the instincts I'd honed since leaving the house I'd grown up in, to set up on my own.

Amy's face darkened and she turned back to the screen. 'I've told you a hundred times, Sarah, university... that's one of the few things Dad was right about. I... I would have loved to be a vet. It was my life's dream for such a long time. I'm not grateful to Dad for much, but he did at least stop me making a fool of myself by applying to study such a challenging subject. He was right – I just haven't got what it takes.'

'How can you say that, Amy? Your grades alone—'

'Being a veterinary nurse alone is more challenging than I ever imagined,' she continued, ignoring my comment. 'Look, Sarah – two other members of the lottery syndicate are also taking holidays. One of the surgeons is going on a cruise... I wish you would trust me on this.'

I opened my mouth to protest but the stiffness that had taken hold of her shoulders stopped me. We shouldn't argue. It was rare that we both had a Saturday off. Tonight we were going to the cinema. My chest glowed at the prospect of Amy's usual excitement over a blue slush drink and ketchup slathered hot dog. Sometimes it was hard to believe she was twenty-three.

But then I was twenty-seven and hadn't even been kissed. Not properly. One-night stands and short relationships didn't count. I meant proper kissing like you saw in the romantic movies I loved watching, where it was savoured on a bench or under a lamppost. I should have had that with Callum but looking back, the spark wasn't there; I never got the sense of wanting a kiss with him to last forever.

'A trip away is exactly what we both need,' continued Amy as tentative rays of sunshine that had snuck through the blinds retreated behind assembling April clouds. 'Especially you.' Her voice sounded thick. 'You've worked your guts out all these years, giving me a roof over my head and so much more – like funding my training to become a nurse at Paws & Claws. Words can't explain how much it meant to me, having this flat, your home to move into when I turned eighteen and could finally get away from *him*.'

'This has always been *our* home – even when you weren't here.'

Her eyes shone. 'Well, this is my small way of paying you back.'

'There's no debt.' I rubbed her arm and crouched down by her side.

She closed the screen of her laptop and turned around, face flushed as I stood up. 'Let me do this on my own. For a change let me take charge.'

But had she checked the reviews on TripAdvisor? And I'd have to find a way to subtly remind her about holiday insurance. The last year or two she never seemed to understand when I was simply trying to help.

I loved Amy more than anything in the world but she'd always be the younger sister who'd run to me when Dad had been mean; the sister who needed me.

'Or are you trying to sneak a peek at exactly where we're going?' Her sharp tone couldn't disguise the twinkle in her eyes. 'There are several islands to choose from and I've finally made a decision. Now go and make those chocolate cookies you promised, whilst I book this surprise.'

'Ooh, an *island*? Thanks for letting that slip.' I chuckled. 'And, um, I might have already seen a few other clues,' I said sheepishly. 'Like photos of a lush hotel with Roman pillars. Waterbeds. An indigo ocean. White sand beaches. Something about tropical massages and Aqua Dancing and all-day buffets offering pyramids of pastries and colourful seafood platters.'

'Sarah! The details are supposed to be top secret.'

'But I'm excited!' I bent down and gave her a tight hug.

'Get off,' she protested and pushed me away. She peered up from under her fringe. 'So, did it look okay? I want everything to be perfect.' She curled a section of hair between her fingers. It was short. Gamine. Brown like mine was without the highlights. It suited her petite figure currently dressed in dungarees over a high-necked jumper. I was taller, like Dad. Her whole look shouted practical.

'Okay? Amy, it looked idyllic. But are you sure about this? I work in the hotel business. My day is spent in hospitality, even though Best Travel doesn't exactly offer five-star accommodation. But you work with animals. You love the outdoors. Hiking. Getting down and dirty with our window box. Spa treatments and fine dining aren't exactly your thing.'

'They could be,' she said in a bright voice.

I raised an eyebrow.

'All right... we both know manicured nails would chip within an hour on me and I'd rather climb rocks than have hot stones placed on my Chakra points. And I'm a little concerned I might get bored. But who knows? I might enjoy the pampering and it wouldn't be a selfless break. Feeling that I was finally doing something for you – that would give me a sense of wellbeing that no fancy massage could ever match...'

Whistling – out-of-tune, as Amy never ceased to remind me – I went into the kitchen. It was only the size of Dad's and my stepmother's en-suite bathroom. Fondly, I ran a hand over the scratched units and gazed at a couple of cracked tiles. I loved every inch of this flat because it belonged to me and Amy.

And Nelly, our much-loved Burmese cat. She was ten now and became more regal as years passed. She padded into the kitchen, sat by her bowl and tidied her tail into a circle around her body.

I took out flour, butter and sugar. 'I can't help worrying about Nelly, if we're away for that long,' I called through to the living room. It was cluttered with Amy's animal ornaments and my beauty magazines, framed photos of the two of us, and several shelves of novels – romance for me, thrillers for Amy. But I didn't mind the lack of space in what was already a cramped room. Those objects were proof of the new, happier life we had now.

'Sarah, I'm a veterinary nurse. I told you, I've a queue of

great people offering to look after her. Or don't you believe me?' There was an edge to her voice.

Of course I did. It was just my habit to worry about Amy and Nelly, my little family.

They were all I needed. Having seen the life Mum led, I'd decided long ago I was never going to get married. The only weddings I wanted to be a part of were the fictional ones in my favourite movies and books.

'I'll still have to clear it at work. I'm not sure how Prue will feel about me taking a month off.'

Just the mention of my boss's name made my stomach knot.

'No one's indispensable. Not even wonderful you,' she called back.

My chest felt warm. Over recent years, Amy had matured and started to look out for me, cooking dinner and mowing the lawn. However, I'd never lose my maternal feelings towards her. When we were ten and six ours was quite an age gap. As was eighteen and fourteen when I'd had to leave her behind with Dad but promised we'd live together again. I beat the sugar and butter, remembering her tears and his folded arms as I dragged my suitcase past the fountain and out of the huge driveway, into the street. I'd finally realised I had to leave after... I swallowed. No. I wasn't going to think about that now.

I let Nelly into the back garden, busied myself with ingredients and cleaned up whilst the cookies baked. Their sweet aroma wafted through the air as I carried them into the lounge, on a tray, with two coffees.

'Good timing,' said Amy and turned off her screen, looking pleased with herself. I put the tray on the table and joined her.

'Is it all booked?'

She nodded. 'A modest deposit paid. The rest is due in the middle of June, two weeks before we leave.'

'Can't you at least share which part of the world we're visiting?'

'That would be telling,' she replied airily and took the largest cookie.

I jumped up and held her right arm firm whilst tickling the armpit. 'I won't stop until I find out, Amy Sterling.'

However, she was as strong as me these days and, giggling, held the cookie in her mouth and forced both of my hands away. I sat down once more. I recognised that expression. She was determined to keep her secret. Sometimes, with my impulsive sister, that could be a dangerous thing, like when she'd agreed to do a charity skydive with colleagues at work. She didn't tell me until the morning of the jump.

'Just a clue. A teeny one,' I said. 'Please...'

'I've never seen you this excited before. Well, not since you were made assistant manager. Oh, and the time you found that fancy moisturiser for half price.'

'It wasn't just *any* moisturiser. The Duchess of Cambridge uses it.' I pressed my palms together. 'At least let me guess... the Canary Islands? Barbados? Australia's an island, right? I mean, you and me – we share most things, don't we?'

'Best buddies, always,' she said solemnly.

It was a promise we'd made to each other, the day after Mum's funeral. And sure enough, we confided in each other about our latest celebrity crushes, about our dreams for the future; we put the world to rights over Chardonnay and Pringles. I knew her favourite colour, favourite food, favourite band. She could always tell when I'd had a stressful day at work and, without prying, would make me a hot chocolate, fetch a blanket and switch on my current Netflix obsession.

Amy laughed and put down the cookie. 'I can't face this interrogation for the next three months. All right. All right – but no more questions after this, agreed?'

'Promise,' I said, beaming.

Her chest puffed out. 'I've booked us the *best* break ever. It's exotic. Luxurious. Our holiday destination is... one of the British Virgin Islands.'

I stared.

'What's the matter?'

'Nothing... it's just...' A lump rose in my throat. 'That really is high-end.'

'And no less than you deserve,' she said quietly. 'But don't ask me which one. You'd never guess, anyway. There are over fifty.' She pretended to zip her lips shut.

My stomach fluttered as I imagined the celebrity treatment and Michelin-starred food awaiting us. I'd have to get my nails done, especially themed for somewhere so grand, perhaps with tiny aeroplanes painted on them. My highlights would need re-touching. I'd treat myself to a new bikini.

'What are you thinking?' Amy asked.

'I'm imagining what it would be like, living in a part of the world like that forever. Away from the grind and dust of London... Only mingling with jolly tourists seeking a good time...'

'I'd prefer to mix with the locals – otherwise it would feel false... manufactured... like moving to Disneyland.'

'Reality is overrated, if you ask me. The ultimate getaway must be working and living on a cruise ship.'

Amy pulled a face. 'I can't think of anything worse.'

I smiled. 'You'd miss saving animals. Doing good. You're not as shallow as me.'

Her voice softened. 'Perhaps my perspective is different because I've had it easier. You had a brutal introduction to reality on your own, aged eighteen. Whereas I've always had you to rely on, looking out for me...'

I'd tried to act as a mum to Amy all these years because I knew how hard life was without that maternal presence.

I shook myself, sipped my coffee and pictured myself on a beach, a daiquiri by my side, wearing large sunglasses and an Audrey Hepburn *Breakfast at Tiffany's* hat. Amy and I clinked mugs.

This was going to be the most perfect holiday ever.

2

Finally the showery spring had passed, yet it was June and still the sky was threatening. I'd been hoping for a few weekends to gain a tan in the local park, before my imminent trip to *the British Virgin Islands*...

I still couldn't believe I was going. My anticipation was building.

Despite the bad feeling it had caused with Prue.

Despite her making it clear I'd have to work all hours when I got back, to make it good.

I unclenched my teeth. It had felt like a long early morning shift. These weeks running up to my break should have been filled with excitement about the trip of a lifetime. Instead Prue had done her best to wear me down. It was true – I should have consulted her before Amy booked it, but it all happened so fast. However, I'd rather her have said no, if I'd known she was going to continually make me suffer for it, with her frequent comments about how I'd have a mountain of paperwork to catch up on when I got back; that I owed her big time for letting me go off during one of our busiest months.

I sat in the poky staffroom at Best Travel and gazed at the half-eaten egg and cress sandwich. It used to be a favourite of Mum's. Very occasionally, she put herself first with Dad and served them, even though his nose would wrinkle. I wiped my mouth and finished my bottle of water. A reusable one, of course – Amy made sure of that. For a moment I wished I'd swigged something stronger, ahead of the chat I wanted to have with Prue before I left to meet Amy for holiday shopping. I'd had another of my ideas on how to improve Best Travel and wanted to run it past my boss. It had kept me awake last night and I couldn't wait to share it, optimistic that this would be the one that inspired her to finally embrace change and would make up for me taking four weeks off.

I tried to ignore the niggling voice in my head, telling me that Prue was being unfair. That I'd never taken more than one week off at a time, in all the years I'd worked at Best Travel. That I was the first to muck in if a member of housekeeping rang up ill. That I'd worked hours and hours of unpaid overtime since I'd become assistant manager.

But it was no good. The frustration within me swelled. My fists formed balls.

I never let on to Amy just how tough it was working for that woman; never wanted to risk my sister feeling guilty about all the years I'd had to suffer condescending put-downs in order to put food on the table. To be fair, Prue had eventually promoted me from receptionist and in my new role I'd learnt loads about the financial side. However, Prue wasn't a dreamer and always knocked back any fresh ideas I had to grow our reputation and make more money.

I felt like a clipped bird.

Please let things be different today.

But if they weren't... I sat up straighter. A month in a luxury hotel was going be an opportunity to find out what it would take to reach the top of my profession. I felt as if I'd put in enough years now, as assistant manager, to take the next step forwards in my career. I'd been researching for several months. It was fascinating. For example, the walls of The Dorchester contained compressed seaweed and cork for soundproofing. Apparently Hitchcock said it would be the perfect place to commit a murder.

I was so used to working all hours but there was no chance this trip would make me feel guilty because I'd be taking notes on the way things were run and still focusing on work. This five-star holiday might set me in a good position to seek a more personally rewarding – and better paid – job once I got home.

'You still here?' asked Prue. She made herself a black coffee and sat down next to me, bringing an atmosphere as sour as the vinegar on her crisps. 'Then I've just got one last job for you, before you knock off for the day – the new family with those bawling twins want to know if we have blackout curtains for tonight. I don't trust myself to give them the bad news, so you'll have to.' She rolled her eyes. 'Honestly. Some people truly believe a hotel should be a home from home.'

That's where Prue and I were fundamentally different – I longed to work somewhere that went that extra mile to fulfil a guest's every need. There was no better feeling than when some little difference you made brightened their stay. In spite of my critical boss, I enjoyed the hands-on aspects of my job so much. I was lucky seeing as I'd only applied to work here, all those years ago, because the position came with accommodation – a perk I was grateful for until I could afford a proper place of my own.

'I'll sort it. No problem, Prue.' I closed my Tupperware lunch box. I pressed down firmly on the lid, clutching the sides as I spoke. 'Could I just run an idea past you that I've been working on – on how we could make the Best Travel experience even more... special?' I couldn't help smiling. 'It kept me awake until the early hours.'

With her hair scraped back into a ponytail, there was nothing to hide the bored expression that crossed her face. Only last month she'd rejected my suggestion that we extend the basic complimentary toiletries range to include a plastic shower cap and sachet of hand cream. Not having much money to spare myself, I knew that for our average customer the small things like that meant a lot. But 'Don't fix what isn't broke' Prue was a fan of the status quo.

Still. I had to give it a go. One thing I'd learnt, since leaving home, was to never give up. Like the way I'd taught myself to hang wallpaper. There'd been tears. Rolls of discarded paper that had gone on wonky. I'd felt so proud when I finished one wall.

I took a deep breath. 'The rooms on the top floor that are slightly bigger... Why don't we trial stocking them with better quality linen, curtains that match duvets, small mini bars and trouser presses? We could charge more and might snag customers wanting a bigger slice of luxury at a lower price.' I leant forward. 'We'd be more competitive against that posh hotel down the road and—'

Prue looked at me and raised the palm of her hand. She was grinning. Hope unfurled in my chest.

Until she started laughing. Tears ran down her bony cheeks.

'Christ, Sarah. What do you think this place is? The Ritz? Stick to what you know best – running the housekeeping team and chasing out late risers.' She wiped her eyes. 'Best Travel is a tightly run ship but not the *Titanic*.'

Neck burning, I stood up. Prue reminded me of Dad. It was her way or no way at all. That frustration, inside me, that had been growing for weeks rumbled like a dormant volcano considering waking up. I pressed my lips together but couldn't stop myself turning at the door.

'What now?' she asked.

I should have left without saying a word.

I should have swallowed my wrath.

Instead I went back over to her.

'Some might say your lack of vision is narrow-minded, Prue,' I said, in a measured tone. 'It could cost you the business. These are competitive times.'

An hour later, still shaking, I met Amy outside the underground station we'd agreed on. She'd managed to get an early shift too. I smiled and nodded in all the right places as she reluctantly fitted on skimpy clothes chosen by me. Blocking out Prue's reaction, I somehow got through the afternoon, eating cake and laughing over a sun cream that smelt like spoiled milk. With relief, I put the key in our front door, went into the living room and collapsed onto the sofa.

Amy collapsed next to me and groaned as she eyed up our bags. 'I'm already regretting buying that bikini.' She linked her arm through mine.

'But the pineapples on it are so cute,' I said. Playfully she punched my arm. I caught her hand and held it tight.

'Thanks, Amy. I know shopping isn't really your thing – like this whole luxury break. You're the best sister ever. And four weeks is long enough for me to convert you. By the time we get back you'll be longing to book your next pedicure and facial.'

'What's the point of pedicures in England? No one's going to see your feet with the weather we've been having. And I've always washed my face with soap and water. I can't imagine a fancy facial really does any more good than that. But... but I'm looking forward to being proved wrong,' she added quickly. 'I must remember to pay the final amount. It's due in a couple of days – as you keep reminding me.'

'I just can't wait for this break,' I said and my voice wavered. I meant every word one hundred times over after what had happened with Prue a few hours ago. I wanted Amy to hug me tight. I wanted to open up and reveal how much I'd grown to detest working at Best Travel.

I'd forgotten what it looked like, to turn white with anger. Prue's complexion soon brought back the worst memories of Dad. She'd slammed down her mug and said I should be grateful. Then she laughed at me for using the word *vision*. Sniggered and said I'd watched too many episodes of *The Apprentice*.

If only I could confide in Amy but I'd spent too many years protecting my little sister, to stop now. 'The accommodation you've booked sounds just like the kind of place I'd love to run one day.' I closed my eyes, picturing the designer executive suits I'd wear, to look the part of operations manager.

'What... this break will remind you of the nine 'til five?'

'Well, I do work in a hotel,' I said and shot her a humorous glance. 'Just imagine the clientele you could attract at that sort of place. I'd offer butlers and personal masseuses and waitressing staff on the beach. This holiday is going to give me a fantastic inside view of high-end hospitality. Don't get me wrong, I… I love my assistant manager position at Best Travel, the job is great… but you know I've been researching working at top-notch hotels. This trip is going to provide me with brilliant insight for interviews. I shall take a notebook and write down everything we experience, from start to finish.'

She gave me a sideways glance. 'This holiday is supposed to be a getaway – a getaway from the usual routine.'

'And it will be.'

'No, it won't. By the sounds of it you're going to spend every hour thinking about the hotel business – namely work.'

'But I'll be experiencing hospitality from the other side of the fence – that's completely new. This is the perfect opportunity to make up for my lack of experience of actually working in a luxury setting. I think I'll write a personal statement, based on this trip, to attach to my CV, explaining what I've learnt from living for a month as a five-star guest.'

Amy raised an eyebrow and gave an exasperated sigh.

'What?'

'Nothing.' She glanced away. 'I've put the oven on for those pizzas we bought.'

'I'll chop up some peppers and mushrooms for the top. We can kid ourselves it's healthy, then.'

Half an hour later we both sat on the sofa again, in our pyjamas, eating pizza and drinking squash. The day's cloudy sky flirted with dusk. I didn't mind. Whilst I loved eating ice cream and favoured my summer wardrobe, the best season was winter and evenings holed up in the flat. We'd drink hot chocolate and watch Netflix in our dressing gowns with a plateful of biscuits whilst diplomatic Nelly would stretch herself across both our laps.

Amy finished her last mouthful, crusts and all. It had been a busy day – although the calorie hit didn't perk her up. Her mood had been more subdued than usual since we got back.

'Good morning at work?' I asked.

Amy's lips upturned. 'The best. You should have seen this owner's face when she came to pick up her dog, Brutus – he's a feisty Chihuahua...' Her eyes twinkled. 'He's been so ill after eating a large bar of chocolate. He almost didn't make it, but turned a corner after a night on an intravenous drip. Mrs Smith couldn't stop crying when he swiped her with his paw like he always used to.' Amy picked up some strands of melted cheese from her plate. 'She's a really interesting woman and works for a company that makes jewellery out of recycled household objects such as knitting needles, cutlery and vinyl records. I'm going to buy something small out of what's left of my winnings. I think it's fantastic, the difference businesses like that are trying to make.' Amy stuffed the gooey splodge of cheese into her mouth and then looked at me, embarrassed.

'I'd better take that plate off you before you lick the pattern off it,' I said and grinned as she pretended to hide it.

'Do you remember when you got back from guide camp, pizza was the first meal you craved?' she said. 'You declared you could never face eating another marshmallow or barbecued sausage again. I was so jealous. Roughing it was – and still is – my idea of heaven.'

'Yes, I had fun on that trip.'

'Did you? Honestly? Ten days in the outdoors, away from your bubble baths and neatly ironed clothes?' Amy stared.

'We slept outside, under the stars one night. I've never forgotten how dark the sky is, away from city lights. So pretty.' I leant back into the cushions. 'It was great, not having to bath every night and keep my hair tidy. Building dens. Learning about orienteering. The sense of freedom was brilliant.'

Amy gave me a curious look.

'But you wouldn't want to go on that camp now, would you?'

I shrugged. 'Grown-up life can become complacent. I need to be more adventurous. That's why it's time for me to really go for a new job. Not that I'm desperate to leave Best Travel. It's not awful,' I said and forced a laugh. 'I'm just ambitious, that's all...' I picked up our plates and hurried into the kitchen before Amy could ask any more questions. I fed Nelly her evening snack and relished the lingering smell of cheese, tomato and oregano. When I returned to the living room, Amy was sitting at the table in front of her laptop. I headed over and she snapped it shut.

'Holiday secrets,' she said and beamed.

I smiled and went into my bedroom to unpack my new clothes. When I came back Amy was still in front of her screen.

'I've just paid the full amount. There's no room for second thoughts now.'

'Good! Although there's no worry on that score – why *wouldn't* I want to go?'

'No reason. I... I just hope I've done the right thing; chosen the best holiday.'

She bit a fingernail. A habit from childhood. She didn't do it often now.

'How could you not have?' I said and squeezed her shoulder. 'Like I said earlier – you're older now... it's time I took some adventures. I'll have fun whatever this exotic stay brings.'

She caught my eye, thought for a moment and gave a thumbs-up.

'And you've put so much thought into next month. It's not as if you've made a spontaneous, last-minute booking.'

Amy's cheeks reddened and she grinned. Looking more like her usual cheerful self, she stood up and gave me a hug.

Acknowledgements

Firstly I'd like to thank tattoo artist Adèle Hudson. The tattoo I had done, on my wrist, in 2018, represented a big turning point in my life, after difficult years, and reminds me daily of where I used to be and where I am now. Thanks so much, Adèle, for your fantastic artistry and friendly, caring manner. And yes, you, Immy and Beki were right, I should have got it done bigger!

I wanted to write a story strongly featuring tattoos as, even though they are mainstream these days, there is still a prejudice out there about the supposed type of person who gets inked. I love tattoos, I love hearing the stories behind them and marvel at the talent of the people who create the designs and bring them to life.

Huge thanks to my wonderful editor, Hannah Smith – for her hard work, efficient manner and sense of humour. I love working with Aria Fiction and must also mention talented Vicky Joss in marketing. Hannah, Vicky, the whole team – you are all superstars for bringing your authors' stories to the world with such professionalism and fun, during the challenging years of 2020/2021.

I must thank my agent Clare Wallace from The Darley Anderson Agency. We speak a couple of times most weeks and Clare is a constant in what can be an up and down career. Thanks for steering me away from some of the wackier ideas, Clare, and for so neatly balancing my desire to follow my muse with commercial considerations. You're a professional rock and one that is set with gems and never ceases to sparkle.

I'm so grateful to all the bloggers who support my stories. Thanks to all those people who take part in my blog tours and publication blitzes, to those who take the time to write reviews or help promote my latest stories. The way you give up your time to do so blows me away, especially during current times. Thanks to Rachel Gilbey for her amazing blogging services.

Martin, Immy and Jay, thanks for being there and for being you. Words cannot convey how grateful I am for how you've been there for me, over the years.

And lastly but certainly not least, readers thank you so much for choosing my stories; for writing reviews or getting in touch with me to say how much you've enjoyed a novel. You are the reason I start the next project as soon as I've written The End. I don't write for myself, I write to share experience and connect with people, in what can often feel like a disconnected world.

If you enjoyed Summer Secrets at Streamside Cottage I'd be enormously grateful for a review on Amazon, it only needs to be a few words long.

And I'd love to hear from you, so if you feel like reaching out you can find me at the places listed below.

Take care and stay safe.

Sam X

About the Author

SAMANTHA TONGE lives in Manchester UK with her husband and children. She studied German and French at university and has worked abroad, including a stint at Disneyland Paris. She has travelled widely.

When not writing she passes her days cycling, baking and drinking coffee. Samantha has sold many dozens of short stories to women's magazines.

She is represented by the Darley Anderson Literary Agency. In 2013, she landed a publishing deal for romantic comedy fiction with HQ Digital at HarperCollins. In 2015 her summer novel, *Game of Scones*, hit #5 in the UK Kindle chart and won the Love Stories Awards Best Romantic eBook category. In 2018 *Forgive Me Not*, heralded a new direction into darker women's fiction with publisher Canelo and in 2020 her novel *Knowing You* won the RNA's Jackie Collins Romantic Thriller Award.

https://twitter.com/SamTongeWriter
https://www.facebook.com/SamanthaTongeAuthor
samanthatonge.co.uk
Instagram: @samanthatongeauthor

Hello from Aria

We hope you enjoyed this book! If you did let us know, we'd love to hear from you.

We are Aria, a dynamic digital-first fiction imprint from award-winning independent publishers Head of Zeus. At heart, we're committed to publishing fantastic commercial fiction – from romance and sagas to crime, thrillers and historical fiction. Visit us online and discover a community of like-minded fiction fans!

We're also on the look out for tomorrow's superstar authors. So, if you're a budding writer looking for a publisher, we'd love to hear from you. You can submit your book online at ariafiction.com/ we-want-read-your-book

You can find us at:
Email: aria@headofzeus.com
Website: www.ariafiction.com
Submissions: www.ariafiction.com/ we-want-read-your-book

🔲 @ariafiction
🐦 @Aria_Fiction
📷 @ariafiction